A TRAVELER'S GUIDE TO BELONGING

BY

RACHEL DEVENISH FORD

Other Books By Rachel Devenish Ford:

The Eve Tree: A Novel

Trees Tall as Mountains: The Journey Mama Writings- Book One

Oceans Bright With Stars: The Journey Mama Writings- Book Two

A Home as Wide as the Earth: The Journey Mama Writings- Book Three

First published in 2015
Copyright © 2015 Rachel Devenish Ford

Cover art by Chinua Ford
ISBN-13: 978-0-9895961-69

No part of this book may be used or reproduced in any way without the permission of the publisher, except in the case of short quotations for literary review or critique.

Small Seed Press LLC
PO Box 7775 #48384
San Francisco, CA 94120-7775
racheldevenishford.com

This book is for my own Isaac.

A TRAVELER'S GUIDE TO BELONGING

PART 1

CHAPTER 1

Later, Isabel's mother would say that her daughter died like a pig on the floor, but Timothy had been there, and he knew that Isabel's death was nothing like the noisy, terrible death of a pig. It happened like this: Isabel was there and then she was gone, gone into the deep black Indian night, gone away from him and her newborn son, gone forever.

The day had started like all of their days since they had moved to the foothills of the Himalaya mountains in the far north of India four months before. Timothy and Isabel lived in a tiny, sun-soaked house surrounded by corn fields. When they had first seen the house, there had been wheat rather than corn, the tall stalks rippling gently as they walked up the curving paths from house to house, climbing stairs on the hillside where there were no roads, until Isabel put one hand on her belly, round with their baby, and declared she had to sit down or she would fall down. Timothy found a chair for her at a small café, then, at her bidding, had walked across the path to check out the little white house. The house turned out to be perfect, the very house where they would live and wait for their baby. They moved in and the wheat grew tall, then was harvested by women wearing punjabi suits with sweater vests, shawls wrapped around their heads. Corn was planted, and it grew, until that day when Timothy and Isabel woke up, not knowing they would be saying goodbye to each other forever.

The morning was so normal. They cuddled in their blankets until finally Timothy got out of bed to make the coffee on the burner in the corner of the room, wincing as his feet hit the cold concrete floor. From the pile of blankets, Isabel laughed at him.

"I was thinking Canadians were stronger than this," she said.

"It doesn't take long to forget the cold," he said, rubbing his arms.

Isabel winced and rubbed her belly. "Ouch!" she said.

"Is he kicking you again?"

"Yes, and it hurts more today."

"Maybe he's wearing boots."

They were used to calling the baby "him," though Isabel hadn't had an ultrasound and finding out the sex of the baby was illegal in India anyway, so really, they had no idea. Still, many women had approached Isabel and told her, "boy," because they said they could tell by the shape of her belly or how she walked, or even what her face looked like. Timothy was hoping for a girl, actually, a girl exactly like Isabel, but he'd take a boy. Getting pregnant had been her idea, just a few months after their wedding, which was heartfelt but wouldn't be recognized by any court at home. They had married in the desert in Rajasthan, where they tied their clothes together in the presence of a hunched, toothless old man with giant glasses, and his wife, even more bent, both of them clapping wildly at the happy marriage, the old man breaking into rusty song while his wife said, "Baba is a good singer, Baba is the best singer, you are very lucky to have Baba here today."

"I need to have a baby soon," Isabel had whispered to him, a few weeks later, in the darkness of their bed. Through the window Timothy could see endless stars; the lights were out for the night, there on the outskirts of the little town where they lived. He traced patterns in the stars with his eyes, unable to stop. He did the same with stones, or patterns in the marble, or the strangely psychedelic tiles in their tiny bathroom.

"Why soon?" he said. He was twenty-three, he'd just left his little brothers behind in Canada, an eight-year-old and ten-year-old who never could learn to knock before barreling into his bedroom. He came to India to experience something of the world, to learn about Indian music, to be the explorer he'd dreamed he was when he was a child. He was in no hurry to have kids.

"Because I just turned thirty-five, Timothy. I wouldn't like to be one hundred years old when my children are twenty."

He slowly turned to look at her. Her face looked like an angel's face, the slight shadows under her eyes and the faint crow's feet scattered in the corners the only indication that she was even a day older than him. Her brown eyes caught at him, and he leaned forward and kissed her.

"Only if I don't have to change any diapers," he said.

She smacked his arm. "You will not be that type of father!"

He laughed. "Ow! If you say so," he said.

She reached up and stroked the side of his face. "Really, though, what do you think?"

"What about right now?" he whispered, and leaned in for another kiss.

"Really?" She sat up and jumped up and down on the bed, and he grabbed her around her rib cage and pulled her back to him.

"Really."

As he straightened with two cups of coffee in his hands, she moaned a little again, and said, "I don't know if that's a kick, Timothy. It's low in my back."

He felt the blood quickly leave his face and then return.

"What do you mean? Should I get the midwife?"

She laughed. "First you must bring me my coffee. And then, yes, let's call Liz."

* * *

Liz told them to wait until the contractions were five minutes apart. And so they spent the day together, walking down the paths between stalks of corn, drinking mango lassis, the yogurt drink they both loved and gorged themselves on. Timothy gave Isabel back rubs when she wanted them, gave her distance when she wanted that. Liz came over in the evening and it all blurred together then, the panting and moaning, the pain Isabel was in, darkness falling outside. The few minutes of holding their boy. And then the worry turning to panic as the bleeding continued and there was so much of it and there was nowhere to go, no doctor to reach for, no ambulance to call. Their house so remote, a thirty-minute climb from any drivable road.

She was there and then she was gone. In the sudden stillness Timothy realized that he didn't even know the precise moment that she left, that's how quietly she slid away from them. All he could hear was the frantic pumping of his own heart, and there was nothing from hers; the quiet thud was gone. His face was still pressed to hers where he was kissing her, whispering that she was going to be okay, until he found that he was alone, talking to someone who was no longer with him. Time seemed to halt.

He blinked and saw stars. He heard the wails of their newborn son, swaddled and in the arms of the landlady, Sunita, who watched Timothy, her eyes filled with fear. The baby screamed because of the shock of cold on the chilly day, the brightness of the one bare lightbulb on the wall after the warm dark of the womb, and the fact that he was now thrust outside when he was accustomed to being inside. He could be comforted by a mother, but the baby's mother was gone. Timothy sat back on his heels in panic. Did he shout? He didn't know. The midwife was still massaging Isabel's abdomen to try to get her uterus to contract and stop bleeding out. Tears were streaming down the midwife's face and Timothy couldn't get any sound out of his throat, tight as it was, to tell her that she could stop working; it was too late.

He looked at his wife's pale face again, the eyes with their translucent lids that had fluttered closed moments ago. Nothing seemed real; just hours before she'd said "I think this is really it," and they had been so excited, like children. They hadn't known they were boarding a train they couldn't escape. He was going to vomit. *Isabel, gone. No.*

He stood. Black and red specks danced in front of his eyes. He walked to the door of the small room with the peeling paint on the walls and looked out at the night. The baby cried harder and Sunita approached him on soft feet. He didn't want to see the baby, he didn't want to talk to anyone; he didn't remember deciding to run but minutes later he found himself out in the night, pushing through wet cornfields. The stalks slapped him on the face, clinging to his wrists as he fought his way through; he didn't plan a direction, he just ran. If he ran, his twisting gut seemed to tell him, it might all be different when he got back. Maybe nothing would have happened yet, maybe there would be a chance to make it turn out differently. As he ran, darkness clouded his mind and his thoughts slowed and became muddy.

He was soaking wet. He didn't know how long he'd been running and walking and lurching. It wasn't raining anymore, but the cornstalks were covered in water from the storm that had swept through a few hours before, so his pants clung to him and he put his palms to his eyes to wipe away water. Stopping wasn't a good idea, though; he panicked again, looking around wildly for something, anything. *Erase,* he thought, sobbing now. *Delete. Rewind.* He would run away, never go back. He would leave this place now that Isabel was gone, he would climb into the mountains. He put out his hands and pushed through the plants again, nearly running smack into the bear that stood only ten feet away. Timothy stopped short and stood very still, holding onto a cornstalk with white fingers.

They'd been told, the last weeks, about bears in these Indian mountains.

"Don't go too far in dark time," Sunita had said with her rich Indian accent, standing at her doorstep with her baby, Beema, in her arms. "You are seeing these marks? The corn is break means bear is coming nightly."

Isabel and Timothy tried to be careful, walking gingerly past the dark cornfields at night, coming home from dinner or late-night music with other travelers instead of by themselves, though they always loved walking alone in the darkness, stopping for kisses along the way.

Now Timothy was facing the bear and he was more alone than he had ever been in his life. *So bring it,* he thought. He hadn't been careful; there wasn't much use in being careful anymore. He had torn right into these fields as though he was looking for the bear.

It was an Asian black bear, and not so big, but standing on its hind legs, holding a stalk of corn in its front paws. The bear ate most of the cob of corn, husk and all, before dropping the stalk. The bear looked at Timothy. Timothy looked at the bear. Drops of cold water trickled down his forehead, into his stinging eyes, and he couldn't raise his hand to wipe them. He couldn't move at all. He stood and watched as the bear ripped another stalk out of the ground and ate the corn from it as well. Its claws left marks on the stalk when it dropped it, long scratches that turned Timothy's stomach. He was going to be sick. Everything had changed the moment Isabel's last breath left her. Now his world was dark, this hulk of bear revealing to him the danger and death under everything. Timothy whispered, "Please," but there was no one to hear him. So he got louder. "Please!" he called, and then he shouted, "No! Get out of here! Just go!" The bear growled a low growl in its throat, dropped to all fours, and walked away from him, heading back toward the dark forest.

Timothy waited until he couldn't see the cornstalks waving anymore, then turned, and there, under the himalayan stars and the bright moon, he vomited in the cornfield. He had been stopped short by the bear. He knew he couldn't run away, he didn't have whatever it took to run into the mountains, whatever it took to be a hermit, to leave his son and disappear. He squatted there for minutes or maybe hours, not even bothering to move away from the puddle of vomit, before he rose stiffly and walked back to the small house in the hills where a naked baby was screaming his hunger and cold in the injustice of a motherless world.

CHAPTER 2

Seven days after Isabel died, Timothy walked down a stone path to a small house surrounded by trees. The baby was tied to his chest and he was breathing hard from the walk. He had been smoking too much lately, lighting one cigarette on the end of another; he was going to need to stop if it made him walk like an old man. The house was white, surrounded by red hibiscus bushes. In Timothy's opinion it was the best house in the valley, with gray stone roof tiles and large windows, and it belonged to Isabel's dearest friend, Anjali, a woman who long ago was from Bulgaria, though she had lived in India, teaching yoga, for many years. She had planned a memorial service for Isabel that would begin shortly. Already a group of about fifteen people milled about in a small clearing surrounded by boulders and tall trees. None of them were related to Timothy or Isabel, none of them were people that he really knew at all.

He hadn't called his family yet to tell them that Isabel was dead. He was stalling, he couldn't bear to say the words aloud. Anjali had called Isabel's parents, who were on their way to retrieve their daughter's body and take her back to France to be buried. Timothy thought if they had asked for the baby he might have just given him to them, he was so overwhelmed and confused, but they were elderly and Isabel had been an only child. Isabel's parents would arrange to get the death certificate for him, and sign the papers needed to show that he had full custody. Isabel's mother had been inconsolable on the phone, asking for all the details and mourning the fact that her daughter had died so senselessly, on the floor, with only Timothy and the midwife to see her go. Timothy agreed with her, it was stupid, senseless, and irreparable. But he couldn't bear her grief as well as his own, so he had handed the phone back to Anjali and gone out to smoke a cigarette.

For the memorial, straw mats had been arranged in a circle and a small campfire burned in the center, dim in the midday sun. Anjali emerged from the house and lit a candle on a stump at the opening of the clearing. She caught sight of Timothy, who had been fighting his urge to turn around and climb back up the hill. He felt a deep, sick anxiety at the sight of so many people. Anjali put her hand to her mouth and made her way over to him.

She reached him in a rush and took him into her arms, making space for the tiny sleeping baby.

"Timothy," she said. "How are you doing?"

She had visited him several times in the last few days. She called Isabel's parents on the phone, she held the baby, she and Sunita handed Timothy cups of chai. He was grateful to her, deep in his heart, though he didn't know if it showed; he was so numb, so tired. He felt exhausted by all of it, the kind of exhaustion that drove him into the ground, that made his heart feel like it was about to stop. It was a tiredness deep in him. It felt like a thirst with no possible quenching.

"I'm here," he said.

"And you brought him," she said rubbing her hand over the baby's curved spine.

"It felt like it would be wrong not to," Timothy said. "That's why I'm late, sorry. I had to wait for Sunita to finish nursing him and then he needed to be changed—"

"Don't worry," Anjali said, cutting him off and putting a hand on his arm. He looked down at her. She was wearing a white scarf around her dark brown hair, with long golden earrings and black kohl around her eyes. She was twenty or so years older than him, ten years older than Isabel. Timothy knew that she hadn't been sure about him at first, didn't know whether he was good enough to be a partner to Isabel, her dearest friend. She had worried that he was too young, that he'd take off and leave Isabel in the lurch. She had warmed up to him eventually. "Many others are late," Anjali said now. "We'll wait a few minutes and then begin. And I have some ladies here to cook for us, so don't leave before you eat something."

"It's up to him," Timothy said, cupping his hands under the baby. Timothy was wearing the baby in a stretchy piece of cloth that the midwife had given to the couple a few weeks before the birth. He had tied it around him several times and folded the baby into it. Liz, the midwife, had to show him almost a dozen times before he could do it for himself.

He saw her then, the midwife, walking down the path, looking extremely nervous. Timothy gave her a brief nod and looked down. The forest floor was covered in pine needles after the heavy rain, which had fallen hard, like pebbles on his roof, all night long. Timothy found a place to stand against a tree, just outside the circle of straw mats. As people trickled into the clearing, they found places on the mats, kicking their shoes into a pile of sandals on the outside of the mats. They sat cross-legged, in a loose representation of a circle, like a slack rope that has been thrown in the air and allowed to float to the ground. People pressed his hands or gave him kisses on the cheeks as they passed. He nodded and tucked his lips up in a ghost smile. Several urged him to join the circle, but he touched the baby and indicated that he couldn't sit. He preferred to be on the edges; he needed some sort of distance to distinguish him from the others.

Timothy and Isabel had been part of the rushing, seething stream of travelers; the international community that moved throughout the world like a school of glittering fish, following the weather, following the music, looking for an open space for themselves, for a simpler way of life. All of the people who sat in this circle were a part of this continuous migration, and Isabel was well known. She had been in the stream for ten years. Timothy was new, practically a baby in the scene. He was only twenty-three when he came to India and met Isabel, falling in love. Now he was left here in the mountains of North India, alone except for his small son.

But Timothy, unlike the others, really knew Isabel. He had been the one who married her deep in the Rajasthan desert, the one who loved the beautiful French woman better than any other. He was the one who would have stayed with her forever.

The rain had brought a chill that wanted to soak into Timothy's bones. He could have used a sweater, or even a vest. Instead, he had a warm sleeping baby. He curled his arms around the outside of the carrier to protect the baby from the cold.

The service began abruptly, and Timothy forced himself to pay attention. Anjali started by telling how she and Isabel met, eight years ago, in an ashram in the south of India. Timothy was fascinated with the story despite himself; he had never heard it before. Anjali wrapped her words up, tears running down her face, then another person told a story about Isabel. Timothy put his hand over his face and rubbed at the hot, tight place above his eyes that had been hurting for days. A Persian man picked up a guitar and began singing. He had long dark hair and a black beard, and wore a *lungi*, a piece of cloth wrapped around his waist like a kind of skirt, with a shirt and Himalayan wool vest. He sang the song "Rainbow Connection," and though it was a song Timothy liked, he felt a bubble of anger that started as a sharp pain in his throat and worked its way down to his chest. *Somewhere I'll find it. A rainbow connection.* Timothy didn't know what it had to do with Isabel. He didn't believe he would ever find a rainbow connection now; he would have been satisfied with the ability to sleep at night, but he didn't hold out hope for that either. The man's voice broke and people on either side of him reached graceful hands out to pat him on the back. He kept strumming the guitar without singing for a moment or two, then soldiered on, his voice warty with tears. Timothy could almost have laughed, but the moment was serious.

The baby squirmed on Timothy's chest, then relaxed back into sleep.

In the circle another man spoke, introducing himself.

"My name's Craig," he said. "I've been friends with Isabel for many years."

Timothy felt a rush of heat in his face. He knew the name Craig—an ex-boyfriend, one who hurt Isabel in those long years in India before Timothy came along. Timothy was simmering, then, trying to listen, but with senses pinging and attention drifting. Crows called to each other in the forest, a pack of dogs howled and fought in the distance. The people in the circle seemed unreal. They saw Isabel's death from a distance, like people exclaiming over an earthquake from miles away. *"The whole room was shaking!"* they said. *"I thought my grandmother's vase would tumble off the shelf!"* Meanwhile, at the center of the earthquake, people were fishing the dead from the rubble. Timothy didn't have any confidence that he would survive this. A multistory house had fallen on him. He was pinned beneath the beams. He was afraid to look at himself, scared to find out what the damage was.

Craig had short, tufty, dirty-blond hair and blue eyes under dark eyebrows. His clothes were white and he drew an invisible circle in the air with two fingers.

"The universe is perfect," he said. "It was Isabel's time to go."

The bubble of anger inside Timothy grew larger, causing his chest to ache even more, almost choking him. *Her time to go.* The words burned his ears, circled his brain, whirling. He took deep breaths, looked up at the trees, at the large pieces of sky between the topmost branches.

The people in the circle were restless now that the man in white had been talking about the perfect universe for more than a few minutes. Below their faces they seemed constructed of bits of scarves, flapping edges of cloth. There were bright and faded colors among them, a patchwork of people sitting in their scraggly line like a ribbon that's been lost in the forest. *Somewhere I'll find it, a rainbow connection...* the lines of Kermit's song echoed in Timothy's brain. He shook his head, tried hard not to focus on any one face. He didn't want to see anyone looking at him, didn't want to meet any eyes. Instead he looked at the small shrine that Anjali had set up for Isabel on a stump at the edge of the clearing. There was a framed photograph of Isabel, surrounded by candles and garlanded with roses. Anjali had asked Timothy for it two days before. In the picture, Isabel sat in a boat on the Ganges River in Varanasi, India, smiling. His stomach felt tight. She was smiling what she always called her big teeth smile. She wore a bright red scarf over her head and shoulders. She was beautiful.

The man in white was *still* talking. Timothy wanted to leave. People had abandoned their rigid, disciplined postures and now lay sprawled out, resting on their arms or lying down with their hands laced behind their heads. And still the man talked. The three Indian women who had been cooking in the courtyard, and now sat back on their heels, chatting while they waited to serve the food. Timothy could hear the gentle rising and falling of their language, words he didn't understand. One woman had something stuck in her finger. One of the others tried to get it out. Timothy felt an urge to walk over to them and offer help. He was great at getting splinters out. He was the oldest son of a carpenter.

"The only imperfect thing is that we don't realize how perfect the universe is," Craig was saying. He smiled at Timothy, pointed at him. "Isabel's son chose to come into the world this way. He chose this life because he knew he could do it without a mother." He smiled. "It is perfect."

The baby asleep in Timothy's baby carrier let out a whining sigh, as though protesting this grave injustice. Timothy felt heat boiling inside of him.

"Bullshit!" he said, his voice echoing in the grove. "This is such bullshit."

Craig stopped talking and everyone looked at Timothy. He was hot from anger, and he felt his face burning hotter still. He was sure he had turned a bright red. "I'm sorry," Timothy said. "Sorry Anjali, but it's such a pile of crap. She didn't want to die, her son didn't want her to die, nothing about this is perfect. It's sad and fu—messed up."

He pushed away from the tree and glanced at the food. It smelled so good, but he had to leave, it was time to go. The two girls closest to him in the circle whispered together, their heads bent tightly together. Craig tried to speak again, but people talked amongst themselves now, stretching, muttering, standing.

"Thanks, Anjali," Timothy said. He turned to go, the baby still asleep but squirming like it would wake up soon. He walked away from the circle, heading for the path up the mountain, but at the last second he turned and approached the three women who still squatted in the courtyard, smiling and talking together, waiting to serve the food. He gestured to the woman with the splinter and she held her hand out reluctantly, her other hand covering her face. It took Timothy three tries, but then it was out. She looked up and smiled a brief, brilliant smile before she remembered to look away.

He turned to go again, but Anjali caught him and planted a hard kiss on his cheek, just above his beard.

"It's going to be okay," she said to Timothy. "You will be okay." He hugged her back but he couldn't even imagine believing that she was right.

CHAPTER 3

Timothy hiked out of the forest after he left the memorial, his feet making their own way on the rocks, almost without thought. He shook his head, fists clenched. The anger inside him was like a tide; his feet struck the ground like hammer blows. The baby stirred and meowed from the carrier, like a kitten. The baby had no mother, Timothy had no wife. *It wasn't perfect!* How could it be? The baby stretched and started crying. Timothy felt a sense of helplessness so deep it almost took him inside it, like a large red ball. It was the sun in a stop-motion movie, sliced from its space in a cut-out sky and rolling down the hill toward him. He walked and imagined how it would hit him, that red ball. He would stick to the outside and roll, bouncing on cars and dogs until they were mashed together.

The real sun had gone down while they sat in their circle, saying nice things about a woman who would never again see the sunset. The trees and hills were black now, against the light. Timothy had reached the chai shop. He nodded at the owner's friendly wave, but didn't move closer. Isabel had loved coming around this bend and seeing the view of the whole valley and all the little houses nestled into it. The curve in the side of the mountain was like a perfect bowl, holding the light. The village where they had chosen to have their baby was called Dharamkot, far in the foothills of the Himalayas. The nearby town was the home of the Dalai Lama and the Tibetan government in exile, but their little village was mostly Hindu with many Gaddi people, an old nomadic tribe with the light-colored eyes of northern Pakistan or Afghanistan. This was where Isabel had said she wanted to make her nest.

The baby was really kicking, making frantic noises. He was loud, like a baby animal. Timothy walked with long strides, desperate to get back to the house and back to Sunita, the wet nurse. He reached the steep part and climbed a stone staircase that had green plants exploding from all the cracks. The rain had been almost incessant lately and this was the first morning of sun in a couple of weeks. Timothy finally reached the house and headed straight for Sunita's door. She met Timothy at the entrance, frowning, shaking her head. She took the wailing baby.

"Too long, *Bhaiya*" she said. His heart warmed as it always did when she called him brother.

"Sorry, *Didi*," he said with respect, calling her older sister, hoping she would let it pass.

She clicked her tongue, then walked into the house to nurse the baby. Timothy stood on the porch and lit a cigarette, trying to avoid the sight of the little house across the path, the place where Isabel and he had lived, where she died. It had been a week, only a week, and he felt that Isabel must walk into the room any minute and at the same time felt that it had been forever that he had been this ghost, the un-man that he had become since she left.

When Timothy had come back from meeting the bear, a doctor had been examining Isabel's body to ascertain the time of death. There were three policemen, another man that Timothy later discovered was the secretary of the Panchayat—the village government—and three men who looked like low-caste laborers. When the doctor finished, the three laborers, looking sleepy now that it was the middle of the night, had gently wrapped Isabel's body in a long white sheet and hoisted her on their shoulders. Timothy was shaking. He shook until his teeth rattled, he grabbed his ribs, trying to stop the tremors that made him feel like he would shake right out of his body. He let Sunita take the baby for the night and he left the house and moved into the room that was next to Sunita and Gopal's little room, across the mountain path from what had been their dream house. The next day Timothy took all the things the two of them had owned and left that house. He never went back. It taunted him now as he looked at it. It felt like a symbol of all that they had hoped for, all that had been taken from them.

He hadn't even met Isabel as much as he was *found* by her, lost as he had been in the train station in New Delhi. It was a year and a half before, mid-March—a hot time to be starting out in India. He was standing in front of a board that had sheets of paper stapled to it, a matrix of names, numbers, cars, berths. The lists didn't seem to hold the possibility of discovery, of finding the right train. Timothy could feel his tired brain struggling to work the visual input into some kind of order, trying and failing. Around him, shorter men pushed in to get a closer look. He was about to give up when he heard a soft voice at his shoulder.

"Do you need help?"

He turned and saw her. Her accent was incredible. She was French, and it was not the French of his country, the wild, new country French with the rough edges, but the soft French of Paris. She pronounced "help" as "elp."

Dark brown hair pulled up behind her head. Dark eyes, so black you couldn't tell the pupil from the iris. She had sunglasses pushed back in the dim light of the station. She looked like a girl in a movie about trains. One of what seemed like several scarves she wore was caught in a breeze from the fan whipping maniacally above them. The gauzy material hovered around her face. She brushed it away.

Timothy didn't know how to answer the question. He had a lump in his throat because she had these little shadows under her eyes and perfect lines at the corners of her mouth. He only smiled and looked back at his ticket. She leaned in and peered at it with him.

"Ah! *D'accord*. Rajasthan Express. It is the very same train that I will board. How wonderful."

Timothy wiped sweat from his forehead, found his voice.

"That's awesome."

"*Challo*," she said. Her meaning was clear, though Timothy didn't know until a later time that it meant "Let's go!" in Hindi. He had to move quickly to catch up with her, after heaving his heavy pack on his back. He looked back down at his ticket, crumbly around the edges because he had handled it so much. When he bought it, three days ago, he set it on the bed in his stark room with the cockroaches in the corners, took a photo of it with his iPhone, and used the guesthouse's slow wi-fi to send it to his sister, Sarah.

"Lucky!" she wrote back.

She couldn't know the truth. India turned everything you knew inside out. At his first sight of Paharganj, the trip had seemed like a terrible mistake. A cow bleeding from a neck wound bumped him with her horns. A beggar with curling legs wheeled himself along on a skateboard, by his arms. Was this even *Earth*, still?

Timothy had boarded a plane in Vancouver, Canada, with the hope of breaking free of the constraint that he always seemed to feel—to fly! To leave his family and their watchful eyes, to see the world. He thought that India would be the place for him. He wanted to study Indian flute and he knew that it was an exotic place, perhaps just wild enough for him.

On arrival, he was instantly overwhelmed. After an incident where he gave a few coins to one beggar child and then eight more showed up out of the night, clamoring and laughing and yelling for money, he nearly got back on the plane. He saw a five-year-old doing flips in the dirt, her little face sweeping the place his shoes had just been, and retreated to his tiny guesthouse room, feeling more trapped than ever. He didn't go home. He bought a train ticket to the desert of Rajasthan, deciding to continue on.

The railway station was seething with life in its dark reaches. On the tracks, rats the size of small dogs. On the platforms, families planted on sections of floor they had squared off with mats. People had their arms flung over bags tied together with string. Real suitcases and sacks, boxes covered with white cloth with an unfamiliar alphabet decorating the outsides. Little kids cried or squirmed or danced away from frazzled parents. Exhausted women breastfed and old ladies lay down with their heads pillowed on their arms. Sweat trickled down Timothy's back, under his shirt as he wove between the mats. The air felt heavy. There were so many people, there was so little comfort. He felt a little bit sick.

Isabel was much shorter than him. At just over six feet tall, he was tall in India. She was closer to the height of many of the other women in the station. Her clothes floated around her. She had that thing that he had noticed about other European women since then—ordinary clothes moved around them in a different way, transformed by the women who wore them. She kept walking. Timothy struggled to keep up. Despite his exhaustion, he felt excited, as if something special was about to happen. Could they sit together, somehow?

They reached the platform just after she brushed past a dozen men in red shirts, who called "Coolie! Coolie!" at her. She stopped, dropped her bag on the ground, and delicately sat on it. The smell of roses came from somewhere inside her scarves. She put her hand in the little purse she was carrying and pulled a pack of cigarettes out, offered it up.

"No, thanks," Timothy said. He had yet to become a smoker.

She lit one and held it carefully, a small bird between two fingers. She extended her other hand toward him.

"I'm Isabel," she said.

He was still fighting with one of the straps of his backpack. He jerked it free and dumped the whole thing on the ground, one rib in his back aching because of too many books shoved in the crevices of the brand-new pack.

"Timothy," he said. "Nice to meet you. Thanks..." They were shaking hands, hers a tiny thing in his. He cleared his throat. "Thanks for showing me the platform."

She smiled, eyebrows raised, put her cigarette to her mouth, and inhaled. She turned slightly to the side to exhale. A large brass pendant clanked against her other necklaces. It sounded like the opening rhythm to one of Timothy's favorite songs, and he started to sing it softly, under his breath. He was already falling quickly towards love, soundlessly and heavily.

"Of course. It is no problem." She stepped back a bit, to get a better look at him. "Timothy."

When she said his name, it sounded like *Teem o tee*. It was something greater coming from her voice box. He was aware that he felt feverish, overworked. That his senses were pinging. Cigarette-less, he cupped his hands in front of him and stared into them. Tired, exhilarated. His heart was thumping as if he'd been running.

They waited there like that, Isabel perched on her backpack, Timothy shuffling from foot to foot. They began to do the normal thing. Asked each other questions about where they were from.

"Canada," Timothy said.

"*Ah, oui? Parle vous français?*"

He ducked his head. "*Non*. From the wrong side of the country."

"Not Québec," she said. "Where they speak some strange wonderful language that they like to call French."

"And you?"

"France, of course. South of France."

A weak-willed fan chugged away above them, pulling the fumes of her cigarette away from her, across the station, into the steel beams, away. Timothy nodded, trying not to appear young and ignorant, although he knew he was both. The strain of it was tightening his forehead. He felt an urge to reach for his flute, to stop himself from talking about Canadian politics, which was what he did when he was nervous. On the tracks beyond the empty space that waited for their train to fill it, another train was parked. People stood in its doorways and stared at the two of them. The station was a cave and they were creatures cut into the walls. Timothy didn't have anything to fear, but his heartbeat was speeding up again. Time and shock and sleeplessness were catching up with him. He saw nothing he could decode. Nothing was familiar.

Isabel stood up and put her hand on his arm.

"Are you all right?" she asked. Her eyes were worried, and he realized that no, he was not okay; he had not been prepared for this.

Before he had a chance to answer, a long blast of a whistle filled the station. The train was coming. Isabel stamped her cigarette out and kicked it on to the tracks. A large rat waddled over to investigate. She grasped her bag with one hand and swung it onto her back.

"Get ready," she said. "Hurry. You must be ready, this will be very serious."

She snatched at his ticket, stared at it. Clicked her tongue.

"*Non*, this is not good. You will sit with me."

His heart was beating quickly again. The train sped into the station and slowed with a creaking squeal. Surely they weren't all getting on this train. People had begun to appear beside him; there must have been two hundred people in their small space. His backpack was on. A man beside him had one of the white boxes covered with writing on his head. He was staring at Timothy. Dark, intense eyes and an eagle's brow. Timothy looked back at him, wondered who he was, where he was going.

The train squealed to a stop and Isabel grabbed Timothy's hand.

"Come!" she shouted, and her voice was there, then drowning in the air, thick and ringing with noise. It was madness. It was a stampede, running with the bulls, a log-rolling festival. This was not the way Timothy had been raised to board a train. He realized too late that he was far too tired for this, but he was caught in a swirling pool of people. They piled in every direction, shouting, arms flying. Timothy was pushed away from the door. He was so confused. Were they *all* getting on this train? Isabel yanked hard on his hand before he was moved away on the current.

She pulled him toward the doorway of the train and he did his best to fight his way through. As he tried to climb the narrow metal steps, other people spilled out, bumping his backpack and whipping him around with the force of their landing. He smelled sweat and garlic mixed with the stale urine on the tracks. He let go of Isabel's hand just before his wrist was bent beyond recognition, but he knew he couldn't let her get away. He burrowed in, finally made it to the top of the steps. He turned and faced the long train aisle, but several men with boxes on their heads were coming down the passageway in the opposite direction. There was only enough room for one person to squeeze through, but three crammed themselves wherever a single person would fit.

Isabel turned around and shouted, "Fourth compartment!"

She turned and tunneled under a fat man's arm to get through. It looked easy for her, but with his height, Timothy was not going to make it.

A woman shouted nearby, her baby being squeezed in her arms. Madness. One innovative foreigner heaved himself to the top of a bunk, then walked along the crowd, his feet landing on ladders or bunks, but occasionally a man's shoulder. Timothy stood for many minutes with his neck pressed to the side of an upper berth, unable to move. Things calmed down, a little. He finally made his way to Isabel. She was busy shooing a man out of the compartment. Next she took his ticket and showed it to another man, apparently trading Timothy's seat for his. The man let himself be persuaded, grabbed his things and held his hand out for Isabel to shake, but she turned him down with sharp words.

The train was moving now. Isabel turned another man away at the entrance to their compartment.

"Ticket!" she said, one hand on her hip, the other held out in front of her. The man tried to push past her, into the compartment, but she stood her ground, and he drifted away. Timothy was still standing, hunched over with his shoulders under the top berth, not sure what to do next.

All the eyes of the others in the compartment were on Isabel as she walked calmly to the window seat and sat down. There were now only the two of them and four others. Timothy stuck his head into the neighboring compartment. There were at least twice as many people in there, resigned, in piles on the floor or the top berths. He pulled his head back into their own compartment.

"Is it okay to tell people to get out like that?" he asked. He wasn't even meaning to say it aloud, but couldn't help himself. The look on the man's face when Isabel told him to go away gave him a sad feeling in his stomach, like when he forgot something after school and went back to his classroom to get it, finding his chemistry teacher eating a bag of Cheetos with orange fingers, reading a romance novel.

Isabel looked up from rifling through her handbag.

"Of Indian trains, Timothy," she said. *"Tu es un enfant."*

His elementary school French was enough to understand that, so he shut his mouth and waded through the legs to reach the seat opposite her, next to the window. He picked up the bag she had left there to save his seat for him, handed it to her. She smiled at him, her mouth sweet, as though she had not just called him a child.

Timothy glanced around at the other people in their little space. They were staring, openly curious. A woman with a dark purple sari, a streak of red color in the part of her hair, rings on six of her toes. Silver anklets. Her feet were impossibly clean. Had she really walked through the same station he had? Timothy assumed the man next to her was her husband. The two men beside him on the bench lost interest in him and started looking at pictures on a mobile phone. Isabel was unwinding the scarf around her neck. She threw it lightly around her shoulders and rested one foot on her seat, knee up, draping her arm around it. Smiled at Timothy.

"Well," she said. "We made it."

Timothy's backpack was next to him. He stood up and squatted to shove it under the bench, winding a chain around it and locking it to the seat legs, then locking the zippers together, like he'd read about in his travel guide. Sat back down. The train beat a rhythm on the tracks; it cracked its way into Timothy's brain. They were on their way to Jaipur, traveling through the dusty central plains of India, on into the desert. Desert was alien to Timothy, so far from his forested island in Canada.

Isabel pulled out a tattered journal and started scribbling in it, not looking up until a man waded down the aisle, calling *"Chai, chai! Garam chai!"*

She set the book beside her and fished around in her purse until she came up with a ten-rupee note.

"Do chai, Bhaiya," she said, when he paused at the opening to their compartment. "Let me buy chai for you, Timothy." It was a statement, not a question. He nodded and watched as she handed the man ten rupees, took two piping hot paper cups of chai, handed one to him. He sipped it, burning his tongue. It was very sweet.

Isabel didn't pick the journal up again. She sipped her chai, gazing out the window. The train compartment was open, no glass on the windows, only iron bars to keep the world out and the passengers in. The two of them sat and drank chai as the train sped through the plains. They watched the light change, soften, watched the sun become a brilliant red ball, falling toward the horizon. The light on Isabel's face was gold, then ruddy and brilliant. Timothy saw stark trees with white flowers at the tips of their gnarled, bare branches. Round haystacks. A different kind of tree, many of them, all in a line. Even the trees were different here; he saw nothing he recognized, and he the son of a carpenter. The train pulled up in villages where more tidy, clean people climbed aboard and tried to find seats. Dusty beggars trailed after their window as the train pulled away, holding their hands out. When the train was still, the air was too. Sweat gathered on their upper lips, under their chins. When the train moved on and wind found its way through the windows, the relief was a song.

They talked, pointing things out as they saw them. Timothy was curious about the round dung patties, rows of them pressed to walls with handprints in the center. Isabel explained—they were old news to her—that the patties would dry and become fuel for kitchen fires, and pointed out the old man squatting on a station platform, large turban and larger mustache, legs coming out of his *dhoti* like bent sticks.

"Traditional Rajasthani clothing," she said. "We're getting close."

They were on the outskirts of the large desert state, the ride was softness and light and the sweet smell of burning dung. It was a thudding in his heart. Her startling smile. It was a trail Timothy had certainly not expected to find himself on.

When she turned her face to watch the fields beyond the window, he could see every line of her profile, how the curves swooped and melted together. He felt so far away from Canada, from the stuck feeling he'd been trying to break free of. He felt a door opening.

Across the aisle, in the alcove berth, a family with two small children sat, bunched together, the kids wound in their mother's sari. As Timothy watched, the man reached out and touched his wife quickly, lightly on the cheek. They settled down for sleep as the sky darkened, the man climbing into the top berth alone.

Timothy and Isabel moved into the top berths when their neighbors wanted to swing the middle berth up, for sleep. Isabel made a nest for herself and spread a blue *lungi* over her arms and legs.

"How old are you?" she asked.

"Twenty-three," he told her.

"Ah! *Vrai, tu es un enfant!*"

No man likes to be told he is a child.

"Well, how old are you?" he asked.

"I am thirty-four," she said, pronouncing it *teerty-four* and the words reached into the air and stirred the space around him. He felt a click, like he had been waiting for them. But she looked like a teenager, except for those shadows under her eyes.

"Too old?" she asked, her voice soft.

"No, not too old," he said. He reached his hand across the space between their berths and their fingers twined together in the darkness.

*

He stood outside Sunita's door and took a long drag of his cigarette. Sunita and Gopal rented out two of the rooms in their old-fashioned Himalayan house, which was coated in cow dung for insulation and painted with white paint. None of the rooms were connected, and the four doors opened onto the courtyard—one to an empty room, the next one Timothy's, then Sunita and Gopal's room, and finally the room that Saasi Ji, Gopal's mother, shared with Gopal's brother.

Blue night was spreading across the sky. Timothy put his cigarette out and ducked under the low eave to enter Sunita and Gopal's room: a single square space with a two-burner gas range on a bench in the corner functioning as their kitchen. Next to the stove was a shelf with all the steel plates lined up against the wall and in the next corner was a wardrobe. On the floor beside the wardrobe sat barrels of rice and *atta*, whole wheat flour that Sunita used to make the chapatti every day. The walls had once been white, but now grime and dark stains from many years were smeared over their surfaces. This was Sunita and Gopal's whole life; nearly all of their possessions fit into this room. The bed was in the corner beside the door, and Sunita lay there, nursing Isaac. Timothy averted his eyes. Gopal sat on the floor with Beema, their own baby, now six months old. Gopal held his hand out and waved for Timothy to sit. There was a plastic chair, but Timothy slid down a space of bare wall, sitting on the floor with his knees up, his head resting on them. He was far beyond politeness, beyond pretending. Sunita and Gopal didn't seem to need it from him. Timothy imagined himself with a paintbrush and a bucket of fresh paint, making the stained walls clean. The only sound in the tiny room came from Beema, the baby girl. Night had fallen. The room was dim. One light bulb strained at the shadows in the corners.

Gopal called through the open door, and his mother tottered in and began to make Timothy a cup of chai.

"No, no, thank you," Timothy said.

His protests were ineffective. Gopal made the Indian tamping motion, his hand pushing down on the air, like dribbling a basketball. *No problem no problem.* Timothy would have a cup of chai, there was no way around it. The quiet rolled up and over him, its purple slant shadowing the room as night billowed in through the door. He heard mutterings from the old woman who was making the chai. She was dwarfed by the wool shawl that enveloped her. Gopal spoke softly to his wife, she replied just as softly, laying Isaac in the corner of the bed, standing. She walked to her baby and picked her up, rubbed her cheek on the little girl's face. Timothy averted his eyes again. The tenderness between the two of them made his throat ache.

The old woman handed him his tea. He sipped it, moved it around in his mouth. It was sweet, very sweet. He stood up, holding the steel cup of chai, careful not to touch the hot cup on its base. He walked to look at the baby, his baby, on the bed. It lay with its arms flung up, elbows at right angles, asleep. Timothy waited to recognize it, to feel like its father. The feeling didn't come.

CHAPTER 4

When he woke, it was dark and early. He had the sick feeling that came from waking up and realizing all over again that Isabel was dead. Someone was pounding at his door. When he opened it, Sunita was standing with Isaac in her arms, her face creased in a frown.

"You take," she said.

Timothy held his arms out for the baby. Since he was born, he had been sleeping in Sunita's bed so she could nurse him in the night if she needed to. The baby was quiet, but its eyes were like bright buttons in its face. It didn't seem sleepy at all. As Timothy held it close, it turned its head, rooted around like a little animal, full of involuntary movements, needy. Timothy found the baby confusing. He was tired. Sleep came late, his dreams kept startling him awake and he lay on the hard bed, staring into the dark. Inside there was rage and pain that sparkled like getting hit in the face and seeing stars. He was afraid even to touch the feelings, afraid of an explosion. He walked the baby back and forth in the courtyard until it finally drifted to sleep as the sky grew light. He lay the little baby on his bed and curled up next to it, asleep as soon as he lay down.

Throughout the day, Sunita took the baby to feed him as she usually did, but that afternoon, Gopal showed up at his open door with a small gas cylinder in his hands. He passed it to Timothy, who took it and looked at it. It was heavy, with a single burner perched on the top that made it a cooking unit.

"What is this?" Timothy asked.

Gopal only gestured at it and nodded, leaning on the door frame, smiling and lingering for a while in the waning golden light of the afternoon, his face handsome and lined, though his eyes were tired. After a few minutes, he left. Immediately Sunita appeared, her shawl tied back from her face and hanging down her back. She had a fresh smear of colored powder on her forehead, between her eyes, showing she had finished making the *pujas*, the devotions Hindus made at their shrines. She was worked up.

"I can't feed the baby anymore, Tim Ji," she said, her high, thin voice cracking over the words. "It is eight days already, and my milk is not enough. I am tired."

Timothy realized what he hadn't before. The gas burner, now sitting in one corner of the room had a purpose. Oh. He sat on the bed, his arms like rubber. Sunita bustled into the room, pulled out the bag with the formula and bottles in it. *Sure, he would be fine.* She told him what she knew of the formula, which wasn't anything. It sounded like she was making it all up.

She glanced once or twice at Isaac on the bed.

"Okay, Tim Bhaiya? Okay?"

"Okay."

He squatted beside the burner and poured water from the five-liter jug into the small steel pot, then lit the gas. Isaac cried on the bed while Timothy waited for the water to get warm. Under the fierce blanket of sound, it seemed to take forever for the water to warm. He seemed to cry more than other babies Timothy had seen. Timothy wondered if he was angry that he had no mother.

He picked the baby up. He was tiny, with black hair and a red face, tiny arms and legs.

"You are eight days old," Timothy told him.

The water was boiling—too hot. Timothy lay Isaac back on the bed. He screamed. Timothy read the back of the formula tin, which thankfully had English instructions. *Blah blah blah teaspoons, blah blah blah water.* He pried the lid off and dug a spoon in, dumped it in the pot.

When he added the water, the formula was too hot. He added cool water, tested it again. Now the temperature was okay, but it tasted terrible. He added more powder, mixed it again, poured it from the pot into the bottle, sloshing it in seven different directions. He closed the bottle and shook it, scooted himself back on the bed until he could lean against the wall. He picked his son up and tried to say soothing things to him. The sound of the baby's crying echoed off the walls. Timothy wedged the baby into his elbow and tried to put the bottle nipple into his mouth. The baby spat it out and turned his head away, screaming even louder. A small puddle of formula wobbled on his chin, then dripped into his red mouth. He blinked and missed half a beat of his wail, surprised. He turned and rooted around for more, but he was tilted too far, trying to suck on the inside of Timothy's arm. Timothy put the bottle down. He turned the baby the right way, picked the bottle up and tried to give it to him again. He couldn't quite get it. Timothy sighed a loud, frustrated sigh. He let the nipple rest beside the baby's mouth and Isaac turned and... somehow it was in his mouth and he sucked away at it.

It was completely quiet. Timothy felt relief like pain.

The baby closed his eyes as he ate. There weren't any tears on his face. Timothy wondered how he could cry without tears—it was like the whole baby became nothing but a wail and now as fiercely as he had been a wail, he was contentment. He sucked at the bottle with his eyes closed. Soon he was asleep. Timothy put the baby to his shoulder and patted the tiny back. The midwife had told him he should always wake the baby if he fell asleep too quickly while he was eating, but Timothy was happy for him to sleep. After a long time of patting, Isaac let out a huge burp. Timothy felt hot liquid cascading down his back. He yelped and it frightened the baby.

"No, no," Timothy said, as Isaac started to cry. "Shhhhhh. It's all right."

He laid Isaac down on the bed and pulled the baby's shirt off. He pulled his own shirt off as well. He curled next to Isaac and pulled the blanket over them both. He tucked Isaac close so that their skin was touching and put the bottle nipple near the baby's mouth again. After four or five tries, Isaac had it. He barely got three sucks out of it before he was asleep again. This time Timothy didn't burp him. He propped the bottle against the wall, and tucked the blankets away from the sleeping baby's face. He settled his head onto his pillow and closed his eyes.

Later, he woke up and blinked. The lightbulb was still on and Timothy was soaking wet. The baby was wetter. It appeared that the cloth diaper the baby wore was useless. Outside, the sky was a greenish black. Isaac was grunting and turning his face from side to side with his little mouth open, trying to latch onto something—anything. Timothy pushed the blanket off of them. It was chilly and the cold air made the baby gasp and cry. Timothy patted around until he found his phone. Two o'clock. *You've got to be kidding,* he thought. Sunita's exhaustion was making more sense. He pulled himself out of bed and rubbed at his face, then started to warm the water for the bottle over the rusty cylinder. Isaac cried harder on the bed.

"Shhhh," Timothy said, walking back to the bed to change the baby's diaper. It was unbelievable. When Timothy opened it, he wanted to put the sheet back over it and pretend he didn't see anything. It seemed that the baby had pooped mustard of a quantity that wasn't humanly possible.

"But you have such a tiny body," Timothy said. "How did you do that?"

He looked down and saw that it was also all over him and the bed sheet and he didn't even have a shower in his room. The shower he used was across the courtyard and there was no way he was walking out there in the middle of the night. He threw things around until he found the baby wipes and got to work, wiping the mustard poo off the baby's skin. A hot shower would be heaven, he thought, but he shrugged the thought away and tied a new cloth diaper on the baby.

Digging around in a pile of clothing, he found a one-piece fuzzy piece of clothing for the baby. His body was so funny, with skinny little arms and legs and such a round stomach. He was red-faced now and angry, screaming for food. It was hard to pull his arms through the arm holes of the suit. Timothy felt like he was going to bend something the wrong way or pull too hard. When he was done, the baby looked like a fuzzy little worm.

"Hold on," Timothy said to the screaming baby. He made a fresh bottle, putting less formula inside than the last time, so it wouldn't be wasted. The midwife had made him promise to make a new bottle every feeding and not to give the baby the leftovers of old bottles. It was ready, he had tested it for warmth and taste, and he was just about to scoop the baby up when he looked down and saw that his pants were still soaked and the bed was still wet.

"Hold up, little bear!" he said to the kid, who was still crying. God. Squalling. In under a minute he had kicked his clothes off and pulled pants and a long-sleeved shirt on. He was shivering a bit, it really was cold in the room. He picked Isaac up, pulled the sheet off the bed one-handed, and threw the top bed sheet onto the bottom. Done. The baby was back in the crook of Timothy's elbow. He took the bottle quickly.

"You learn fast," Timothy said. He felt a rush of pride, but sadness and loneliness were right on its heels. He rubbed at his forehead and closed his eyes. His throat ached. He heard the wind in the corn and it sounded like waves, reminding him of the ocean that he grew up next to. He wondered if he would ever see it again, or see any of those soft places of mild sunlight. India was a hard place with no extra padding. The bed was hard, the plastic chairs, the rickshaws, the floor. He hadn't found softness in a long time. He hurt, all through. His back ached from hunching over and holding the baby. His butt hurt from the hard bed. His clothes were in a pile on the floor; there was a half-drunk bottle of formula in the corner; there were wipes in the pail, water and formula slopped by the gas cylinder. His mother would be horrified. Timothy was horrified too, but how could he clean up with the baby's scream like an air raid in the mountain valley. *Why do people do this?* he thought. *What's all the fuss about babies?*

He still hadn't told his mother that Isabel had died. His mother had given birth to five kids at home, with her mother, husband, and midwife lingering nearby. She sang during her labors. Timothy was never invited into the birth room—his mother was very private— but he heard through the closed door. The family had a little farm on Vancouver Island, in British Columbia, Canada. Timothy lived there all his life until he left for India and the earth seemed to flip around until the sky was underneath him, like the sea—everything he thought he had known about the world proving to be untrue in this alien country.

Growing up, the farm had been the whole world to him. It was only a family farm, since his dad's real job was carpentry. Timothy's mom did sell eggs— Timothy fetched the egg containers and ran them out to the people in cars who would stop to buy them— and she was always cooking or baking or gardening. The kids ate like half-starved wild beasts and then scrambled into every tree they could find, swinging in and out of the barns and inventing worlds and galaxies in their heads. Timothy's father and uncle owned a carpentry business together, making custom kitchens and bathrooms. Timothy's uncle and aunt lived on the same piece of land as Timothy's family, their house just visible from Timothy's kitchen window. It was across one of the ponds that were like mirrors all around the land. You could get to Timothy's uncle's house by going around the pond or by walking over the bridge, stopping to drop stones in the water on the way. The four cousins were all boys who came and pulled Timothy away to play war games in the stand of birches north of the pond. They had a favorite game to play on the bridge itself, hanging over the edge of the railing to see who could hang the farthest without falling in. The game always ended with a splash and a lot of laughter. Timothy was often the one who came home wet after they played, his jeans and hair streaming water.

He played with his sister, Sarah, as well. Sarah was eleven months younger than him, nearly his twin, and early on the boy cousins liked to play "boy against girl" games, but after a while of Timothy sticking up for her, they discovered that Sarah was really good at devising traps and doors and even boats out of fallen wood and driftwood that they hauled back from the beach. She used ivy as rope and sap as glue for traps that never caught anything, but looked awesome. The six of them were pirates, they were kings and queens, they were pioneers. A few years after Sarah was born, Timothy's mother started having babies again. Three more boys were born in the family, making Sarah the only girl in a giant extended family of boys. It had been an incredible place to grow up, he knew now. Because he lived on an island, he was always confident, somewhere in a small, subconscious part of his brain, that he could travel in any direction to find the ocean. Always until this moment, marooned in the mountains in a small cold room with a tiny baby.

He lifted the baby to his shoulder and began to thump gently between his shoulder blades. He swallowed hard, two, three times. He thought of his mother and closed his eyes to imagine her, but her image seemed so distant. She was always thin and very tall. She had filled out some in middle age, but she was still so straight and tanned. He imagined her standing in the garden with that big hat on her head, when she could remember to wear it, her blond hair all threaded with grey, her eyes when they looked at him clear as water. As a person she was more light-hearted than Timothy ever had been— joyful and easy-going. She never worried too much about mess or clutter, was incredibly absent-minded, and loved the beach more than any place in the world, more, even, than the garden.

She couldn't understand what Timothy was doing in India. Breaking free, he had told her when he left home, and then there he was, free and alone, and even he didn't know why he was still there. The boy cousins would have been shocked if they saw him sitting on the hard bed feeding a baby. They weren't the type to want to wander the world. Two of them were in business with his dad and Uncle Jeff. Two were still in school. Timothy's Uncle Jeff was the business mind of the carpentry business. Timothy's dad was the designer and made the cabinetry himself.

In junior high, when Timothy started playing the flute, the four cousins frowned over it, discussed him being a flute-playing boy with arms crossed over their chests. They came to an agreement and decided to rough up anyone who teased him. Timothy was gifted and went farther and farther with his instrument, rather than it being a short-lived obsession as his father had hoped. He so impressed the bored band teacher at his school that the teacher began to give him extra lessons, always with a sort of awed surprise, as though he couldn't believe Timothy actually existed.

Timothy eventually decided to major in music in university. All during junior high and high school, he played the flute and he ran. He ran 5k and 10k races, he played music and read books, and that was his life. He and Sarah stayed up into the summer nights, long after the little boys had gone to bed, sitting on the front porch his father had added to the house a few years earlier. Timothy played classical, but also played flute adaptations of Radiohead and Bob Dylan while Sarah drew page after page of sketches. If she was working on a painting, she pulled out her easel, pastels and oils, turned the bright outdoor lights on and complained about the way they changed the colors, frowning over her work, always so focused. When they leapt off cliffs into the cold rivers in the summer, she checked the rocks from every angle until she found the best place to dive from, and then she flew like a cormorant, tucking her feathers in to stab the water almost without a ripple. Before starting a painting, she made at least twenty sketches. He had never been as focused as she was. He was a wanderer even in music, threading his way through the space of notes and chords without a clear direction.

Timothy thought about the frantic blinking messages he was sure were in his inbox, shimmering with anxiety. He hadn't charged his phone, it sat with its screen dark, unused, in his backpack. Sometime in the next days, he would have to plug it in and make a call to them to tell them that Isabel had died. They felt so far away. He didn't want to bother them with it. He felt responsible, that they would be angry with him, even though he could tell himself rationally that it was ridiculous.

After a few minutes of patting Isaac, Timothy heard a small but satisfying burp. It was dry. Timothy used the corner of his shirt to wipe a tiny bit of formula out of the corner of the baby's mouth.

"Good baby," he said, as he settled Isaac beside him on the bed. "Talented baby."

He got up to switch off the light before they slept again. He lay down, made a little hammock for the baby with his arm. He pleaded silently with the kid, *please go to sleep quickly*. The baby rustled his legs for a while, and then there was quiet.

CHAPTER 5

Prema had come to India for freedom, but it seemed she was thwarted at every turn. She explained this to her father on the phone, standing in the corridor of her uncle's house in Pathankot, Punjab, desperately needing privacy and feeling close to tears. She took a deep breath and tried to stay calm and rational. She knew rationality was what would sway him, not crying or making threats.

"You're right," he told her. If she closed her eyes she could picture his office in Vancouver, Canada. She felt a wave of homesickness. "You need to take a trip," he said. "Go to the south, see some of the beautiful Indian sights. You need to do some more investigation before you come home. I know they're terrible, they boss me around too—"

"It's not that they're terrible," Prema broke in. She couldn't explain the closed-in feeling.

"No, I know," her father said. "Trust me, I know exactly how you feel. But it's time for you to spread your wings a little. Go fly away, but take a train. It's better." Prema felt her heart lift and she broke into a smile. This was why she had called him. Her uncle was not going to allow her to get on the train herself; it wasn't done as a single woman in India. She knew the only thing she could do was talk to her daddy and hope that if she laid out her feelings he would come to his own conclusions. She could almost taste her freedom. But he was still talking. "I spent a great deal of my life on the train. I had to, traveling to see relatives. Much of the Indian population spends great amounts of time on the train. Clacking along." He made a familiar noise, the sucking of his tongue against his teeth. Prema was very used to that sound, as her parents used it to describe anything from mild irritation, to thoughtfulness, to disgust. "You be careful, though."

"I will, Daddy!" she said. "I promise."

"Give the phone to your uncle."

Taya Ji and Tayi Ji, her uncle and aunt, were going to be angry with him, angry with her. She wanted to ride Sleeper Class, the train car with the open windows and nothing but bars for protection, with people flowing in and out as the train moved along. There were thieves and men who took advantage if you weren't careful. She knew all of this, but she still wanted to go. Her family in India was horrified. They were well off, they wouldn't dream of taking a Sleeper Class train unless it was an absolute necessity.

"Take the AC car," Uncle had said. "Two tier or three, it doesn't matter."

"No, tell her to take the plane," Auntie said. "There are cheap flights and all."

Prema knew what she wanted. But in the end, to get it, she had to make a phone call home and have her father intervene. She quietly crept out of the room as her uncle began shouting into her phone. She made an "Oops!" face at the maid who was cleaning the floor in wide circles as she squatted next to a bucket with a rag. The maid smiled a small smile and kept cleaning.

Prema was in India on a quest for spirituality and for ancestry. She planned to spend several months traveling India alone. She wanted to reclaim the part of herself that belonged to the homeland. She was supposed to be free, with room to move—it was the whole point of being alone—to discover the part of her that everyone else in her family seemed to reject in themselves. Her parents? They didn't actually reject being from India, but they did seem contented and secure in Canada, like they didn't feel any of the longing she had for the Motherland she'd never known. Prema's mother and auntie talked of little more than India, but if they missed it so much why didn't they return more often?

Prema was Canadian-born—brought into the world in a gleaming hospital in Vancouver. Her father's hospital, actually. He worked on the seventh floor, in orthopedic surgery, and when his wife went into labor he skipped down four floors, excited to see the new daughter he was waiting for. He had one son and one daughter already, and Prema would be the last, he thought contentedly as he swung the doors open and found his wife in the last stages of labor. He'd already had the vasectomy. They were unheard of in India, since it was the woman's job to see to her reproductive frugality, but he was a modern man, a successful Punjabi doctor in Canada, ready for any new innovation. That was what he told all the relatives, for years and years, as well as Prema's elementary school, junior high, and high school friends. Dr. Singh's vasectomy was famous in the west side of Vancouver.

Prema had grown up with her older brother and sister, riding bikes around the neighborhood, playing video games and going to school with clothes that were perfectly in style. Her siblings squirmed with embarrassment when the family turned Indian in public, if anyone packed a tiffin, or if the old aunties were there, waddling in bright, colorful *shalwar kameez*, holding each other tightly by the arms. But Prema always thought the aunties looked wonderful. She loved the Punjabi suits the uncles wore. And at her eldest cousin's wedding, she thought her mother looked like a queen in her sari, thick vermillion in her hair part, bangles nearly to her elbows.

In college, Prema took to wearing saris herself. She lurked around the shops in Vancouver's Little India, flipping through stiff silks and simple cottons. She remade herself, literally wrapping herself in what her father had given up by moving to Canada in his early twenties with his young bride. The only part of wearing saris that she didn't like was trying to walk past her mother and her Bhua Ji, her father's sister and mother's best friend, without being seen. The two of them always sat in the living room, right near the front door, tea in front of them on the short table. They raised their well-manicured eyebrows at her in unison.

"Prema, dear," her mother would ask, as Prema tried to slither out of their line of sight. "What are you doing?"

"Going to school, Mom!"

"What are you wearing?"

"Come have some chai," her aunt would add. "Don't bother the girl about what she's wearing," she would say to Prema's mother in a voice that Prema could hear clearly.

"I'm wearing a sari, Mom. Why shouldn't I?"

"Well, your blouse is not matched properly, for one thing. And, look Leela, she's folded it all wrong."

And the two of them in their house dresses hurried out to the hallway where she still stood with the front door open.

"Mummy, just let me wear it the way I want to," she protested, as they unwound her and her mother placed a couple of fingers over her bra to tug the sari blouse farther down.

"This is not possible, Prema. You cannot wear sari any which way you please."

"She needs a pin, Bhabi," her aunt murmured.

"I'm late for class," she said. But neither of them listened and she stood there, waiting for the pin, flicking at her auntie's glass bangles idly while she was tucked and folded and clucked over. She seethed as she missed the bus by inches. *See*, she muttered in her head. *This is why I need to go to India.* She said it to all of them, but silently. She said it in the dark as she was falling asleep.

When she could get out of the house without encountering anyone—on the mornings her mother drank tea at Bhua Ji's house—she still wore saris. She hennaed her hands and feet, on her own, which didn't look as good as she thought it was going to. In her third year of college, she shaved her head and wore something that looked a little like a monk's outfit, and this caused her mother and aunt to flutter their hands over their faces and cry, and her father to stop and look at her in the hallway, really look at her, and ask if everything was all right.

No, everything is not all right, she wanted to say. But she didn't want to hurt her father's feelings. He was part of the problem. He, his wife, his sister and her husband had all converted to Christianity when they were in their twenties, and to the many Punjabis in Vancouver, this meant they were practically non-Indians. They were the only family Prema knew who didn't have a picture of Guru Nanak over the mantel, the only family who didn't go to temple and went to church, instead. When she was really little, she didn't know the difference. Recently, she had stopped going, and it wasn't a matter of belief so much as culture, as she tried to explain to her dad, standing there on the stairs. She could smell her mother cooking downstairs, frying onions in *ghee*.

"I don't get why I'm the only one who sees it, Dad," she said. "It's like you're eating cardboard instead of a good supper. You think it's modern, but it's just ugly, it has no roots where we have roots. There are chairs in rows, for goodness sake. Why can't we sit on the floor?"

"I think you romanticize it," he replied, holding one hand on the wall above his head, stretching it. He had begun having some pain in his surgery arm, which worried him, and even now, talking to him, Prema could tell that the lines in between his eyebrows had nothing to do with her. She sighed.

"It?"

"India."

She didn't know what to say to him. She felt angry about how his heart had left his country, how all their hearts had. How so many of her friends, her cousins, her brother and sister said, "I would never be able to live in India," and then laughed, because with their births they were assured they would never have to. They were all soft.

"Prema," her father said. "If you really want to go, you can go. Take a break from school. I won't try to stop you."

And about eight months later, she made her way through security and boarded a plane, ready, really ready for the missing pieces of her life to fall into place. Ready for all of the belonging that she had been waiting for. Ready to put the image of her weeping mother and Bhua Ji behind her.

Her uncle and aunt were angry, as she'd thought they would be, but they showed it in funny ways, transferring their anger to Prema's father, as though he was to blame for her train trip. The day she came home with her ticket safely tucked away in the zipper pouch of her hiking backpack, Tayi Ji silently piled enough food for six people onto her plate. Prema watched in alarm as the pile grew, raising her eyebrows at her cousin, Pooja, who sat across the table from her. Pooja swallowed a laugh, which sent her into a coughing fit.

"Excuse yourself, Pooja," her mother said, then went on as Pooja stumbled from the table. "What I cannot understand is what he expects her to eat, Pati," she said to her husband, Prema's uncle. "No one in the south knows how to make a decent *dahi curry*. The food is falling down from lack of flavor." She bustled back into the kitchen.

Prema's uncle raised his voice to answer her. "Are you planning to feed her enough this evening to last the following months?" he asked his wife. Tayi Ji popped back into the room, her face furious. Prema sank down in her chair and put a spoonful of dahi curry and rice into her mouth. She closed her eyes at the burst of flavor. Her aunt was an excellent cook. In her uncle and aunt's household they used spoons because they were wealthy and it showed that they were rich, maybe? Prema didn't know. But at their first meal together, she had been proud to show off her skill at eating with her hands and she had been stared down by her auntie, as though she was shoveling cockroaches into her mouth, rather than rice and curry. Since then, she used a spoon.

"Do you know anyone in the south?" her uncle asked her now.

She swallowed and sipped at her water.

"No," she said. "I'm going to travel to a few cities, then go to Goa. I'm sure I'll meet some nice people."

"What, people you meet on the train only? Strangers? Foreigners?" her auntie asked.

Prema shrugged, and her aunt hurried around the table and hugged Prema close.

"Her father has spoken," Prema's uncle said, with a shrug that meant Vijay Singh had clearly lost his mind.

At mention of Prema's father, Tayi Ji went into a tirade of Punjabi which Prema only slightly followed. She tuned them out then, imagining herself on an Indian train, meeting new people, eating with her hands, seeing things she had only ever imagined.

CHAPTER 6

Tomorrow is the first day of September, Timothy realized one morning. The fog was draped around the valley below, cradling the little houses and large boulders on the hillside. Above, the sky was clear. Perhaps the fog would burn off and the clouds disappear in a rush of steam. His baby was six weeks old. Timothy shivered. It was chilly. He took his chai from the bench in Sunita's room and sat on the cold stone step outside with his thoughts and his baby. He had swaddled Isaac in blankets and hoped he was warm enough. A man passed on the path, heading up the mountain with three donkeys in front of him. He waved a stick beside their faces to keep them moving, shouting choppy words. "Hoy! Chal! Ha!" The donkeys were carrying heavy loads, with vegetables tied to them, bottles of water in boxes, even a gas cylinder for a stove. Timothy felt badly for the donkey with the heavy gas cylinder. Rough luck. They climbed all the way past him, jingling, their hooves making sharp clacks on the rocks.

Timothy and the baby had managed the first night together, and then they had survived the night after that, and all the ones after, until this day. Isaac was already six weeks old. Timothy sipped chai. Isaac opened his eyes without warning and stared at him. Timothy put his cup of chai down and tucked the blanket a little closer around the baby's face. He wiped at Isaac's rumpled mouth, curved so much like Isabel's. The baby rooted at the blanket, turning his face for a breast, squinting his eyes shut because of the bright sky overhead. Timothy didn't see any of his own face in the baby; he could only see Isabel.

Three weeks ago he had finally called his parents. He plugged in his phone, turned it on, and discovered that his mother had been in a panic and had done everything to find him but fly to India. She even called the embassy, which didn't help since he'd never bothered to register with the embassy and they couldn't know where he was.

"Isabel died after she had the baby," he said. He didn't know how to make the words come out of his mouth. They were flat, toneless, quiet.

The silence was so deep and long he thought she'd fallen into a pit, walking out in the pasture with her cell phone. He could picture it, he could almost smell summer in Canada when he heard the sound of cows around her, but the picture in his head was wrong. Something was wrong with the cows. He frowned. What did their cows look like again? He'd been gone two years: it was a long time.

"Three weeks ago," he added.

Still she didn't speak. Moments later, his dad was on the phone, clearing his throat to get ready to speak. *His* voice had Timothy smelling new wood in the shop in the middle of the farm, where saws and lathes were barely ever at rest.

"Son?"

"Dad." He started crying then.

"Are you all right?"

"No, no I'm not."

He had figured out what was wrong with the cows in his head. They were Indian cows, Brahmins with their humps, rather than the long-lashed Jerseys that Timothy's family had.

In the background, he heard his mother's voice.

"What about the baby?"

"He's fine," Timothy said. "The baby is fine."

They had talked twice since that first call. His mother wouldn't let his silence go.

"I still can't believe that you didn't call us," she had said during their last call. Timothy felt uncomfortable. He didn't know what to say. He didn't really know why he didn't call them either, except that whenever he thought of it, his stomach tightened into a gigantic knot.

"Should I come?" she wanted to know.

"No, I'll be fine. You shouldn't come." He couldn't see what good it would do.

"Can you come home?" she asked.

"Probably soon," he had said, turning the cooker off, since he was finishing up with sterilizing bottles. She said a lot more, about how he was in shock, that he sounded strange. That she was really, really sorry, and then her voice was thick and wobbly. He tried hard to listen, to not drift into daydreams with his mother's voice in his ear. It was so hard to focus these days, the sleepless nights all piled up until he felt like he'd been tired forever. "But," he interrupted her, "I'm going on a bit of a journey with the baby. We're going to see some other places in India before we come home."

She hadn't thought that was a good idea, of course. But he knew what he needed. He murmured his understanding, and they had hung up after making a date to talk again in a few days' time.

He finished his chai, then tied Isaac into the baby carrier on his chest and walked down the monkey path that threaded through the forest toward McLeod Ganj, the official Indian town of the Tibetan Government in Exile, on his way to buy a train ticket. He chose the monkey path to show the monkeys to the baby, who seemed more alert these days. But Isaac was held tight against Timothy's chest, and he fell asleep almost right away. The monkeys jumped around from tree to tree for Timothy's eyes alone.

It felt as though he was heading to the big city, after all those weeks of being constrained to his side of the mountain. In reality, McLeod Ganj was small and congested, with tour buses that held their breath to squeeze through too-narrow streets, losing side-view mirrors as they scraped past unwieldy buildings. Coming out of the forest and into the city forced him to blink and gather himself.

He walked down to the temple road to buy a train ticket from a travel agent. The office was quiet and the agent, an efficient woman in her early twenties like him, managed a small miracle as she booked a ticket for the last week in September. Aside from the quotas reserved for elderly people, tourists, and birds, it was the last ticket on that train. He thanked her and left the shop.

He stood staring at the ticket in his hand, then was distracted by a parade of robed Tibetan Buddhist monks, coiling downhill in a dark red stream, heading toward the temple. One young monk dropped his prayer beads and an older monk paused to pick them up with a flash of saffron as his robes opened. He gently dropped the *mali* into the younger monk's hands and they continued on their way.

The buildings in the town were built of concrete and stone, and at any spot Timothy could see prayer flags twisting overhead—brightly colored ones as well as flags that were old and faded and looked as though they had withstood a few years of monsoon. Strong Tibetan incense filled the air, accompanied by recorded chanting that echoed off the buildings as sellers attempted to lure the many tourists into buying a version of their chanting CD. An old Tibetan woman sat on a folding chair, dressed in a traditional dress and striped apron. She manipulated her prayer beads without looking at them, chanting under her breath, while at the shop next to her a Kashmiri man selling carpets and shawls gazed at the street over her head, eyes open for rich-looking tourists. His eyes skipped right over Timothy.

Timothy was in a hurry. He wanted to get home before Isaac woke up, now that the ticket had been purchased so quickly. He could avoid having to feed him his bottle on the side of the street, or beside the prayer wheels, or on the path beside the monkeys.

A young beggar woman approached him, hand out, baby on her hip.

"Brother, something. Baby hungry."

He shook his head at her, but she followed him, repeating her four words until after a while he dug in his pocket for a five-rupee coin. She took it between her first finger and thumb without comment and dropped it into a drawstring bag she wore around her neck. She turned and walked away to look for someone else on her never-ending search.

Timothy was haunted by questions lately, some of them hovering around his mind vaguely without ever becoming clear, some of them easier to define. Why was he born in Canada and these people born here? Why had he had a mother when his son didn't? The questions pressed in on him in the early hours of the morning, when his mind was vulnerable and confused.

The sky didn't seem to be the same color in India and Canada. In his memories, his island was sparkling, green and blue, the sunlight like sparks on the water. In India, the edges of the world were tinged with brown and saffron. Red was draped over the landscape in a transparent haze. The sun was a cadmium ball before it dropped into the horizon. Nothing matched with what he had always known to be true.

The street was busy with auto-rickshaws, cars, motorcycles, cows and people. Dogs darted in and out of the kicking feet of people. Timothy walked a path the size of a tightrope on the right-hand side of the street, ignoring the calls of people selling wall hangings, jewelry, beads. He dodged into a tiny grocery store to buy milk, bread, bananas, and formula. The baby wrap kept Isaac tight against him as he squeezed through little aisles. He put the groceries into the backpack he carried and held the book in his left hand, the dozen eggs he bought in his right.

He reached the end of the street, where he could choose to turn and go down the mountain to the big city of Dharamsala or climb farther up into the remote hills for his own village of Dharamkot. He looked around for an auto rickshaw, feeling exhausted and cold. He shivered, watching the shiny bare heads of nuns and monks who hurried past him. His own head was warm, despite the chilly day, because of his thick ropes of dreadlocks, looped and fixed on top of his head.

"Dharamkot?" he asked, leaning into an auto rickshaw, a small black three-wheeled vehicle which was open in the front.

"Yes," the rickshaw *wallah* replied. They wrangled over the price cheerfully, and then they were on their way.

Timothy set his groceries down on the seat and held Isaac tightly against him, trying to absorb the bumps of the road into his own thighs and spine so the road would rock the baby gently and keep him asleep. The baby squirmed for a minute as he felt the change in motion, then relaxed into a limp bundle again, his small red mouth falling open. The road was lacy with potholes. Judging by what Timothy could see of the sky, rain would come soon. He hoped the sky would stay closed until they were in the house. After that, it could do what it wanted.

They passed a Tibetan monk whose skirt brushed the muddy ground. The monk pulled a fistful of his robe to lift the hem above the old smashed vegetables scattered on the path. They had fallen from a vegetable cart and been left alone, there, the leaves and stems of *ghobi*, bits of *palak* that shed away from the tight bunches. In this season, the vegetables looked tired and limp. Timothy was tempted by the round glowing pomegranates on one vegetable cart, but needed to beat the rain, so he didn't stop. A few melons were squashed and spread over the road. A cow stood, stupefied, directly in the path of the rickshaw, as though this was a pasture from her genetic memory. The rickshaw driver leaned on the horn, waiting for her to move, edging ever closer. Across the way, a bull bellowed, wanting her. She knew what the bellow meant. She whirled and clattered away, down the hill, nearly knocking over an old Tibetan woman toiling up the hill.

Timothy used to believe that the world was a romantic place. He didn't know what he had thought he would find in India, but he hadn't expected this explosion of suffering. Everywhere he looked, there it was. It was in the missing hands of the lepers, the crow that had its head taken by a rat, the puppies scrounging in the trash. He knew the truth when he saw it. The world was war, grief, blood. People constructed the slightest scrapings of beauty over the top of this sorrow. Even sex was painful, even sex could lead to grief; a female dog eluding the pack.

Surely he would go crazy, thinking this way. He took a deep breath, leaned his head against the seat, pulling it back up when the rickshaw dove into a pothole with violence.

Isabel would have helped him. She lived in India for a long time, she had a different perspective. "It is not new," she would tell him. "The suffering was here in the world all the time. Your home was in a very nice part of this earth."

It hadn't comforted him, really, when she said things like that. The fact that he had lived his peaceful childhood in a delusion that it was "normal" was enough to throw him off, to tilt him under the world as it slid and crumpled around him. But Isabel had lived simply, with joy in tiny things. She was a cool lake, something you fixed your eyes on when everything else was dry and tasted like dust.

His dreadlocks were hitting the roof on the side of the rickshaw. They had grown so much in the past year, as though Indian air was a super growth fertilizer for them. They were halfway down his back now, catching on things when he wore them down. He wouldn't cut his hair, though. He didn't know if he would ever cut it now. It held too much of her, the beautiful year all entwined into it, like a history.

Timothy looked at his sleeping baby as the rickshaw continued up the broken road, up, up into the mountains. This boy had entered the world of suffering without even meaning to. Maybe he had been waiting for her—he knew her womb and was waiting for her arms— but instead found a skinny boy who could hardly bear to lead him farther into the big screw-up called life.

They arrived, finally, at the point where the road ended and the rickshaw couldn't go any farther. Timothy paid the driver and set out to walk the rest of the way. He was on the far curve of the mountain and he made his way into the valley along the stone path toward the center where his house was, almost parallel on the hillside. The fog was drifting in, white paste oozing around the trees, heavy and dense. He could barely see the people coming across the mountain toward him. He reached the steps to the house and saw Gopal coming down with the cow, bringing her in from grazing. When Timothy saw Gopal's smile, some of the ink on the edges of his vision dissolved. He had been so alone with dark thoughts these weeks, but Gopal and Sunita had helped him journey out of the murkiness of his grief. Moving the cows or goats, cooking the rice, making the chai, washing the laundry. Sometimes Sunita sang while she washed the clothes—she charged less to do it by hand, though she always put the diapers in the machine—and Timothy lay back on his bed and let the sound wash over him. People had so many little things that kept them moving along.

And other travelers had been so kind. People who had known Isabel, people who hadn't. They came, bringing him food or Bhagsu cakes, the little chocolate and caramel squares with a shortbread crust. They sat in his room, on the floor or the bed, played with Isaac. One older man from Austria came every day, his white hair wild around his face. Sam Baba. And every day he brought a gold box with two pieces of Bhagsu cake in it, one for him and one for Timothy. Timothy made cups of tea, and the two of them sat and drank tea and ate the sweet cakes, neither quite sure what to say. Timothy liked the old man; he was simple and kind. He lived on the other side of the canyon and he walked an incredible distance to get to Timothy. He spent his days walking from hill to hill. Having left his other life behind in Austria, he walked and kept strong on Himalayan air.

Then there were the sisters from Mexico City. The sisters had names that always escaped him, though there were only two of them. They were young and lovely, one with dreadlocks coiled around her head, the other with a shaved head from her meditations in the Buddhist meditation center. They sat together on the bed when they came, murmuring over Isaac, taking turns holding him, each impatient to get to her turn. They didn't look like any Mexicans Timothy had ever met. They were tall and blond, though they had dusky skin, brilliant green eyes. When he remarked on this, the one with the shaved head laughed, her eyes crinkling in a gorgeous way that made him look away.

"You are familiar with Mexican Indians," she said. "But Mexico was colonized by Spanish, remember? In Mexico City our Spanish roots are still very strong." He smiled, embarrassed by what he still didn't know about the world.

And there were the three Israeli families who lived nearby, filling a guesthouse and sharing a kitchen. Whenever he passed by the tall building they lived in, they were sitting outside, the kids spilling over rocks and into holes. They called to him to *come over, eat something!* The mothers all looked at Isaac as though they would like to pick him up and breastfeed him immediately. They sat Timothy down, passed him salad made with tomatoes and cucumbers, gave him bread and hummus, talked over him in Hebrew while he kept a close eye on Isaac, so near to the whirling children, the mother that held him clutching him tightly while shouting instructions to her kids. Timothy didn't understand, but he understood the tone: "Stop throwing rocks, don't do that to your sister, gentle near the baby."

He saw these people and many others. They reminded him of life, they kept him out of the deep hole of despair, but still he felt like there was a wall between where he stood and where they were. It was transparent—he saw them shouting to him from the other side.

I can't quite hear you, he tried to tell them. *I'm far away.*

They reached their room and Timothy walked to the stove to heat the water for Isaac's bottle. Isaac still hadn't woken up, so Timothy peeked into the carrier to make sure he was still breathing, and found the baby gazing up at him.

"What?" he said. "How long have you been awake?"

The baby stuck his bottom lip out, the saddest face, as though he would cry.

"No, no. Shhhhh. It's coming."

Isaac was rounder in the face now. Sunita and Saasiji wouldn't stop smushing his cheeks, pinching them and then kissing their fingers. He was cute. The black sheaf of hair, the dark eyes. Small boneless nose with nostrils that flared so alarmingly when he screamed. Little red mouth. It was straight from his mother's face, that mouth.

Timothy was such a pro at bottle making by that time that it was ready within minutes. He took it to the bed like usual, unrolled the baby from the mass of stretchy fabric, and sighed with relief. They were both slightly damp with sweat. Isaac took the bottle wildly, shaking it like a deer that was about to get away.

Sometimes Timothy dreamed of driving. He was in a car from childhood, the old station wagon that was already old enough when they bought it to draw looks on the highway. His father was driving, but they were on the right hand side of the road, auto rickshaws weaving straight toward them. It was all wrong, the landscape flashed between the unpaved roads above McLeod Ganj and their country roads on the island. They avoided disaster only narrowly, again and again. When Timothy woke up, he was sweaty and nauseous. This was how he felt whenever he thought of home. Something had skidded in parts of his brain, crumpling it like paper. Until it felt right again, he knew he couldn't go back.

But he couldn't stay at Sunita's house, either, because the police had started pawing around, scraping at the old ground of Isabel's death, wondering if they could get anything out of it, whether money could end up in their pockets.

Sunita was nervous. So nervous she shook when she talked about it.

"You must leave," she told Timothy last week.

She was convinced that they would try to take Isaac. Timothy wanted to ignore her, but when he saw the worry on Gopal's face, he decided to believe them. He had the train ticket that would carry him away. Not toward the airport, not toward home, but farther into India, into the very heart. He had a score to settle with this country.

There were so many questions.

He had married Isabel. He made her marry him, though certainly she wanted to. He couldn't imagine being any more in love than he was at that moment, when he woke up after the first time with Isabel beside him, curled like a small girl, tiny crow's feet at her eyes like small fans, her eyes tightly shut in sleep.

He knelt down when he asked her. He had known her two weeks, she was his first girlfriend. She laughed and gasped, then cried. They had a tiny ceremony with the old Indian couple who lived down the street. The old woman reached down and tied Timothy's lungi and Isabel's sari together. It didn't take much to convince Isabel to be his wife. She was like a flower, and some of the men in her life hadn't treated her gently. Timothy hated them then and he hated them still, with a burning that seared the inside of his stomach.

Isaac was finished with the bottle. He burped after about a hundred pats on the back, and the two of them walked back outside. The rain clouds passed without even letting their water go. The evening was clear as glass. The air was beautiful and cold when it was like this, when the fog lifted, or before it settled. Sometimes there was frost on the ground in the morning, now that it was so close to September. Timothy got a shawl from the house, sat on the ground with Isaac, and watched the stars come out.

*

It seemed like no time passed before Isaac was two months old and it was the evening before their train journey. Timothy was taking Isaac to Varanasi first, to visit a place of old fears and try to reconcile them. He had to stay in India, though his mother really didn't understand.

"Why can't you come home?" she asked him on the phone. She was still only forty-five, having had Timothy at age twenty, and she was a person who had never been crippled by fear, who had barreled over all the obstacles in her life. "You must be running out of savings by now. You should come home before you get into trouble."

"If I leave," Timothy told her, "Isabel will be swallowed up by all the rest of it. She'll be gone."

She was silent.

"Can you try to understand?" he asked.

"I can try," she said. "Send some more pictures, please. I loved the one of Isaac with the little hat on."

He did send pictures, right away so he wouldn't forget. He scrolled through the pictures on his phone, then picked a couple and messaged them to his mother. They struggled through the weak signal, but eventually they went through, and he got a message from his mom right away: THANK YOU!

When Isaac was asleep for the night, Timothy stood on a plastic chair and pulled the nails out of the pictures on the walls, then began to pack them and the other decorations away. He had put Isabel's pictures up during a storm and a power cut, a few days after he first started bottle-feeding Isaac.

He paused for a moment, holding the wooden elephant with the marigolds carved around its ears, then rolled everything up and wrapped it all in the tablecloth, and he put the whole package carefully in his backpack. He sat down and leafed through Isabel's journal, sitting with his back against the wall, smoothing the pages with his palm. He could read bits here and there, where he understood a couple words of French, or where she had written in English. He saw the word Timothy scattered everywhere in the last two thirds of the book. In the last third, the word *bebé*, over and over.

"That's you," Timothy whispered to his sleeping son. He put the journal next to him on the pillow and went to sleep.

In the morning, Timothy stood up and put on a jacket and a scarf. He walked to the door and opened it. The sky was still completely dark, it was still before five. He hadn't slept well, dreading the trip ahead. He could see the outlines of shapes against the few lights that were on, but not much else. He sat on the step to wait for the light. He was packed and ready, his strange bottle system for the first train ready in a new backpack. There were enough bottles for the trip, with pre-measured formula already in them and a giant bottle of water to fill each one when it was time.

He went through the rest of the morning in a dream cloud, finally walking to Sunita's room for a last chai. Sunita banged the chai pot onto the counter with tears in her eyes. This place, this little village was where Timothy's future had been ripped from him, and another, alien, future given. Still, he would miss this mountain. He would miss playing family with Sunita and Gopal, chai in the morning, Sunita bossing him around.

When it was time and they said goodbye, Sunita wiped her tears with the back of her hand again and again, quickly, as though she was not crying, as though she didn't want to admit it. She pulled her shawl over her head and around her face. Gopal gripped Timothy's shoulder with a strong hand. Timothy felt that he had been nothing but misfortune to them, but they were treating him like a brother. Gopal's mother put colored powder on Timothy's forehead, touched his head, and said a few words in Hindi that Timothy did not understand, but that touched him deeply anyway. He reached down and touched her feet, knowing that this was what the young did for the old in India, not sure if it was okay for him to do, but wanting to anyway.

He stood. "Thank you," he said, again and again, like he forgot all the other words. "I'll be back," he said, not knowing if it would turn out to be true. He got in the taxi that would take him to the train station, five hours away. He waved through the windows until they rounded a curve and couldn't see the little family anymore.

PART 2

CHAPTER 7

Prema arrived on the train platform in Pathankhot with excitement building in her stomach, launching off her sides like wild birds, bigger than butterflies. Tayi Ji leaned on her neck, brimming with the kind of love Prema tried to receive but that truly made her squirmy. Her aunt was crying, of all things. She straightened and squeezed Prema's hands and cheeks, bangles tinkling. She put one hand on Prema's waist, giving it a squeeze for good measure.

"I am not happy," Tayi Ji said.

Prema smiled. There was no one in the world like her aunt. Prema picked up her backpack, but her uncle called a porter over. Prema looked at the porter, then looked at her aunt and uncle and sighed. She handed the backpack to him because what could she do? The old, thin coolie with cheekbones like knives wrapped his *gumcha* around his damp head and easily lifted her rather heavy pack onto the padding formed by the red scarf. He stood, silently waiting, while she adjusted her *dupatta* and gave the last kisses.

"Why are you going this way?" Tayi Ji demanded.

"Hush," Prema's uncle, her Taya Ji, said to his wife. "Her father has given consent."

Prema wanted to say something now, something along the lines of, "I'll be fine," but she had learned that words like that were the gateway to another round of fierce Punjabi/English sentences, crying, and recriminations. She glanced toward the train. It would leave without her if she didn't go now, and she would be left with all the squeezing. Taya Ji didn't want to leave their SUV in the parking lot, so they were saying goodbye at the entrance to the train station instead of the platform.

"Please say goodbye to Pooja for me," she said. Pooja had wanted to come, but Tayi Ji wouldn't allow it. Prema thought her auntie believed traveling on trains alone was catching, though Prema thought there was nothing her very proper cousin would have rather done less.

On the platform, she found that her train was already waiting, holding its breath. The coolie walked straight to her car and climbed aboard. He located her seat and gestured for her to sit, tucking her bag beneath the bench. Taya Ji had paid him, but the slender man waited for a tip. Prema put a ten-rupee note in his hand. He looked up, eyes wide, then left quickly, and she realized that once again she had tipped too much.

She sat down, playing with the ends of her *dupatta*. The old coolie hadn't look like he should have been strong enough to lift her backpack, not with all the books she had packed. She was surprised when a young white traveler with dreadlocks entered her compartment. Somehow she hadn't thought that foreign travelers like her would be on the train. She hid her surprise. She was good at hiding things. She had to be, growing up like she did, in so many worlds, in the world of school, of church, of the Sikh kids, the few Hindu kids, all the others, the non-Indians, the artsy kids she hung around with in high school, dressed like gypsies, her mother would say, wrinkling her nose. In high school there were the art and photography rooms, and the dark room, which was almost never used anymore because they had digital SLRs by then. But Prema still loved the darkroom, the way it was the perfect place to hide and make photos come out of nothing, she loved the squeak of the chemicals on her fingers, the way she blinked a lot when she stepped out into the light.

She missed Canada. She had been in India for two months already, strictly with family, practicing the Indian side of her nature with difficulty. It wasn't the food. It wasn't the hygiene. (And although the streets had trash scattered for miles along them, she could have eaten off Tayi Ji's floor.) It was the feeling of being absorbed by India, of fading away like a leaf on a brightly patterned carpet. She felt that she couldn't even tell who she was anymore. She hadn't been there long before it all started to choke her--the lack of open space, the way people always asked her why her short hair looked the way it did, people fingering her lip ring, suggesting they could take it out for her (*much more beautiful*). Crowds everywhere, having to wear a *dupatta* across her chest and around her shoulders on a hot day because she needed to be a good girl. All the noise. Not being able to go anywhere alone unless she ran away without telling anyone and then submitting to being scolded later. Some of what she saw was beautiful. It stunned her, made her cry for no reason whatsoever, because it felt like something she should know and understand, but didn't. She recognized other things, things from her own life; she saw her aunts and uncles from Canada, her parents, in the streets and marketplaces. She saw them everywhere, she was becoming acquainted with all the things that made up who they were. But what she never found anywhere, no matter how hard she looked, was herself.

The boy walked into the compartment she had already settled herself into and he had to duck to avoid hitting his head. He had one of those heads of thick dreadlocks that she always found incredibly attractive in college. Brown dreads, a little curly at the ends. She had barely admitted to herself that she liked them, back then. She was too busy figuring out colonialism and the collective shame of non-resident Indians, who, rather than being proud of their rich, old heritage and beautiful accented English, were busy trying to assimilate. To fade away, fade into a foreign society. Everyone was being torn apart, Prema would tell her Hindi teacher after class. The traditional parents, the kids trying to attain distance from them even while they loved their big amazing families. And there was the large, unwieldy homeland at their backs, a whole block of cultures and religions nobody understood.

She was too busy being emphatic to admit that of all the people she met, she liked the free-spirited hippie artists in class best of all.

He lifted his legs to avoid knocking into the legs of the auntie by the aisle and walked to the window seat, opposite her, which for some reason was being avoided, and heaved his backpack onto the seat.

"Sorry," he said, to no one in particular, and she knew. The accent, the long "O" in "sorry," the unnecessary apology, the mark of the traveling Canadian to anyone who was familiar enough to recognize it. He was from where she was from.

She watched him from behind her book, one hand tapping against her cheek. He had been there for maybe ten minutes before she realized that *he had a baby tied to his chest.*

She looked at his face again. He had light blue eyes and he was looking out toward the window. He watched the water sellers on the platform and glanced at the five-liter jug of water at his feet three or four times, then bent over to tip it and check the level of water still inside. There were deep shadows under his eyes, and he looked as if he could use more weight; his skin was stretched over his face. His dreadlocks were looped and tucked in some way that made half of them stick up at the crown of his head, while half of them cascaded around his shoulders. He had a beard that was in between short and long. Lips that were tucked in at the corners. Sharp, wide cheekbones. He looked at her then, and she quickly glanced back down at her book.

The train began to move. She looked up at the train station rolling by. This was it. Her first train in India.

Her father had prevailed and now the train rolled out of the station, leaving the water sellers and beggars behind, leaving the dirty, urine-soaked station and the large rats. When her father told stories of train travel in his youth she had formed a picture in her head of what it would be like. The station hadn't looked like the picture she had made. Everything in her head had been shinier, somehow. But there were families propped up against each other on the floor, and that was beautiful, children leaning in their mother's laps. And the train gathering speed. Now they were out of the station and quickly into the lowland plains of the province. Rolling away, across the great country toward New Delhi.

She glanced at the boy again. His eyes were turned to the plains they were passing as well, the remnants of the city, until the clicking of the train swept them away from even the outer edges and there were only fields and trees, villages with small concrete houses. It was early morning, still cool, with the sun not yet strong enough to blast the color out of the landscape. Prema saw gentle colors, orange and blue and green. It had rained the night before and the trees were still wet.

The baby in the wrap on the boy's chest began to squirm, and he gently pulled it out of the carrier. The Tibetan woman beside Prema jumped in surprise. She had been earnestly knitting and Prema supposed she hadn't seen the small arm peeking out of the cloth tied to the boy's chest. The first thing Prema noticed was how young the baby was. It couldn't be much older than a month or two. The boy grabbed his backpack and quickly unzipped it, pulling a bottle out, one-handed. He began to feed the baby, who let his or her eyes drift shut.

"That's a good idea," Prema said.

The boy looked up, startled.

She went on. "Bringing the bottles already prepared."

He looked at her for a minute. "Wow, where are you from?" he asked.

"Vancouver," she said. With others, she would have said 'Canada', but she was almost sure he was Canadian as well.

"Really? That's amazing. I'm from the Island."

"We're neighbors," she said. "I can see you have quite a story. I'm just not sure whether it's polite to ask about it."

He smiled and looked down at the baby. His face grew sad. He looked out through the bars and she wondered whether she should ask her question again, or just drop it, but then he spoke.

"What do you want to know?" he asked.

Prema thought it should have been obvious. She closed her book and sat forward with her chin on her hand.

"Is the baby your brother or sister?"

His eyes grew large. He adjusted the baby, making his head more secure, propped at a better angle. "This is my son." He glanced at the baby, as if checking to see if it was true. "Isaac."

When he said it, Prema felt a swooping in her stomach, like something inevitable and sad and terrifying had entered the train car.

"Oh," she said. "You look very young."

His lips tightened. He smoothed the baby's forehead with his free hand, licked his finger and tried to scrub a piece of food or dirt off. Prema felt the woman beside her stiffen. She glanced at her. The woman's face was shocked, watching Timothy groom the tiny baby on a train car. She noticed Prema looking at her and spoke to her in Hindi: "Why is the baby out without his mother when he is so young?"

Prema told her she didn't know and looked back at the boy. He was watching the two of them silently. The train moved steadily on.

"His mother died in childbirth," the boy said.

Prema gasped and put one hand over her mouth. Tears sprang to her eyes. She had always cried easily.

"I'm so sorry," she said. "That's horrible."

He nodded with tears in his own eyes. Prema softly told the Tibetan auntie that the baby's mother was dead. A line formed between her eyes as she clicked her needles along the row of stitches. Prema heard her begin to chant softly in Tibetan.

"I'm Prema," she said to the boy.

He nodded and swallowed, rubbing his hand over his face. "Timothy," he said. "And this is Isaac."

"It's nice to meet you both," she said.

"You too."

The air outside the window was bleached now, by the sun, full of dust. Prema adjusted her *dupatta*, red today, and sat back against her seat, wondering if she could take the conversation farther. The boy picked his baby up and held him to his shoulder to burp him. The bottle looked as though it might have teetered and fallen, so Prema leaned forward to catch it, just as the baby gave an impossibly large burp. She laughed and sat back. Timothy smiled at her, then checked his shoulder and made a face.

"That was liquid," he said. "Will you hold him for a minute?"

She took him without really knowing where to put her hands. Her oldest cousin sister in Canada was pregnant, but she was the first of the cousins and Prema hadn't held many babies this small. When she was younger, she had her own babysitting club, like the books, but no one would join and she was the only member. The young Indian mothers loved her, she would work just to sit in their houses and hold their babies, eat dinner over there, watch TV. That was a long time ago. In between then and now there was university–a giant childless institution of thought and study. She sat back and looked at the baby. He had very black hair; she could almost have mistaken him for a light-skinned Indian child.

Timothy was digging in the small bag at his feet. He pulled out a long white *gumcha* to wipe his shoulder, and Prema noticed all the bottles in the bag with pre-measured formula in them. Ready for water, she supposed.

"Wow, you're even more prepared than I thought," she said.

He squatted down on the floor to shove his big backpack under the seat. It was too fat, but he smushed the top down with his hands and punched it under. He sat back on his heels, red-faced, and looked up at her.

"I can't take credit," he said. "My friend Sunita thought of it."

Prema wondered about his friend Sunita as Timothy reached out to take his baby back and tucked him in the crook of his arm. The baby looked around with wide eyes, then crossed them. Prema heard the chai man in the corridor. Ah!

"Do you want a chai?" she asked, delighted. Her India dream was coming together now. Chai on the train. The air on her cheeks hot, like oven air.

Timothy looked up, frowning. He looked at her strangely for a minute, then said, "A chai would be nice."

"Do chai, Bhaiya," Prema said to the chai *wallah* as he skirted around the post and appeared in their compartment. She took the two tiny steaming paper cups and held one in each hand. "How do you do this?" she asked Timothy.

"You can set it there," he said, nodding at the little table between them. "I'll get it when it's not so hot."

He watched her as she set the cup on the table and she nearly fumbled and dropped it. But she didn't, and only a few drops spilled. "Sorry," she muttered.

"Do you live here?" he asked.

"Me? No," she said. "I live in Vancouver. Just visiting. I've been with my auntie and uncle and cousins in Punjab." She took a sip of chai and nearly scalded her tongue right out of her mouth. "Now I'm running away, thank God," she said, when she recovered.

"You didn't like it?" The baby was nodding off in Timothy's arms. Timothy was sitting cross-legged on the bench, his sandals sitting on the train floor. His eyes were very blue, he held himself very quietly.

"No, I liked it. I love them, you know. They're amazing. I'm so lucky to have a big amazing Indian family. But they are... intense. There's so much attention on me, even more than at home." She shivered. "It was hard to get away, to be honest. They didn't want me traveling alone like this. It's not done here." She moved her shoulders in circles, took her *dupatta* off them and dropped it in her lap. "But I did get away. My father finally told them to let me be."

"Wow, it really bothered them?"

"I know, right? It was the Sleeper Class thing. But I wanted the Sleeper Class—the stories of my father. You know? When it's so hot on the train that you the air will stop your breath and then it stops in the desert and sits on the track for hours and you feel like you'll die because there's no breeze, and then it starts up again and it's heaven?"

Timothy looked at her for a minute, then glanced down at Isaac and adjusted the baby's head so it rested in the crook of his elbow.

"I don't think I'm looking forward to it as much as you are," he said, then smiled, his eyes crinkling at the corners. When he smiled, she could see that he was funny and nice, but also very, very sad.

"I can help, if you need help," she said. She drank the rest of her chai and crumpled her paper cup.

"Thanks," he said.

"Where are you headed now?" she asked.

"Ah... Varanasi," he said.

"Really? I'm going there too."

"Oh, so we'll see each other there," he said.

She nodded, her eyes on the sleeping baby. Timothy cupped the baby's face with one hand and left his hand there. He turned to look out the window, so she did too. They were in open fields. Men and women bent in half while they harvested wheat. They were evenly spread throughout the rows, like chess pieces, colored flecks in the dun-colored fields, wrapped in saris or lungis with bright scarves on their heads to protect them from the sun and keep dust out of their hair.

Prema had the feeling that she was the only person in the world who had ever really noticed the field workers, how they looked almost like birds with their dipping and swaying. Beside them, egrets hopped and ate the bugs the workers' long scythe strokes exposed to the sun. One woman stood and wiped her forehead with the back of one hand, then folded her body back in, swung her scythe. She was out of sight quickly as the train barreled past her. Prema put her face to the bars on the window and tried to see back to her, but they were in a new field, with more people who circled around a large sheaf of wheat, and more egrets swooping in and landing, their long necks moving quickly in their search for bugs, beaks flashing into the field near the workers.

Another field. A worker swung the scythe and startled an egret, and a whole flock of birds lifted and there! The sky was filled with white birds. They followed the train and suddenly Prema's eyes were filled with tears.

CHAPTER 8

Timothy reached Varanasi a couple days later. He and Prema had waved goodbye to each other in the Delhi train station, she hurrying off into the bright sunlight surrounding the taxis outside the station. She was planning to visit more family in Delhi. Timothy immediately boarded a train to Varanasi. The next morning, exhausted from the long trip, he checked into a guesthouse in the old city. For the next few days he split his time between feeding Isaac and wandering the tiny streets of the ancient city and the steps to the river—those that weren't still covered in mud. The noise of the pressure washers ground into the air as men worked to clear the mud that was left on the steps when the river receded after the monsoon.

One morning, when Isaac had fussed so much Timothy's jaw felt permanently clenched, Timothy took his baby for a ride on a cycle-rickshaw, a man-powered tricycle with a seat. The other rickshaw passengers stared at them and Timothy stared back. Men and women in brightly colored clothes, sitting tall on the slanting seats like proud eagles with strong brows and intense eyes. Timothy felt that their eyes burned into him, a tall gangly kid with dreadlocks piled on his head. A man who looked like a sadhu, but had a tiny baby wrapped up on his chest.

There were kites strung in the wires above his head. He tilted his head back to see them more clearly. Hundreds of kites were caught like flies in an electrical web. And the wires! It was a ceiling of wires. Flightless kites in powerless wires, in this city that so rarely had constant power. When he looked down again, Isaac was looking up as well, but staring only at Timothy. The baby gave him a startled, involuntary smile as their eyes met. Timothy smiled back.

Isaac was just over two months old. It was tentative, the thing that had developed between Timothy and the baby, a sort of uneasy peace. Timothy wasn't sure what it was. He was unsure of many things, of what it meant to be related to someone, of what it meant to love. When Isabel died, all his definitions seemed to unravel. He had lost so much more than only a person; he truly didn't know how the world was supposed to work anymore.

Should he like Isaac more than he liked other people? They had bonded, but the baby was changeable and irrational and sometimes when Timothy was exhausted he wondered why God didn't make kids more consistent if he wanted people to take care of them.

Timothy leaned down to smell Isaac's head. The smell of his head was one perfect thing in a difficult place. Varanasi was beautiful and painful at once, an ancient Hindu city on the banks of the Ganga, the holiest river in India. Timothy wondered if Isaac would see it in his dreams for the rest of his life. Would Isaac remember the ancient maharaja-era buildings, the gentle orange rays of the rising sun that stroked the water, the towers and people who came every morning to bathe? Would he remember how the river was tired and overused, like so much of the earth?

When Timothy had arrived with Isaac, a traveler told him that if he really wanted the baby to be strong, he should feed him Ganga water in his bottle. Timothy sat on the *ghats*, the steps to the river, with the man, and watched a dozen water buffalo take a bath, a small boy poo on the steps, a crowd of laundry *wallahs* wash saris and stretch them out on the *ghats* to dry.

"No... I don't think so," he had said. The man had looked at him with pity. Timothy wondered later whether Isaac would blame him one day, for not feeding him Ganga water. If Isaac ended up in a dead-end job, would he blame it on missing out on the blessing of holy river water? He hoped not.

The rickshaw was taking them nowhere. Isaac had been fussy all night, but up here, above the crowds, he was quiet, so they simply rode. Timothy thought the baby liked to preside over the city. The two of them sat, drifting on a slow tide of rickshaws and motorcycles in thick traffic. The two of them with nowhere to go. The sari shops were lined up in one steady row on this street, saris glittering and rippling in a faint, brief breeze.

"Look at the saris, Isaac," Timothy said.

The baby stared at his father's hairline. He preferred staring at Timothy's face over most things, mostly at his hairline, like he couldn't quite control his eyes enough to direct them to Timothy's eyes.

Timothy stepped off the rickshaw at the entrance to the main ghat, adjusting the baby wrap so Isaac was sitting comfortably. He had tried once to tie the baby so he was facing outward and could see, but while they walked, so many hands reached for Isaac's face, he never did it again. Instead, he told Isaac what he saw, keeping up a running commentary, lapsing occasionally into a dark, deep silence.

He stopped to buy a small clay bowl of *mithai dahi*, sweet yogurt, from the *dahi wallah*. The street was full of strong smells that made his breakfast experience unusual. He could smell the old milk in the gutter, fire, incense, something rotten, and cow shit farther along the path. He ate the thick, sweet yogurt with a wooden stick, scooping it out of the rough, unfired clay bowl, which was meant for only one use.

He thanked the *dahi wallah*, as he always did, and the *dahi wallah* threw his bowl into a corner, where it broke and slid down, leaving a trail of white yogurt on the wall, which was blackened with smoke from many fires. Eventually someone would come and clear the broken bits of pottery away.

Timothy started walking, Isaac still staring upward, at his hairline, or at the tallest corners of the buildings; the lines where they met the sky. The old city was made of buildings that had grown so close together over the years that the narrow winding alleyways between them were very, very tiny. The gullies, they were called, narrow enough that if a herd of water buffalo came along, Timothy knew by experience to pin himself to the wall to avoid being knocked over. The buffalo were so solid, so heavy, that a human was like a rubbery bowling pin in front of their innocent, dumb faces.

"Listen, son," he said. "It's not even a contest with a water buffalo. Always give way."

His very next step was into a large pile of buffalo shit. In the city an unending parade of cows and buffalo had created an obstacle course made of large piles of poo on stones that became very slippery. Timothy had never been very good at watching his feet when he walked, so it was hard to avoid stepping in it sometimes.

He felt assailed by it, the shit in his flip flop, the kind of thing that could defeat him on what was otherwise a promising day, now that the fussiness of the morning had passed. He took some deep breaths while Isaac watched the sky, and decided to go down to the river to wash his foot. He took long steps down the hill toward the *ghats*, past the flower sellers, avoiding the eyes of the beggars.

Isaac was not the reason Timothy felt assailed by life. It was death and the off-balance way his baby was being parented, and the feeling he had of being too young, too stupid. Those things had taken their turns landing blows, and Mother India had laid a good one on him, too.

He walked down the steps toward the torn umbrellas that were like colorful pointed stars in the morning light. The *ghats* were wild and teeming with people. Just down the river, men were frantically burning bodies alongside the local fauna: dogs, crows, and cows that roamed the steps, often chased away but always milling around the humans. Varanasi was the most auspicious place for a Hindu to be cremated, and the burning *ghats* sent up black smoke all day and all night long. *Ghat* children skipped over the steps without care, selling flowers and candles to the thousands of pilgrims, their parents nowhere in sight. Timothy held Isaac closer, one arm around the baby wrap. He descended to the bottom step and dipped his foot into the water, swishing it back and forth until it was clean. He watched the filth lift off of his foot, dissipating with the rest of the detritus that ended up in the river—the ashes, the dead dogs, the human remains.

After Timothy and Isabel had found each other and married in Rajasthan's bright desert, she had brought him to Varanasi, city of lights. Benaras was the old name for it, thick and steamy with spirits. The place terrified Timothy. His newly found love was so big and all encompassing. The heaviness of human sounds and smells in Varanasi was too much for him in his extra-sensitive state. It nearly did him in. She brought him here after the desert she said, because they needed water. He didn't feel that he needed anything or would ever need anything again, but he was willing to go wherever she wanted to go.

"The river," she had said. "We need the Ganga."

She forgot to tell him that the river was a place to die. That all of Hindu India longs to be cremated at the Ganga's edge. She didn't understand his fear and avoidance, his horror of the burning *ghats*. They had arrived in the city early one morning after a night on the train. The train was cold, icy wind whipping in through the open windows. Timothy had barely slept, unable to get to his backpack for more clothes on the crowded train. They walked out of the station into an Indian morning with the scent of burning dung in the air, and the kaleidoscope of smells that characterized India, incense on one breeze, frying food on the next, urine on the next. A never-ending pummeling of the senses. The desert had been quiet in comparison to Varanasi's stir. Timothy blinked in the light after the dark station.

Isabel knew where she wanted to stay. She seemed excited at being in the city, humming under her skin. Timothy hovered beside her, almost a foot taller than her, while she talked to the rickshaw drivers.

"Atman Guesthouse," she said. "Kedar Ghat."

They were led to an auto rickshaw that beetled in the early sun. Timothy and Isabel slid themselves in, hunched with their backpacks in the small space. The driver started the tiny three-wheeled vehicle up and zipped through the city, weaving in and out of oncoming traffic effortlessly. He steered around cows and men on bicycles. Timothy began counting cows on the street. He reached twenty before giving up. At one point the rickshaw driver pulled to the side of the road and two men jumped in on either side of him, lacing their arms behind his shoulders. There wasn't enough room on the seat for more than half of their butts, but they balanced perfectly. They spoke loudly, the three of them, gossiping in Hindi, Timothy assumed. The two men jumped out at another point in the road, the rickshaw pausing only long enough to let them leap clear.

Timothy glanced at Isabel to see what she thought, but she was gazing into the street, a soft smile on her face. She had these eyes with darker skin on the rims, like natural eyeliner. She had a fine, dark fuzz, on her temples that Timothy thought was beautiful. He squeezed her hand and she looked at him and smiled, her dimples like deep holes in her cheeks.

"Was that a free ride on our dime?" he asked.

She smiled a little wider, but nudged his ankle with her foot. "Shhhh."

He peered out of the rickshaw, past her swinging earrings, trying to get a sense of Varanasi. The sun was getting stronger. Men swirled streams of some dough into hot oil, then fished them out with a sieve. Men squatted outside shops, or leaned on walls in what seemed like exaggerated poses. There were thin men in *lungis* with *gumchas* on their heads, men in long, seventies-style slacks, slightly flared at the bottoms. Men everywhere leaned on one another, draped themselves over one another's shoulders, stood looking at traffic with arms looped around one another's necks. They sauntered down the street, holding hands.

"Where are all the women?" Timothy asked.

Isabel snorted. "At home, making *roti*," she said. "Cooking food, washing clothes."

"Oh, there's a woman!" Timothy said.

"You sometimes see the women," she said. "But you will see many more men."

The rickshaw took a steep dive into what looked like an alcove, but opened up into an alley. They buzzed along until they couldn't go any farther.

"Now we walk," Isabel said.

They paid the driver and left the rickshaw, backpacks on again. Timothy was lightheaded from lack of sleep. Everything was violent, the sun, the dust, the people everywhere. It crashed around his ears, shaking his brain. Finally they stepped out of the small alleyway and into a quiet courtyard. A man jumped up from a plastic chair.

"*Namaste*, Didi!" he said. "Welcome!"

"*Namaste*, Uncle," Isabel replied, smiling. "*Aap keise hai?*" How are you?

"*Tik hai, tik hai.* Come, come! Your room is prepared."

"Ah... the same one?"

"Of course. Why not?" he said.

The man spoke with a large wad of *paan*, the mixture of betel nut and spices that men and some women around India chewed perpetually, wedged into his lower lip. He had to tilt his head back to get his words out without losing the wad, slightly muffled words at that. He pulled out a large book, adjusted a pair of glasses that perched on his face. He was short and round, with intriguing tufts of hair over his ears and in his ears. He wore a button-down shirt and lungi, with an impressive belly rounding his shirt out over the lungi.

Two handsome boys lounged against the wall, staring at Isabel. Timothy was doing his best to stare back, let them know that it wasn't cool to gawk at her, but they completely ignored him. The proprietor barked a few sharp orders around the wad of *paan*, and the boys scrambled for the bags. He turned his head to the left and sent a stream of red juice through his teeth into a potted plant by his foot. Timothy watched the betel nut juice soaking into the leaves and dirt of the plant, nearly missing his wife as she left the courtyard and headed for the stairs.

"Timothy!" she called.

He ran to catch up.

"You are very fortunate," the proprietor said. "The man who was in this room moved out only this very morning."

"Oh, I am blessed," Isabel said. "I have a gift for rooms." She craned her head to see Timothy, trailing behind on the stairs, which were dark and narrow, *paan* stains spread along the walls. "Timothy," she said. "You must see this room. It is *incroyable*."

The uncle turned around, facing Timothy. "All the travelers are desiring this room," he said. "It is the very best in the city." He turned and kept climbing, huffing a little.

Timothy watched Isabel's ankles as they climbed the last set of stairs to the fourth floor. They came to a small door, where the hotel boys waited, panting and wiping their faces. The uncle made a big show of unlocking the door, then swept it open.

It was a small, ordinary room. There was a small double bed, barely big enough to hold two people, a shelf built into the wall, a table with two plastic chairs. It was like any other guesthouse room they'd ever been in. Timothy glanced at Isabel, but she kept moving, walking straight to one of the two large windows at the other end of the room.

"It is the view," she said, breathing her words like a prayer.

"Come to the front with your passports after you have refreshed yourselves," the uncle said, making another sweeping gesture at the tiny bathroom.

"Sure," Timothy said, seeing that Isabel was lost at the window.

The uncle turned and closed the door as he left, scattering the boys who were still standing at the entrance. Timothy went to stand beside Isabel. Outside, the Ganga was a brackish mass of waters piling on waters, pulling the remains of the city towards the far off sea. Tiny ripples on the surface winked in the sun.

Timothy had seen rivers. He had hiked in the Rocky Mountains, swum in the Gulf, fished the Fraser with a tiny campfire to roast the fish. This river didn't even seem like a cousin of the blue or green rushing water from his childhood. This river had so many human remains that it was no longer only a river. It had become human itself, a large, engorged human, hungry and tired.

This is what he thought, standing there, remembering all the things he had heard of this place, remembering that when he heard of this place he had decided never to come here. Isabel turned to him, her hair messy in its knot at the back of her neck. Her long dark eyebrows were raised at the corners.

"We are so blessed to have this view," she said.

Timothy watched her, absorbing her enthusiasm, but feeling none of his own. She turned back to the view and he put one hand on the back of her neck. He was troubled already. Shaky, unsteady. Something that had always held him together was being pulled out of him, the cotton innards of a rag doll. He had no doubt that the river could finish him off, could pick at his bones. He didn't feel blessed that they would have it there, breathing at them in the dark.

And it almost did finish him off, because three days later Isabel woke him up before dawn for an early morning boat tour of the river. They tiptoed down the stairs, to the courtyard and woke a sleepy boy to open the gate for them. Isabel tripped along the *ghats* ahead of Timothy in a long red skirt and black tunic. She had some kind of brown scarf, shot through with gold, wrapped around her twice to keep the chill off. Timothy followed his gypsy bride into the boat.

Just by knowing her, he was being turned inside out. His love for her had grown to fit the inside of his body perfectly, so that there wasn't room for anything else. He was uncomfortable around sorrow, death, the world of the river.

But there they were, stepping into the boat. As the boat *wallah* pushed off, the sun began to rise.

"Perfect," Isabel breathed, looking all around her with delight.

The boat man plunged his oar into the water, coaxed the boat along. Hundreds of people bathed at the river's edge, standing on the steps in saris and lungis, pouring water over themselves in libation, pouring water into the river. Timothy couldn't figure out what was happening to him, why the devotion he saw hurt him, why watching a woman make a lather out of soap and wash her arms and legs with it made tears come to his eyes.

Isabel caught sight of him and pressed her hand to her heart. Timothy didn't know what she imagined was happening to him, but on the train to the city she told him about Varanasi syndrome, about people losing their minds on the steps to the river.

"It becomes too much," she said. "They grow crazy. Too much, the gods, the people, the animals. They lose themselves in it."

Timothy felt that he was tipping, now. Careening toward the edge of losing it.

The orange light of the sun made the people unearthly. His breath came in shorter gasps. By this time the boat had traveled along the river far enough to be past the main *ghat* and close to the large burning *ghats*. Dead India on fire, ashes spread far along river banks, clinging to the steps, making its way to the ocean. Hindus looked for improved karma through this burning, for escape from the endless wheel, the *samsara* that kept them turning helplessly from one life into the next. They hoped for a better life next time, better chances. The ultimate hope was for the wheel to come to a halt, to finally rest. So all day the fires burned as old people and sick people died in the city, brought by their relatives from places near and far. The burning *wallahs*, the caste of men who did this all their lives, heaved the bodies onto piles of sticks and set them alight.

It took a long time to burn a body.

The boat *wallah* plunged one oar into the water and steered the boat right into the smoke.

Isabel saw it coming. She shook her head, hard.

"Naheen, Bhaiya!" she said.

But he ignored her and the boat moved into the space so close to death, right next to the piles of wood and ashes, where crows circled, wheeling deliriously overhead, fluttering to land and pull at flesh and take off again. A thin man jumped from a stone landing and thudded into their boat, landing like a crane.

"Namaste!" he said.

He launched into a tour guide's speech about cremation in the holy city. Isabel again tried to argue with him, telling him that they didn't want to hear it, but she finally grew quiet when she saw he wasn't paying any attention. He kept talking, his words rising and falling like the water lapping at the edges of the boat. They were caught there.

Timothy was trapped. A crowd of people stood on the platform, a little apart from the pile of wood and limbs that were burning, orange flame licking into flesh. The dead man was young. The burning had just started. Suddenly, a woman broke into the crowd, screaming. There was a scuffle. She collapsed and wailed and two men came, lifting her by an arm on each side. She fainted, and they dragged her away by the arms. A child with a shaved head stared with large eyes, then burst into tears, calling "Amma, amma!".

"Ah," the man who had invaded their boat said. "She has followed her husband down to the *ghats*. Women are not allowed at the burning *ghats*. This is why. It is not a time for screaming, but for peace."

The woman's head lolled as she was being half-carried, half-dragged away. Timothy couldn't look. He couldn't be there, watching. He stood. He turned and dove into the water to get away. The water was cool, not cold. It felt surprisingly clean. He came up flailing, on the side of the boat away from the burning ghat. In a couple of moments his old swimming skills came back to him, as though this river was no different from a river or lake in Canada.

There was a part of Timothy that wanted to swim down, all the way to the bottom, to just keep swimming down, but he turned. He used all those summer nights in the local pool, all those weeks away at the lake to propel him along the river, back to the main *ghat*. His chappals were gone. He felt like parts of him were being broken off, like his shoes. His money and passport soaking in the small bag he carried them in. Pieces of his identity, wet and soaking. Water streamed from his eyebrows over his eyes in sheets. He dove down again, kicking with all his might.

Under the water it was very quiet. A welcome quiet, the kind you don't want to end.

When he surfaced, he looked for a place on the steps to climb out. A spot opened up, somewhere there might be room for him. He aimed for it, swimming through rotting garlands of flowers.

When he reached the steps, he crawled out like a baby. He threw up on the bottom step, retching until nothing else would come out of him. The woman washing her clothes farther along looked horrified. He scooped water onto the step to wash his vomit away.

He crawled up to the third step and sat, shivering. Not because of the cold but because of the horror, the stink of death.

It was the sharp teeth come to find him. His grandfather falling down in a field one day, dead.

It was the summer he was twenty-two. Timothy's uncle and father had taken a tractor out to the field to bring his grandfather home. Timothy watched from a distance. It was a strange sight, the two men lifting a third, like a baby, his limbs dangling as they put him in the tractor.

His father was quiet for a long time after. At home, Timothy's Opa lay on the bed in the spare room as if he was sleeping, covered with a crocheted afghan. Timothy's Oma sobbed in a chair beside the bed. He sat beside her, holding her hand as she clutched his tightly. He had always been a sensitive kid, now he was a sensitive man. He breathed her sadness right in, watched as she climbed up onto the bed beside his Opa, lay right there like she could put her heartbeat into his silence.

The next day they took him. A hearse and a coffin, cool corners of a hole in the earth. The scraping of a shovel against stones.

I don't know this, he thought as he sat there on the *ghats*. I don't know this public grief, the heat of fire. People grieving in the sun, no hair left on their heads. I don't know this.

This is what he knew of death: you fold it up and put it away, you hide it under the earth. He didn't know the brilliant flare of fire and sun, orange cloths draping the body, watching every part burned away.

When Isabel finally found him, he quickly wiped at the tears on his face.

"How can you leave me alone?" she said. She stood on a step above him, frowning, her arms crossed around her ribcage. She was beautiful and angry and sad. Timothy stared at her.

"You swim away and leave me with that horrible man."

"I had to," he said, beginning to feel angry. He could feel the heat in his face. "You brought me there. You knew what it would be like, but you still brought me."

"*Non*, I didn't know the boat man would do this thing."

She had draped her scarf around her head, now she put on her sunglasses. Timothy felt he couldn't see her properly. She waited on a step above him, and he slowly stood up so he didn't have to twist his neck to look at her.

"How could you not know?"

"All the boats don't visit the burning *ghat*, Timothy. You—you can't ever know what will happen here."

He shook his head, turned back to the river. It wasn't only death. It was knowing that everything was different than he had thought it was. The whole earth had shifted on its axis when Timothy arrived in India. He took it for granted, maybe everyone did, that some things were basically the same everywhere. But things were not the same and there was no telling what was real.

Isabel walked down to him and put a hand on his shoulder. He laid his cheek on her hand.

They walked up the steps slowly, surrounded by people, but alone together. Old women changed out of wet saris into dry ones, showing no concern for the moment when their breasts were bare to the sun. Babies splashed in their mothers' arms in the ashy river that had felt so clean. Saris were draped like banners across the *ghats*, drying in the knife-edged rays of the sun. The sun was no longer orange. It was a bright, burning yellow.

They took a cycle rickshaw back to their guesthouse. Timothy took a shower, ate a thali. He went to the room with the windows that opened to the river. He didn't come out for three days, except to eat. Isabel lay beside him in the bed, touching his face as he slept far too much. As soon as a train was open, they left for the north. They went to Manali first, with its crisp mountain peaks, then to Dharamsala, where Isaac was born.

Timothy had needed to come back to this city that almost undid him. The city that was filled with the things he didn't understand about the earth, that he didn't understand about India. He had tried to avoid the death and sorrow, but they caught up with him anyway, taking his wife from him forever. Maybe it was stupid to try to resolve it, but he had to try. He was a ghost in the ancient town, looking for redemption, for understanding in its stone walls.

CHAPTER 9

Prema woke early after her first night in Varanasi and left her guesthouse to meet Timothy at the chai stall. She had gone back and forth about whether to contact him when she arrived, but late in the afternoon she sent a text telling him she was there. After a couple of hours she got a text back; a picture of the chai stall, the place he sat every morning. "Assi Ghat," the text said. "You can't miss it." She met the early morning with its clang of metal roll-up doors as men threw water into the street and swept the dust and trash away from the front of their shops. The air was cool and fresh. She reached the steps to the river at the *ghat* with the sun barely above the earth. Assi Ghat was one of the last *ghats*—sections of steps leading from the river—before the city tapered away. The *ghats* were divided into territories: Assi Ghat, Kedar Ghat, Harishchandra Ghat. The old part of the city was oriented by the ghats; you knew where you were in relationship to them. Prema's guesthouse was in Assi Ghat, where many travelers stayed.

She spotted the chai *wallah* and walked to sit beside his stall on a high section of stairs, under the wall that held the city up and away from the river.

He greeted her and she ordered a chai in Hindi.

"Am I your first customer?" she asked.

"*Naheen*," he said, with a swift shake of his head. He pointed to a cow on a nearby stair. "She is always coming first."

After she met Timothy on the train, Prema had spent a week in Delhi, visiting cousins who lived in a fancy apartment with tall ceilings. Delhi had been tree-lined and restful after Taya Ji's house. Her cousins mostly left her alone, working during the day, when she had the house to herself, with only the maid moving quietly from room to room, sweeping and plumping pillows and rearranging the magazines that Prema's cousin Navital spread carefully across the coffee table. Prema was almost lonely after the clutter and noise of her uncle's house. She tried to make conversation with the maid, following her from room to room, practicing Hindi, asking questions about her life. The maid answered in short sentences and spoke an unfamiliar dialect Prema could barely understand. The maid was shy and nervous, pulling at her *pallu*, draping it over her head when she talked, putting her hand over her mouth when she smiled at some ridiculous thing Prema said to make her laugh.

Naval and Krishna took Prema out to nightclubs and fancy dinners. They all said goodbye nicely, but Prema thought that she would probably forget much of the visit within a year. Nothing had happened. No adventure had come her way.

She was only halfway through her first cup of chai when she spotted Timothy, tall, wiry with his dreadlocks looped on top of his head, and the baby carrier wrapped around him. Her heart sped up a bit and she cursed herself and this unexpected crush. She smoothed her hair, the section shaved up the side, her bangs that slanted across her forehead. She tugged on one brass earring and with that, there he was, standing in front of her, looking very sleepy. He smiled up at her, wiping at his eyes.

"*Ek chai, Bhaiya*," he said to the chai *wallah*, who poured the chai and then left his pot on the fire to peek into the cloth that was wrapped around Timothy.

"Sleeping," he said in English.

"Now he is," Timothy said. "He wouldn't go back to sleep last night, though. Kept me up for hours." He sat down, very carefully, beside Prema.

"You made it," he said, and she nodded. It did feel like she had made it. They sat there in silence while he drank his tea, faster than anyone she had ever seen before, and ordered another. She thought about her rich cousins in Delhi, and how much more comfortable she felt here with the simple chai *wallah* and Timothy with his sleeping baby. She felt pounds of tension rolling off her.

"How's it going with the little one?" she asked.

"He's fine. Not sleeping well these days. I think he's teething or something. But we have a routine."

"Yeah?"

"Yeah. When he's really awake in the morning—usually before the sun comes up—I feed and change him, then I come here to drink chai until he falls asleep. Except that he fell asleep on the way here this morning. And then he'll sleep for a long time and I can sit and drink about a million cups."

"Very quickly," she interjected.

He smiled, dimples forming in his cheeks, looking down at the second cup, which he had tossed back quickly. "Yeah, I like to drink it fast."

"Do you have a throat made of leather or something?"

"I used to drink hot water before I sang," he said. She lifted her eyebrows, wanting to go more into that, but he went on. "When he wakes up we walk back to our guesthouse," he pointed back down towards the big street in Assi Ghat, "it's just over there—and make him a bottle in the kitchen. I feed him in the courtyard while the cleaning *didis* pinch his cheeks. I tell him they're his Indian aunties..." he broke off, looking embarrassed. He turned toward Prema with those startling blue eyes. "Sorry, This is probably totally boring to you—"

"No, no! I like to hear about it. I've been curious about how you're making it work."

"I talk to very few adults these days. There are some travelers that I see around here, but they're all studying Indian classical music and have their heads all wrapped up in it. They wouldn't want to hear all the sorry details about bottles—" He frowned. "I wouldn't." He peered into the cloth that sheltered Isaac from the light of the rising sun. "Did I tell you that I'm a music major?"

Prema shook her head. What had happened to him? On the train he'd been mostly silent and tense, but the words were pouring out of him today.

"I am," he said. "I'm taking a 'break.'" He changed the subject quickly. "It's too hot in the day for us to be out much. I think we need to leave Varanasi soon, but we have a mission before we can go."

"Really?" Prema said. She caught the chai *wallah's* eye and held her finger up for one more chai.

"And another for me," Timothy said, laying his cup beside him.

The river flashed like a mirror in the bright sun. Soon the sun would be high over head, and this little stall in front of them wouldn't give shade anymore. She drank her cup of milky sweet tea, while Timothy tossed his back like a shot.

A cow approached them and Timothy leaned toward it. "This cow," he said, "is the friendliest cow in Varanasi." The cow put her head on Timothy's shoulder, then in his lap, almost pushing him over, rubbing her horns against his arm. Timothy asked for another cup of chai, then poured some out for the cow to drink. He scratched around her horns. She tried to put her nose in Isaac's face, but Timothy pushed her away gently. "Get your own baby," he said. Prema smiled as the cow slowly plodded down the steps toward the river.

"Come throw your cup," Timothy said to her then. He stood with their clay cups in his hand and Prema followed him to a large wall. He handed her a cup, then threw his against the wall, where it smashed into pieces. He nodded at her. "Your turn."

She threw hers and it smashed with a satisfying crunch. She smiled.

"We do that every day, too," he said. He paused. "Tomorrow, Isaac and I need to take a boat out onto the river. I promised I would hide his eyes if the boat *wallah* bring us to the burning *ghat*."

Prema could see Isaac moving his mouth in his sleep. His eyes moved under his eyelids, as if he was dreaming. Timothy touched his cheek very, very gently. The baby's cheek was soft and curved, his eyelashes dark against his face. Timothy turned to Prema, his eyes intense, almost feverish.

"Will you walk with me today? I need to take the boat tomorrow alone, but I want to prepare, to see more of the city before we go on the boat—"

"Wait, wait!" she said, laughing, uncomfortable with how mournful his words were. "You sound like you're expecting this to be your last day!"

"I can't be entirely sure that it won't be," he said, his voice glum. Then he finally cracked a smile as he glanced up at her.

She took her time changing her clothes for the walk through the old city. She looked for clothes that she wanted Timothy to see her in, but wouldn't be too conspicuous. She chose a long baby-blue *kurta* over flowing black pants, and she wrapped a scarf around her head. Checking the mirror, she knew it was a lost cause; she would stand out no matter what—an Indian girl walking through the city with a foreigner who had a baby.

She met him at his guesthouse, just around the corner from hers. It had a nice courtyard, unlike her sterile hotel-like place with the dingy rooms. She waited in the courtyard for him, watching a butterfly land on a fake flower again and again, completely fooled by the bright pink of the flower. Timothy appeared in front of her while she was still watching the butterfly try to get nectar from cloth. She looked up when she saw his legs come into her line of vision, feeling sad for a reason she couldn't name. He was wearing a clean white shirt and loose pants with Isaac in the baby carrier on his front.

"Ready for our pilgrimage?" he asked. He seemed feverish to Prema. There was something wild in his eyes. She was worried about him, she wanted to stick close and make sure he would be okay. A long walk in the heat of the day didn't seem like it was going to make his feel any better.

"Are you feeling up to this?" she asked as they began to walk.

He laughed briefly "As much as I'm up to anything," he said.

She put a hand on his arm for a moment, then dropped it. The gully was cool and Prema thought it felt alive, the way stone did sometimes when it was breathing with the stories of the many thousands of people hidden in its walls, between the cracks. Timothy stopped beside a *paan* stall and they watched the *paan wallah* work. The man picked up a smooth green leaf from the pile fanned out in front of him, plopped some creamy white paste on it, spooned a little scoop of betel nut and tobacco in the middle. Then he opened several unmarked tins, added this and that, folded the whole thing into a little present and passed it to the man who stood nearest to him. The man popped it into his mouth and held out some money. The busy *paan wallah* tossed the coins into a pail and started with the next leaf.

"How does he remember what's in all those tins?" Timothy asked.

"What *is* in all those tins?" Prema said, which made Timothy laugh a real laugh. She felt heat come to her face as she smiled. The way the *paan wallah* flourished his hands when he selected a leaf from the fan, when he tossed the white paste in an arc, directly into the center of the leaf, brought a wave of nostalgia to Prema.

"Have you ever chewed it?" she asked Timothy.

"Yes, once or twice," he said. "But it makes me jittery. Have you?"

"My mother had words with me before I left," she said. She tapped her forehead with one finger. "Maybe one day it will be my final act of defiance. I think my mother is worried that I'll come home with *paan*-stained teeth, or no teeth at all."

"Like her," Timothy said softly, gesturing toward an old woman who was waiting for *paan*. She had elbowed her way to the front and was scolding the man behind her. Prema could see that she had only two or three teeth in the front of her mouth, and those were red and crooked. Prema shuddered.

"She's lovely, but yeah, I'll pass."

They walked on. The walls rose steeply above them like the stone walls of a canyon. Cows pushed past the many people who scurried along the flag-stoned ground. Prema stepped carefully to avoid the large piles of poo. Waves of smells drifted along, arriving one after the other. Poo smells, then incense, then something cooking, then roses. She turned to look when she smelled the flowers and saw a flower *wallah* outside a *mandir*, a temple, hawking garlands of marigolds, jasmine, and roses. Timothy stopped and dug in his pocket. He bought each of them a garland of marigolds.

"It's an auspicious day," he said, settling the garland around Prema's shoulders.

Everywhere they looked, devotion obscured nearly everything else. Timothy stepped into a *mandir*, leaving his sandals at the entrance. After a minute, Prema followed, feeling uncomfortable, like she was a tourist to someone else's religion. The *mandir* was shaped so that they entered at the back and was tiny, just a small space cut into the city walls. At the front, a man rang the bells to wake Ganesh. Near the altar, four women sat with *pallus*–the loose fabric at the ends of their saris– draped over their heads. They rocked back and forth, chanting. Prema watched for a moment, but it felt too personal to watch. She felt unsettled. She ducked back out into the gully and watched a mother dog with four tiny puppies that were already showing signs of mange. Timothy joined her again in a while. He took deep breaths, clearly upset.

"Are you okay?" she asked, putting her hand on his arm.

"It catches up to me in the strangest places," he said. He took one more giant breath and let it out slowly. "Well? Onward?"

She followed him again, wondering what the "it" was, but she thought she knew that it was sorrow and grief.

The two of them wandered all day. They walked quietly through the noisy gullies, stopping when either of them saw anything of interest. Prema touched the walls with her hands; Timothy stopped to talk to mangy dogs and feed them *puri* from a nearby shop. They talked to three Japanese girls who cooed at Isaac with delightfully excited faces. "Oh!" the travelers said, and reached out to stroke the back of his head. Timothy didn't say anything about the baby's mother, and Prema realized that people must assume that *she* was Isaac's mother. She felt uncomfortable. Why didn't he explain? Then she thought of all the questions he must have heard, all through India. He had surely grown tired of them.

Timothy stopped in front of a bangle shop and looked at the rows of glass bangles that sparkled from floor to ceiling, in every color imaginable, from very plain to shimmering with fake jewels.

"After our wedding," he said, "Isabel really wanted to wear bride bangles. She bought them at a place like this, red and white, layered up to here." He gestured to his elbow and paused. The man at the bangle shop stepped, barefoot, to the edge of the mattress on the floor, which was covered in a white sheet.

"Something?" he asked, gesturing inside.

Prema shook her head, "No, thank you, Ji."

Timothy went on. "She wore the red powder in her hair part, too, you know. Every day after we were married."

"She lived in India for a long time before she met you, didn't she?"

"About ten years, coming and going a bit, but mostly in India, yes."

"I can imagine that she saw many newlyweds—it must have seemed right to her."

"It did seem right. She looked beautiful. Some people, well, mostly her parents, didn't feel that we were really married because we married each other without the law being involved, but when people say that I think of the red powder in her part, her bangles, proclaiming to the world that she loved me every single day that she was with me. That makes me feel better. We were married, I couldn't be more sure of anything."

He turned and kept walking. Prema felt uncertain, she thought she had said the wrong thing, but she didn't know what the right thing would have been. She stopped short at a shop with rows of plastic jars filled with colorful Indian candies. She called Timothy back.

"Timothy! Come here... I love these!" she said, excited. "I've grown up with candies like these—oh wait, I've never tried these ones!" As soon as she pointed to a jar, the man sitting cross-legged behind the wall of jars picked it up and opened it. He handed her a little pile of the anise seeds coated with candy and silver, then gestured for Timothy to hold his hand out and gave him some too. But he didn't stop there. On and on he went, handing them samples of some tiny things that Prema couldn't name, spicy mixes, breath fresheners made of betel nut, salted mango. A couple of things made Prema cringe when the flavor hit her tongue, some of them filled the corners of her mouth like secrets. She bought tins of breath freshener for her mother and auntie.

They walked, they walked, they walked.

Timothy leapt to one side to avoid a herd of water buffalo doggedly making its way through a gully. He turned and warned Prema, but she was already pressed to the wall, watching them and laughing. Their faces! Water buffalo had the best faces, with jaws that chewed like the hands of a clock, around and around in a jerky circle.

Twice during the day they ducked into a restaurant and asked for a bottle of water to be warmed for Isaac. Timothy fed him and changed him into a new diaper. Timothy didn't seem to notice the stares the three of them got from people at nearby tables, who sometimes turned all the way around in their seats to watch him with the bottle. Prema was getting her fair share of stares— she assumed they thought she was the mother, allowing her husband to feed and change her infant without helping at all. She tried to be as cool about it as Timothy, but inside she was burning up.

Toward the end of the afternoon, when they had left the gullies and wandered out into the larger street, Timothy stopped to join a group of men looking at a car engine. One man leaned his elbow casually on Timothy's shoulder, drawing him in. Prema was struck by how different it must be to travel this country as a man, to join the large clumps of men in the parks, on the street, the ones who watch and shout helpfully from the fringes. It would be fun, she thought, feeling envious.

They started the long walk home, choosing to walk on the *ghats* on the river rather than back through the gullies. Along the way they stopped to watch a makeshift cricket match on a large platform that separated one set of stairs from another. Some kids had propped a piece of discarded styrofoam on top of two sticks to form a wicket, but the wind kept blowing the Styrofoam off, wrecking the game. The kids were little, maybe six and seven years old. Timothy searched around by the boats until he found an old board, from a broken-down box or a boat. He walked over to the wicket and replaced the Styrofoam with the board. The boys broke into shouts and cheers, dancing around, some of them singing and swinging their hips—wild *ghat* children. Prema laughed and laughed. As Timothy walked back to her and the boys went back to their game, she saw that he was laughing too. It changed his face completely. An auspicious day. It occurred to her that she felt she had known him for months, though she had spent less than two days with him altogether. He didn't look feverish anymore, but as the smile left his face, she saw that he was exhausted. She was tired too. She wondered if Timothy was purposefully bringing himself to the brink. His face looked grey.

"Has our pilgrimage been a success?" she asked him, holding one hand up to shield her eyes from the sun as she looked up at him.

"We submerged ourselves in India for most of the day. So..." he shrugged and pulled his dreadlocks off his neck, then dropped them. "...yes." He looked down at her, then gazed farther along the *ghats* that stretched like a long fat snake along the riverside. "The city took us in for a while." He laughed again, quietly. "But still it held us on the outside—how does it do that?"

"You feel that too?"

"Me? Yeah, sure—I've lived in India for a nearly two years now... not so long. But some of these guys—" He gestured at the *ghats*. "There are westerners who have been here longer than they can remember. Some have even taken the robes of a sadhu. But they're still foreigners in the unforgiving eyes of mother India. The people are all around them, like a wave, but the wave doesn't take them in."

"It seems like it must... eventually."

"No, I think India holds even itself at arm's length. People consider the people in the next state to be foreigners. But travelers, well, they should know this: They may love India, they may adore it, but they will never belong here. It's like we've been embraced and rejected, all at once. And Isabel told me that the sad thing is, India will be in our skin and our eyes and our thoughts forever, we will never be rid of her."

Sudden tears filled Prema's eyes as she struggled to keep up with Timothy's long legs. They left the wide space of the ghat platform and had to move to separate stairs, hers above, his below. He glanced up at her and went on.

"It might be different for you, though. Maybe the place recognizes your blood."

She blinked tears away quickly and swept one hand across her face. "I don't think it's any different—that's what bothers me. I thought that I'd be like a long-lost daughter..." they halted to let a boy wander by with a herd of water buffalo, fresh from washing in the Ganga. Men beat laundry on the laundry stones. The sun disappeared behind the high walls of the buildings that edged the *ghats*. Timothy watched her.

"No, no. It's okay," he said. "That's what I'm learning, slowly. You don't have to belong, to own anything, to have even one piece you can call your own. Even if you're always on the outside, you can still be in love."

CHAPTER 10

Timothy was ready to get home, and so was Isaac. The baby was hungry and Timothy was out of formula. They reached the guesthouse just in time, and after Timothy heated some water in the kitchen—which he now used, rather than always having to ask for hot water—he walked up the stairs slowly, feeling relieved at the thought of being in his quiet room for a few hours. In the morning they would re-enter the thrum and howl of all the people out there, but for now—quiet. It was a relief to get Isaac out of the baby carrier and unwind himself from the long, stretchy piece of fabric. He took his shirt off and stood under the fan to dry the sweat that trickled down his back.

He sat on the bed with Isaac and the bottle and watched Isaac's mouth close around the nipple. He thought of the next day and all the days stretching into the future and felt himself beginning a familiar cycle of worry, but then something new happened, something that had never happened before. Isaac pulled away from the bottle to smile at him with sweet sleepy drunk lips. Without knowing how it happened, Timothy felt some closed chamber of his heart springing open and filling with pain and love. He smiled back.

The baby had dirt in the creases of his arms. When the bottle was empty, Timothy burped him and laid him on the bed, then went to turn on the hot water in the bathroom. It took a while to warm up and he waited, watching to see if his son would smile at him again, and if it would make that slightly painful feeling bloom in his chest again. But the baby was quiet, staring at the line where the shadow met the sun on the wall.

Timothy stood and filled a bucket of water in the bathroom. He peeled Isaac's shirt and diaper off. The baby's limbs were so tense, moving constantly, his fists never relaxed all the way, except when he was sleeping. He looked even tinier naked, with a swirl of hair on his back, tiny folds in the back of his neck that made him look like a little old man. Timothy lowered him into the bucket, waiting for the screaming to start. Isaac had never liked being bathed. But this time he was sitting slightly forward, and it seemed that he liked it. He didn't throw his arms out like he was falling, and though his eyes widened with shock when he felt the water on him, he didn't cry.

"That's right, little bear. It's just water."

Isaac studied the water. He moved his arms as if by accident, then did it again. Timothy was almost sure he was doing some infant version of a splash.

"Don't get any in your mouth." Timothy kept his voice soft. He held Isaac with one hand and used the other to smooth soap over his little arms and legs, his belly. All over him. He was so slippery, Timothy had to be careful not to let him go sliding into the bucket. Isaac's eyes were huge and serious in his face. He opened and closed his mouth, which looked so much like Isabel's mouth.

"No way kid. You can't taste this stuff. It'll rot your insides."

The tiny narrow bathroom was filled with the smells of soap and damp baby skin. Timothy washed his baby slowly, taking his time. Isaac finally cried when Timothy washed his hair, building up to it with shaking lips. His wail in the tiny tiled room was impossibly loud. Timothy finished up in a hurry, then took Isaac out and dried him. He lay the baby on the bed and took his own quick bucket shower, throwing the small pitcher of water over himself again and again, pouring water over himself like a maniac.

When he was finished, he dressed in clean clothes and found a clean shirt for Isaac. Timothy hadn't eaten since lunch, but he was too tired to leave the room. They fell asleep on the bed just as darkness was covering the sky.

When they woke in the morning, after a midnight waking and feed, the sky was still dark. Timothy stepped over the sleeping boys who worked in the hotel to heat some water in the kitchen. Back in his room he sat on the bed to feed Isaac, hunched over, feeling like he hadn't exercised in years. Soon his back would be curled like a leaf. Isaac kept falling asleep and Timothy kept waking him, poking at the baby's little chin with his fingers. He was too sleepy to eat. Eventually, Timothy gave up.

Somehow they made it out the door. Timothy walked to the *ghats* to find a boat. The *chai wallah* was still closed, this early. Timothy tried to keep calm, but he was shaking. All the fear from the last boat ride rushed over him. The sun's first touches burned white in the darkened sky, lightening the corners. Light shifted and the sky moved and they were walking quickly toward the *ghats*. Timothy took the steps down, his breath coming quickly. How could he be so afraid of a river? He knew, though, that he was afraid of the great suffering of the river, of the death here, of what he would find, of being adrift, of seeing what he couldn't fit into his heart, sodden with grief already.

Seven or eight men strode toward Timothy and Isaac. Their alarms were going off.

"Boat? Boat?" they asked.

Timothy stared them all down, silently rejecting the ones who glared back just as hard, their brows a heavy shelf over burning eyes. He chose the first one to give up and turn away, the shyest one. Maybe he would listen to Timothy when Timothy asked him to stay clear of the burning *ghat*.

Small *ghat* children tried to sell him candles. One small girl stood with candles in leaf plates in her hands, staring at him. Her hair was in a ponytail with wisps that had fled confinement, giving her a halo of amber-colored hair. A trail of snot formed a line from her nostril to her upper lip. She was barefoot. As Timothy watched, she balanced her leaf plate of candles of one hand to wipe at her nose with the back of her other hand. He bought a candle for Isabel.

He stepped into the boat very carefully, balancing around his sleeping baby. The boat man pushed off. They floated on the river with nothing more than a wood shell beneath them, separating them from the heavy contents of the river. Women and children were never burned and neither were cripples, untouchables, or animals. They were thrown into the river with weights tied to them. The river was filled with those who used to be living.

The sun had roused itself and the buildings were beginning to glow. The boat was small and shaped like a long leaf. The rhythmic strokes of the boat man calmed Timothy. He whispered to Isaac to hide his fear. It was a pretense because Isaac was fast asleep.

Timothy could smell the burning, dung and seared flesh on the wind. But the boat was still far from the burning *ghat*. Timothy turned his attention to the *ghats* nearby. An entire family walked down the steps to the river, every one of them wearing red. When they reached the water, they began to take it in their hands and splash it over their heads and upper bodies. Nearby, two old women spread thick soap on their arms and legs. Old men offered libations, scooping water into small brass jugs and holding them at chest height to pour them onto the river again and again.

The boat man kept rowing, oar stroke after oar stroke. They moved along the river softly, like angels. As the light became brighter on the ancient buildings, with their towers and arched windows, the sounds of the day—the creaking, the bustle, the laughing and splashing and music from temples in all different directions—washed over Timothy until he felt the spark of creation. He sat up straighter, in the dawn. There were beginnings here after all, not only endings. They were like seeds inside him.

They passed a boat filled to the brim with Korean tourists. They swiveled toward Timothy's boat as it passed. He was startled to see that each one of them without exception was holding a large camera, the words *Canon* and *Nikon* jumping out at him from the black bodies of the cameras. He heard the digital shutter sounds as they captured him, just one more sight on the river. He laughed out loud. Now each of these people owned something of him. On the *ghats* a monkey and a dog played together like friends. These were good things, life things. Timothy wished Isaac was awake, that he could see all of this.

The boat man drew closer to the burning *ghat*. This time Timothy had no escape open to him. He couldn't jump into the river with a baby tied to his chest, even if the same panic overtook him. He looked at the boat *wallah* and the man gave him a gentle smile, sweeping his hand across the length of the *ghats*.

"Ganga means... life," he said. He didn't seem to have any nefarious plans. He was simply rowing, his arms bending and dipping in a soft, silent rhythm. They passed a man with a television blaring in his small rowboat. Timothy stared at him with an open mouth. The man offered to sell him a DVD, but they were already past, even if Timothy had wanted one. In the distance, past the burning *ghat*, a crooked building jutted out of the water, leaning like a tired old man. Young boys leaped from the steps into the water that slowly gathered itself and moved along. On the far bank, the land was empty and the plants looked lush.

They were very close to the burning *ghat*. Timothy's nerves felt stretched to breaking. He felt like he could hear Isabel's last breath, could see her life pouring out of her with all that blood. The smoky swirl of crows drew near, but instead of moving closer to it, the boat ducked away and around, closer to the leaning building. Timothy kept his eyes on the old building as they came close. He saw men in the spaces between the columns on the partially submerged building. It must have been an old temple, now halfway under the water.

"Temple," he whispered. He lit his candle with a match he had bought from the girl and set it into the water in its little leaf boat. He whispered a prayer as he watched the candle float away, a prayer for love and help, though he only slightly understood to whom he was calling, and he didn't even know the words. What was this feeling? He was submerged in it, like the temple in the water, dying in the suffering he saw all around him, unable to run free, the waters heavy and laborious around him. Humanity deep and needy. The river, the *ghats*, were writhing, seething with it. From beginning to end, the babies, like small roses being bathed to the ashes tossed like petals. Human beings, created things, rushed along regardless of the shortness of their lives, barely able to acknowledge how many others there were on the earth, people just like them. There must have been something more, something immovable, that didn't writhe and eat and search. Who was that prayer directed to? He sat on the boat with Isaac, looking up at the sky, wishing someone would show himself, wishing he had a window or a door to walk through. He rubbed at his face and tried to see the floating candle, but it had been carried too far away to see.

He left the boat fuller than he had been before, and yet he was starving, his stomach ready to eat its way through his shirt.

He walked up the dusty steps with Isaac, up to the main ghat, just as an ominous rumble of thunder sounded, its bass creeping under the dirt. There was the thunder in the distance, a metallic smell in the air, and then a wave of hot, damp air. Timothy covered Isaac's head protectively with his hand. He stood at a samosa stand and ate two samosas, one after the other, fresh out of the hot oil.

The drops started to fall as he walked from the samosa stall to the center of the dusty street. The drops cracked into the dust, heavy and large. This was serious, then. The rain was going to hurl itself into the city. Timothy was far from his guesthouse, and he knew from experience the gullies were lethally slippery when they were wet. It was better to take a rickshaw down one of the main streets. He arranged the loose ends of the baby wrap so they formed something like a rain hat for the still-sleeping Isaac, already covered with the stretchy fabric.

A rickshaw *wallah* spotted him just as the rain started in earnest and the wind started blowing. It was a downpour. All around, people scurried to cover their piles of tomatoes or peas, bangles or tiny idols, to fix tarps securely. The man cycled his rickshaw over to Timothy and slapped the seat behind him. He was middle aged and ropy, with the hollow eyes and cheeks of someone who didn't get enough food or sleep.

"Can you drive in this?" Timothy asked.

"*Kya?*" The man hit the seat again, hard, with a flat hand.

Timothy shook his head and climbed up.

"Assi Ghat," he told the *wallah*, and he supposed the man understood, because he nodded.

The rain was collecting on the streets now, forming puddles. The air heavy and grey, a curtain between Timothy and the rest of the world. He had never seen rain like this before in Varanasi. Maybe he hadn't believed rain came to cities this way, he had believed it would respect the human endeavors of buying and selling in places where some people had no shops, only a square of tarp on a debris-strewn road. But here it was, reminding them that they were specks in a grand wilderness. People ran to put their things away.

The cycle *wallah* fixed his *gumcha* more securely around his head, climbed onto his bike, and started off. To get the bike going, he had to stand on the pedals, leaning on each in turn with all his weight. He expended this incredible effort as though it was no big deal at all. Soon his thin legs were pumping as fast as they could go. The rickshaw jounced steadily down the road, tangles of electrical wire following overhead, water pouring from the sky.

The cycle *wallah* careened around the big traffic circle, narrowly avoiding a stranded ox on a piece of dry ground. They had barely gotten anywhere yet, and already Timothy was soaked through. The roads were clear, all the saner people had decided to wait out the storm. At first the cycle *wallah* weaved around the puddles, but that became impossible, and then he drove straight through them. They passed a group of kids who leaped and danced in a puddle that had become a small lake, shrieking their hearts out.

Women ran down the street with the ends of their saris draped over their heads, wet cloth clinging to their legs. Men walked with water sheeting over their brows. Isaac was getting wetter and Timothy began to worry about cold. They were still far from the guesthouse, but he couldn't stop now because they were wet; they needed a warm shower and dry clothes. They drove into what looked like a small puddle, but it turned out to be a pothole, and they hit the bottom, hard. The cycle *wallah* pushed them out of it, but Isaac startled awake and began to cry a thin scared cry. Timothy tried to rock and shush him, but Isaac kept on crying in his wet baby carrier.

The rickshaw *wallah* looked back over his shoulder at the two of them. He smiled a gentle smile and then did something that Timothy couldn't have dreamed up. The rickshaw *wallah* began to sing.

Timothy would never have known it from looking at the thin, tired man, but he had a powerful voice. He sang and Isaac continued to cry frantic, miserable cries. The *wallah* looked back at them as he sang what sounded like an Indian folksong, glancing at the road in short spurts that made Timothy nervous. But the sound of his voice fell and rose and echoed on the watery street as they sped through the new landscape. His voice mingled with Isaac's cries and the chaos of the falling water, the puddles they cycled through, deep enough to reach the man's feet as he pedaled. His voice climbed notes like tiny steps, then bumped back down and ran back up the steps again, as he sang the old song.

It was the smell of water and dust mixing together that finally broke Timothy down. Tears started behind his eyes as he listened to the high-pitched keening of his son and the full-throated voice of the man spinning the pedals, the ropy muscles in his legs shiny with rain. The tears filled Timothy's eyes and found paths down his cheeks, already wet. He didn't bother to wipe them away. The rickshaw *wallah* gazed back at him, singing, and Timothy cried and held Isaac in his arms with all his desire to keep him warm, keep him safe.

When they arrived, Timothy felt reborn and shaky as a baby himself. He had nothing in his life to compare to what had just happened. He paid the rickshaw *wallah* too much money, and the man held the wrinkled bills up to his forehead for a moment before putting them into a small plastic bag he folded up and put in the pocket of his shirt, next to his chest. His shirt hung open and Timothy could see the thump of his pulse near his collarbone, ridged like a small mountain range. The man pedaled away, still singing, and Timothy watched from the doorway to his guesthouse, waiting until he was out of sight before walking into the guesthouse and up the stairs to his room.

CHAPTER 11

It was difficult to get Isaac warm when he was hungry. First Timothy had to wait for the water to warm up. He ran down to the kitchen with the wet baby to warm the water for formula, then raced back upstairs and stripped his and Isaac's wet clothes off. Isaac's hands and feet felt cold and he was screaming, a clang like alarm bells, his wails and the cold raising goosebumps on Timothy's skin. There seemed to be no room for error, no time to do things slowly, in this new life of his.

Someone was tapping on the wall behind the bend, wanting the baby to be quiet. Timothy felt heat rise from his belly to his ears and forehead. He felt jittery with anxiety, with the impossibility of his job. Why didn't they just come and help him? His throat felt thick and painful.

He splashed them both with the warm water and dried off quickly, then wrapped the baby in a towel and himself in a blanket. They sat in their usual spot, on the bed against the wall. Isaac screamed and fought, but finally took the bottle, his whole body tense as he tore at the bottle. Timothy felt the baby relax as the warm formula began to fill his stomach. He stared at the wall. He had accomplished what he came here to do, but he felt old and alone, despite the fact that he was only twenty-four, despite having the best intentions, despite all the carefully chosen prayers when he was a kid. He was alone with a baby in a country that had swallowed him. The people! The people all over the earth, the mystery of all that they were and all that they did, the knowledge that they were there swelled in him until his skin was tight with it, ready to be popped like a balloon.

He wanted to call Prema, he realized. He had to find someone, another human being, someone to talk to, maybe not about the boat or the rickshaw *wallah*, but about non-important things, things that weren't as important as life and death.

As though he had willed it, his phone rang from the one table that sat across the room, a red plastic thing that wobbled if he tried to actually use it for anything. Isaac was asleep, so Timothy carefully laid him on the bed and put a blanket over top of him. He held his blanket up around him while he walked to the ringing phone. But the screen showed that it was his mother. He pressed the button to answer.

"Mom?" he said.

"Hi, love. There you are." Her voice had a tiny break in it from a delay in the reception.

"Yeah, I'm here."

"How are things?"

He never knew how much to tell her. What could he tell her about this day at all? The boat, the rain, the skinny impoverished rickshaw guy singing to him? The cold wet baby, the angry neighbor who thumped on the wall and the way Timothy thought he could happily punch him in the face?

"We're okay. I think Isaac might be teething, though."

"Really? It's early for teething. But then, you were an early teether."

"He drools a lot, and he's fussy at night sometimes."

The rain was finished, outside, and a trio of small birds that looked like sparrows sat on the ledge outside the window.

"Timothy," his mother said. "Please come home."

He sighed. "I can't," he said. "I don't have a passport for Isaac."

"Get one. You can't travel around without a passport for him. It's dangerous. You have the birth certificate and death certificate, right? Just take it a step at a time."

He was silent, watching the birds as they hopped along the narrow ledge. One seemed tired, standing hunched over, feathers still wet.

"I can't explain it, Mom. We're not finished. We need to be here for a while longer, to finish what we're doing here."

Isaac sighed and murmured in his sleep, then made short, startled sounds like he was having a bad dream. Timothy went to him and gently rested a hand on his tummy, and he stopped and smiled absurdly in his sleep. He was so cute. Timothy felt a sharp flash of love.

"I'm worried about you. I think you need to be around family, Timmy."

"You could come here."

"I can't, love."

"Then I guess we're in the same boat." He smiled to think of how untrue it was. Her boat was a sleek white ferry on blue water, under sparkling blue skies. His was an old Ganga boat in the smoky red morning. He walked to the window and put some old Parle G's, Indian biscuits, out on the ledge. The birds hopped away when his hand loomed on the sill, but he barely withdrew before they attacked the biscuit crumbs. He heard his mother take a sip of something and swallow it. Her tea. It would be late there, it was noon where he was, and she would be drinking Celestial Seasonings peppermint tea before bed, as she always did. The moment was so clear to him that he closed his eyes and felt that she was sitting across from him, her knees up as she sat looking out the window on the sunroom couch. Moonlight on the fields. He opened his eyes and saw his three birds with one more as well, pecking at the biscuits and beyond them the river.

"How is Isaac?"

"Other than the teething? He's fine."

"I loved the pictures you sent the other day. Is he doing anything new?"

"New? No."

"Timothy!"

"What?"

"Surely you can dig up a few details for your mother."

"Oh." He thought for a minute. "He's doing this weird thing where he stares at me all the time, now. He just looks at me for a long time."

"Oh, Timmy, I love that age," she said.

He could picture her so clearly, holding her hand to her chest, leaning back to pull at the strings of the afghan that sat on the back of the couch.

"What are you drinking?" he asked.

"Peppermint tea," she said.

"Of course." He paused. "It creeps me out when he does it. When he stares at me."

"Why on earth would it creep you out?" she asked.

"It feels like he's trying to make me feel guilty."

Silence again. A crow landed on the ledge, frightening the four small birds away. It took what was left of the biscuits in only a few seconds, then flew off. Timothy wanted to tell his mother that there were worlds and worlds separating his crooked shifting ground and her memories of sweet babies.

"That worries me," she said, finally.

"I—"

"Listen to me for a minute. He doesn't know. He doesn't blame you for losing his mom. He's giving and looking for love, for connection, the way he's meant to. Those stares are some of the most important moments in his world. There's nothing quite as magical as the love that flows out of those eyes. They are so wise, so kind. Take that love, Timmy, and give some back to him."

"It just makes me feel uncomfortable." He was embarrassed.

"This is officially about a lot more than you."

Now that the crow was gone, two of the other birds were back, but there were no more biscuits. One bird hopped in through the window, right onto the table, looking around for more, black eyes full of hope.

"I know," Timothy said. "I wish you could come and stare at him in the eyes."

"I would love to do that. You know, Timothy," she paused for a long time. "Something your father and I have talked about… if this is too much for you, if you want to go back to school… we could take him. We could raise him."

Timothy caught his breath. "What?"

"Just, I know it sounds crazy, but you seem overwhelmed. You're so young and alone. Just keep it in mind over the next while."

They didn't talk much longer. Timothy felt stunned when he got off the phone. Give Isaac up? Maybe that would be best for Isaac. He looked at his baby, asleep on the bed. The thought of uninterrupted sleep was so beautiful it was almost painful. But could he go from being Isaac's father to being like his brother? What would he do if he gave Isaac to his parents? Could he keep traveling? Would he want to? His head buzzed with questions and it took him a long time to go to sleep.

The next morning, he fed and dressed Isaac and put him in the carrier, then walked down to the *ghats* to look for Prema. She had texted that she would be at the chai stall, and sure enough, there she was, chatting with his chai *wallah*. As he drew closer, he saw the exact moment when she noticed him. He waved.

She stood up and walked toward him, and he saw again how pretty she was, beautiful even, in a stunning effortless way, but he blinked this out of his mind quickly, with the same trick he had used when he was with Isabel and saw a pretty girl.

"How'd it go?" she asked, when she reached him. She kept her hands in the pockets of her knit sweater.

"I'm finished," he said. "I can leave Varanasi now."

She looked confused. He realized he hadn't answered her question.

"It went well," he said. "I didn't jump out of the boat."

She laughed, and he knew she thought he was joking.

They had been drifting back toward the chai *wallah*, and he held his hand out for the chai the man had already prepared for him. It was hot, he smelled the strong smell of cardamom and tasted just a bit of the hot, wet clay of the cup as he put it to his lips. His shoulders relaxed and he sat on the steps, Prema settling herself beside him.

"Do your legs hurt?" she asked. "From the other day when we walked all day?"

He hadn't thought about his legs. He unbent them, testing. "Not really."

"Mine do. You must be in better shape than me."

"Yeah," he said. "I lived in Dharamkot for nearly a year. I climbed hills almost every day." He smiled at her as she stretched her legs out and screwed up her face in pain.

"You need to climb more mountains," he said.

"Trust me, I know," she said.

He looked out at the morning light on the river and felt a sudden swell of happiness. "I can't tell you how relieved I am to be finished with what I came here to do," he said. "I'm thinking about moving on."

"Really?" She was smoothing her hair. It was really short on one side of her head and longer on the other. Really cute. She fiddled with the hair behind her ear. "Where are you thinking of going?"

"We're going to try Goa. I'd like to get him in the sea. We're ready for the beach. Some sun, a little ease." He paused, imagining the sea. He had wanted to go there with Isabel, but that wasn't possible anymore. "I should get out of here before I lose my mind completely."

"Hmmm," she said. "It must be nice to have such clear goals about what you want to accomplish in India."

He had to laugh; the person she was describing was so utterly different from him, wandering, lost, in a country that wasn't his.

"Clear goals? No." he said. "It's all about survival. Maybe they're clear, but they're not logical. To take my baby on a boat ride. Wow, I'll never be a grown-up."

"It's probably overrated," she said, smiling at him. Her nose wrinkled a bit when she smiled. She had very white teeth that flashed against her dark skin.

"Do you have goals for being here?"

She was instantly serious, she looked down at her empty chai cup, then back out at the river. "I wanted to find myself in India, but now I think that goal is too big. I still want to understand... well, it doesn't make that much sense, but I grew up believing in God, and I think I still do, but I want to know if I can find a shape of faith that I understand here. Do you know? The shape of it? In Canada it doesn't make sense to me. It can't reach me," she touched her heart, "here."

He watched her for a moment without saying anything.

"Let me know if you find it," he said.

She looked at him, a soft smile curving her mouth. "I was thinking of going to Goa too. I wanted to see a few more things here, but maybe we could go together. Are you going to take the train?"

He nodded. He didn't know what he thought about taking the train together. It seemed unsettling, somehow, but it wasn't that weird, travelers always met along the way and traveled together.

"I could help with the baby, if you needed to go to the toilet or something."

He nodded. That would be amazing. He remembered the train car where he met her, how he needed her help even to eat something. It wasn't easy to eat a *thali* on a moving train with a small baby.

"Okay," he said, feeling like he had forgotten something that was bothering him, not quite able to put his finger on it. He sounded reluctant, even to himself. She looked down at the steps, then up at him again, a crease between her eyebrows, but she didn't say anything. She took a sip of chai.

"Jailbreak, kid," he said to Isaac, who was sleeping very deeply, curled up on Timothy's chest. "We're getting out of here."

CHAPTER 12

Prema followed a butterfly into an ashram because she didn't have anything better to do. Timothy had decided to stay inside with the baby because he wasn't feeling well. He didn't want to do anything at all, he told her. He wanted to move on. Prema had picked up train tickets, and they were breathing in her pocket, whispers of another long journey through ancient fields. She had time and nothing to do with it, so she wandered through gullies, drinking cups of chai and sampling Indian sweets. Her mother's were better, she thought. She felt a strong wave of homesickness. She missed her mother and the way she smelled in the mornings, drying her hair in the kitchen, combing oil through it as it fell around her waist. For a long moment she was saturated with longing for home, but then she spotted the butterfly.

It hovered over half a discarded sweet that was sitting in the gutter among the hundreds of red splatters of *paan* that had been chewed and spit out. She paused to look at it there, a pale blue butterfly lost in a city world, and it fluttered up to her hand. It perched with delicate feet on her wrist for a moment, but when she spoke to it, it flew off down the gully, its fragile legs landing momentarily on a windowsill. So she followed it.

She hadn't told Timothy everything when she spoke of her desire for God. Sometimes the longing was like an inner thirst that was so deep she thought she would faint with it. She could imagine herself as a whirling dervish or a nun in a cloister. At home it had her waking in the night, thinking she needed something: another drink of water, or a slice of pizza from the place down the street, but she knew it wasn't food or drink that she wanted. She sometimes thought she would pass out from wanting more, wanting to understand. She loved the faith of her parents. But sitting in chairs listening to the teaching whims of some man with a pulpit left her absolutely dry, blew her flame right out.

Her ancestors were shaped by India, following Guru Nanak, who was followed by nine more gurus and the final Guru, the Sikh book of scriptures. On this trip she had come searching. She had gone to see the Golden Temple, and though she had found it beautiful, she knew she was no Sikh. But she knew that the seat of spirituality was in the East—even Christianity had formed in the Middle East, she told her father, not in any cold northern place. Thomas the disciple had brought the words of Christ to South India, so there were Christians in India as well as Hindus and every shape of Hinduism possible, statues of gods falling out of every crack and cranny. There were Jains, of course there were Sikhs. There were Muslims in crisp white and pastels, the women in black. She had never seen so much religion in her life, and she admired the devotion as she sat on the *ghats* and watched people pouring out libations. One person ate only vegetables for their religion, another slaughtered goats in the street. On taxis and rickshaws, paint and stickers proclaimed the religion of the driver, stating who the driver *was*, not only who he worshiped. *Jai Ganesh, Shiv Krupa,* the signs said. She only needed to look behind the head of a proprietor in a shop, to the altar behind him, to know what family he was born into—whether Sikh, Hindu, or Muslim.

She had visited Hindu temples. She had walked into churches and found the same chairs as at home, pointed all in one direction. She loved the devotion of Hindus and the God of Christians and all of it made her feel as though she was insane, as though there was no place in the world for her to lay her head. What if she just gave it up? She was coming to the point where she wasn't even enjoying India, she was so desperate to find something, to find truth or a way of living that showed her something real, something lasting. And then there was Timothy, taking up whatever of her thoughts were left over after her desperate search. Maybe this was why she had been led to India. Or maybe there was no purpose in anything at all.

The butterfly was something beautiful, something light. She watched as it fluttered from spot to spot, and she followed along, wishing her heart could lighten in the shape of its airy flight. It led her in a chaotic zig-zag pattern, through the gullies and out blinking into bright light. Piles of trash smoked along the road, and she covered her mouth with her *dupatta*. At one intersection it took a sharp right, so she followed it again, looking up to see a dozen boys flying kites over ancient temples in a large, dusty field. "*Arrey baba!*" one boy yelled. The kites filled the sky, whipping each other, scourging the air. There was no sign of the rain that had descended so suddenly yesterday. The earth had gulped it down and the sun had already dried the field so that clouds of dust rose under the boys' bare feet. At that moment Prema wasn't wondering how she fit. She was only walking, for once, not thinking. Only following a butterfly.

After she passed the field of boys with kites, she reached a gate. She watched the butterfly float right through the bars, but when she wandered up to it to peer through the heavy bars, she noticed that the lock wasn't actually holding the gate together. There was a sign that said, "The Dwelling Place," in English, propped on the gate, seemingly as an invitation. She pushed the gate open and walked through.

The scenery changed immediately and drastically. She stepped into a softer, quieter place. Large trees spread their branches overhead, soft grass was under her feet. A pathway of slightly more trampled grass ran on ahead and the butterfly was off into a hibiscus bush whose red flowers nodded at Prema. She followed the path, wondering whether she was trespassing, what this green world was, where the path was taking her.

She came to an old building that had layers of flaking paint, different color levels telling of past years. She heard voices and continued around the corner of the building, stopping when she saw what was before her. A group of people sat under a large tree beside the building, eating from plates in their hands. They sat on mats on the grass, mostly foreigners, travelers like herself, grouped in a loose circle with pots of food clustered in their center. She wanted to duck back, but a girl had spotted her and was waving her in.

She was nervous—*what if this was a cult of some kind?*— but she had come to India to find out about all things that existed under the sun, so she wandered in through the bamboo gate as she tucked her hair behind her ears.

"Come, come! Sit down." an old man called out to her. He was dressed in the orange robes of a sadhu. He had a kind face, so she slipped off her *chappals* and sat beside him, tucking her legs under her. She was wearing a red skirt under a black *kurta* today, with a saffron *dupatta* looped around her shoulders. She tucked her skirt so her legs wouldn't show and smiled at the man, then at other faces around the circle. A girl a bit older than Prema approached with a plate of food balanced in her hand.

"Would you like to eat?" she asked. "I just dished this up."

"Are you sure?" Prema asked. "I didn't mean to just crash in on you here."

"Oh, this is what this place is for. It's an open lunch and you're making it more delightful."

Prema laughed. "Well, then, if that's the case, sure."

"All right, let me get a plate for myself and I'll come and join you and Govinda Baba."

Prema took a bite of the rice and *subzhi*. It was good. She took another bite.

"I'm Govinda," the old man told her. He was not from India and she was curious about him.

"I'm Prema," she told him.

"Ah, beautiful name," he said. "And if I'm not mistaken you have been brought up somewhere else?"

"Canada, yes," she said.

"A long time ago I was from Canada," he told her. "And how are you enjoying the mother India?"

The girl who gave Prema the food had come back to sit beside her. She had a bottle of water and two steel cups. She sat, her hair swinging down and hiding her face for a moment before she brushed it away with the back of her wrist.

"How is it?" she asked. "I cooked today and I can never be sure how it's going to work out until we're all putting it into our mouths."

"It's delicious," Govinda said, and Prema nodded with enthusiasm, her mouth full.

"Thank you," the girl said. "I'm Ruth, by the way. From Australia. And you?"

"Prema," she said. "From Canada."

"How did you find us?"

"I — well, I followed a butterfly," Prema said, laughing.

"I love you already," Ruth said.

Prema was surprised and laughed again. She looked around the circle. A slender woman was pouring chai from thermoses into small white cups. A young traveler with a shaved head was pulling his sitar out of its case.

"If you don't mind me asking," she said, "what is this place?"

"A Yeshu Ashram. A Christ Ashram," Ruth said.

Prema felt her jaw drop. "Are you serious?"

Govinda nodded.

"She's absolutely serious," he said, "definitely, completely, and utterly."

"What does that mean? Jesus ashram?"

"It's like other ashrams," Ruth said. "It's a place for study and meditation.

We contemplate the life of Jesus and offer teachings and meditation."

"Are you doing a teaching right now?"

"Oh, no, this is just lunch!" Ruth had been sitting on her knees but now she settled onto the mat, pulling her legs in front of her and stretching her bare feet. Prema looked around again.

"Do all these people live here?"

Ruth looked up and adjusted the scarf that was tied around her hair, fiddling with the fringe on the edges of it while she shook her head.

"No, only a few people do. A lot of these people are our friends, not all of them follow Christ or come for teaching, but our friends wander in and out of our lives." She nodded at Govinda. "Govinda Baba is a fixture. He's been in Benaras for nearly forty years, right Govinda Baba?"

"Longer than I can remember," the old man said.

"I'm sure you remember every bit," Ruth said.

"So—you live here?" Prema asked them. She couldn't imagine living here, and for a minute she felt like she had turned into one of her cousins in Canada. *India? I could never live there.*

"Yes, for now," Ruth said. "With my husband and kids." She pointed out two children sitting with crayons and paper under the tree. "But what about you? What's your story?"

"I can't even remember my story, that's how shocked I am that you're here. I feel like you're just what I've been looking for."

Prema found herself telling Ruth all about her family in Canada, her lack of satisfaction and her quest in India, coming here to figure it out. She talked about how frustrated she was in the worship of her parents, so un-Indian. She told her about meeting Timothy and about his baby.

"He sounds like an amazing person," Ruth said, playing with the cup of chai the slender woman had set in front of her, smiling at Prema as she gave her one as well.

"I can't describe him. I've never met anyone like him—he's so serious and really grieving, but so thoughtful at the same time. And the way he is with Isaac..." She didn't know how to describe Timothy. Something about the way he seemed so determined, though he was obviously hurt and alone. Govinda had wandered away and was standing with some chai and a large slice of the cake that had been brought into the courtyard.

"It's egg free," Ruth said, noticing where Prema's eyes were.

"You have an oven here?" Prema asked.

"It looks like a big tin box that you set on top of the gas cooker," Ruth told her. "It's a big crazy thing, a space ship, but it works really well." She played with the ends of her scarf again. "You're welcome to stick around if you're keen, you know. Come to meditation if you want."

Prema felt a lurching in her stomach. "I'm leaving in a couple days. With Timothy. We're going to Goa."

Ruth nodded, her eyebrows up. "Oh. Wow."

"We're just friends, though. I'm helping him out."

"Be careful with that," Ruth said. "People who are hurting often hurt other people without meaning to."

"Oh—I don't think Timothy would."

"Well, we have a meditation tomorrow. You could come then. And the invitation stands. We even have a room available in the ashram." Ruth stood up and stretched, then walked around the circle and started to pick up chai cups. Beside Prema, a girl was lying back on her mat, staring up at the trees overhead. People sat and talked, the man with the sitar played a *raga*. One man drew in a sketch pad, another worked on macramé.

Prema tipped her head back and looked at how the light was streaming through the windows on the second floor of the old building. Birds landed in the trees and called out to one another, and clouds cruised through a blue sky. She knew she could learn here, she knew this might be the answer to her deep need. But Timothy and Isaac had appeared in her life, and Timothy was so lost. She thought of his eyes on that first train when they met, or after their walk. She thought of him alone and she knew she couldn't leave him that way. She was getting on the train. There might be answers here, but she would be leaving them behind.

The next day she walked home from the meditation slowly, thinking about all she had to accomplish before they would be ready to go to Goa. Not so much, really, she needed to give her clothes to the laundry *wallah* and send off some postcards, go for one last photo journey around the city. It was still midday and she stopped for a lassi, thinking about the meditation and the deep peace she felt all through her. The lassi was thick, almost as thick as yogurt, but more fermented, with bits of pistachio on the foamy top, and served in a clay cup. Prema took the wooden paddle spoon the proprietor was offering her and dug in.

They hadn't done all that much, during the meditation. Prema had come prepared for some kind of teaching, with a new blank notebook in her bag and her best pens in the small zip-up case she always carried with her, like the good university girl she was. But there wasn't any teaching, and no spiritual secrets were shared. There was a lot of silence, and in the spaces between the silence, the guide, Ruth's friend Lindsay, spoke the words of scripture.

Though the mountains fall into the sea,

And in the silence Prema dove around in her head and out through the branches of the tree.

A very present help in trouble

She thought about the old words and how somehow they were reading ancient thoughts that still made sense, though she was reading along on her iPhone. She thought about King David,

Therefore we will not fear

And she thought about Timothy, lost and trying to be brave, his mountains having fallen into the sea. And though she felt so much peace, though she knew that the place could be an answer for her, she knew she would go with him, to help however she could.

She was finished with her lassi. She handed the empty bowl to the boy who was sweeping up, and picked up her skirt to walk along the gully to her room, to drop off her laundry and gather her things together to leave again. Overhead, women threw water out of their windows and called to one another, and on the street a small goat that was tied to a pole gave a startled bleat when her leather sandal came too close to him. Prema felt closer to finding answers, though they still seemed to slip away when she turned to look at them.

CHAPTER 13

Timothy stood at the open door at the end of the train car, the baby fast asleep and secure in the carrier on his chest, his little head soft under Timothy's palm. It was hot outside with dry heat like an oven. Trees sprawled into the sky in distant fields. Reality was sinking in more and more these days. *She wasn't coming back.* What he had now was what he had. He had always known it in his head, but even now the rushing landscape pushed the knowledge a little deeper into his heart.

Women walked along the road beside the train, saris pulled halfway over their faces, each with one hand holding a large pot balanced on her head. They made it look effortless, they walked with a gentle sway.

He talked to his sleeping baby. "She had dark hair like yours. Really dark. And dark eyes like yours too. The only thing you have that looks like me is that cleft in your chin. Your bum chin." He paused. "That's what your grandma always called my chin. A bum chin." His thoughts reeled around him.

It was like this. She gave birth quickly and the placenta tore away. She bled, all her blood spilled around her and we couldn't stop it.

It was like this. She left you, kid. I'm so sorry.

It was like this. She was floating and I couldn't hold on. She slipped through my fingers.

It was like this. The midwife did her best to save your mother and was left sobbing at the end.

It was like this. She kissed you over and over until she had no strength left. She was white, like a flower, floating away on the rapids. Sunita didn't take you from her until she couldn't hold you anymore. We were walking her to the door to try to get a taxi to the hospital when she collapsed. We didn't know what to do. We didn't know what to do!

She was dead. She was dead. And she wasn't coming back.

He kissed the top of the baby's head. "I'm so sorry, Isaac," he said.

Back in his compartment, the lunch *thali* was getting cold. Timothy had started eating earlier, then not been able to finish when Isaac started crying. Now he sat at the tiny table and dug his fingers into the rice. The hot dry air rushed through the window. He mixed the *dahl* and vegetables with the rice, finally looking up at Prema. She had been watching him, but she looked away when his eyes met hers. She had on a *shalwar kameez* and *dupatta* again, her train clothes. She tucked her hair behind her ear.

Isaac was still asleep with his mouth hanging open, the little innocent looking gums exposed. Timothy put another handful of food in his mouth. The woman sitting next to Prema was holding her handbag in both hands, watching Timothy eat.

"You look really sad," Prema said.

He looked up at her. She sat with one knee up at the window, resting her elbow on it. Her hair whipped around in the breeze from the window. He had a friend on this train.

"I'm having a rough day, I guess," he said.

"Want to talk about it?"

Did he? Not really. He also didn't want to be rude to his only friend.

"I was thinking about Isabel."

"Tell me about her," Prema said. She had a book open, but she shut it and put it into the small bag that sat beside her on the seat. She closed the bag and smoothed it with one long brown hand, looking at him with her soft, bright eyes. Timothy thought about what to tell her.

"I was thinking about how different life was with her. Traveling. It didn't matter if people stared at us, because we were familiar, we knew each other. But we were foreign enough to each other to always be interesting. It was amazing." He put more food in his mouth, chewed and swallowed it. "She could have had me forever. I never would have left her."

Somehow it seemed important to tell Prema this.

"We met on a train and got married in the desert. She wore a red sari. She was my first girlfriend and then I married her right away, right after we met. But I knew she was the one."

"Wow, you married your first girlfriend? Not that I can talk, my dating life has been... sparse." Prema smiled.

"I was clueless about girls in high school. They were always giggling and traveling around in big groups."

She laughed softly. "It's true. Girls do that."

"I didn't get it. The other guys seemed to understand girls fine, the guys who mocked my flute, who called me gayboy. Those guys were like those birds you see on nature shows, the ones who click and whistle to call the female birds, hopping around. They all knew the dance. I didn't know it. I didn't understand the competition, the insults, I don't seem to have a lot in me for acting or pretending. So I played music, that's basically all I did. That was my life."

"Music."

"Yeah. Like my flute was a part of my body."

"You were a different kind of bird."

He watched her eyes, saw her eyelashes like shadows on her cheeks, her eyes dark and full of understanding.

"Sure, but the female birds didn't stick around to listen."

"They—" she stopped and started over. "What happened after high school?"

"I got a scholarship to UVic. Climbed into more music, harder and harder stuff. In university we played louder and faster."

"How did you end up here? Did you finish school?"

He shook his head no and thought about it. What was the door to India? It was death, of course, the same door that had him catapulting along on the train right now.

"My grandpa died in my third year and I took time off for the funeral. I had already been having trouble with the pressure of playing faster, better, longer; all the exams, my grades. I couldn't make myself go back to school, could barely get my fingers to move on the flute. My professors gave me time, but I didn't want to go back."

"Wow."

"I know, and everyone was like, *of course you knew your grandpa would die, old people die. How can you be freaking out over a grandparent?* But it wasn't so much that he was gone. It was the shape of his body once he was no longer it in, how he was dragged away without agreeing to it. I don't even know if it was my grandpa dying that did it. I didn't love playing anymore, it felt like so much work. My mom said I was depressed, that's all, and I needed to take some medication and go back to school, but I decided to leave, instead."

He looked through the window and was somewhat surprised to see India rushing by outside. He had been so absorbed in talking about Canada that he had forgotten where he was. It was raining on the plains now. They passed tiny shops in shacks. The sky was big and grey.

"I packed and came to India. When I was here, I could play my flute again. That was after I met Isabel, pretty much right after I got here. I would play, she would dance. She brought it out of me." He was silent. Isaac started to wake up, so Timothy wiped his hands on the thin napkin that came with his *thali*. It tore with the slightest pressure. He pulled out the bottle he had prepared and took the baby out of the sling, settling him in the crook of his arm to feed him. Prema cleared her throat.

"Do you still play?"

"No, not since she died. I haven't been feeling like it... and I don't have much time."

Isaac had his eyes closed, eating. The family that shared the compartment with Timothy and Prema were all avidly watching.

"I would have stayed with her for life," Timothy said again, without looking away from Isaac's face. "I suppose I did."

He looked up at Prema. "I mean, it wasn't perfect. Nothing is."

He looked away, out the window, thinking. There were things she did that annoyed him. She laughed at him sometimes, and he didn't like being laughed at. Sometimes she teased him about the difference in their ages, calling him cute, and she was always stronger in India; she understood everything and he understood nothing. You couldn't exactly call it a fight, though. He knew he annoyed her, too. She liked to plan things well and he had never been a good planner. He took a deep breath, seeing her so clearly; her eyes and her black tangle of hair. He missed her so much.

Isaac pulled away from the bottle and opened his eyes, blinking at the light. Timothy smoothed Isaac's hair, feeling the small baby head, round and warm under his hand. He felt the soft place where his skull hadn't grown together yet. He closed his eyes and leaned his head against the seat. Prema came and took Isaac out of his arms.

"I'll take him for a while," she said. "You rest."

He could hear her talking to the baby as she walked down the aisle with him, but it was faint, because he was already falling asleep.

Timothy woke up feeling like his mouth was a desert and the train had been running over him, but after he had chugged a liter of water, Isaac had been changed, and he had stretched a little in the aisle, he felt like a human again. Isaac had another sleep, and another feed. Each hour on the train seemed to last a day. Prema read her book and looked out the window, resting her chin on her knees with her feet up on the seat.

"Do you miss home?" she asked later.

Home was tricky. Timothy sat Isaac on his lap to burp him. He put one hand against the baby's chest, his thumb and pinky fitting under his tiny arms. He patted Isaac on the back. Home. Wet grass, hot wet pavement after a summer rain. He could smell it. Hills, the ocean always there somewhere nearby. Firs and pines everywhere the eye could see. Sister, mother, father, brothers. Isaac burped.

"Yes," Timothy said. "I do."

In his backpack he had the death certificate and a birth certificate that could help him to get a passport for Isaac, a step toward going home with his baby, but he was crumpled and soggy like a wet newspaper and how did a wet newspaper get himself to the embassy? He had come to India to find missing pieces, but more had shivered away, like those ashes that floated away from the burning *ghats*, drifting on the wind.

He stared through the bars that lay like long arms across the window. The day was drawing to a close, the light had turned rosy. The train pulled into a station for a brief stop, then slowly rolled forward again. Two young guys hauled their chai thermoses down the tracks and away from the trains, back to wherever they came from. A man poked his head into the compartment and asked whether they wanted dinner.

Timothy laid Isaac across his knees and looked into his baby's face. The hot orange-tinted air blew past the windows with their iron bars. The baby stared at him with those intense eyes and this time Timothy forced himself not to look away. He watched the baby and the baby watched him with his large, brown eyes. And then Timothy felt it—a warm rush of love from the baby. Isaac looked at Timothy as if he was the whole world, and instead of shrinking away or feeling terrible about being the only parent the baby had, Timothy let himself fall into that love. It surrounded him. Isaac's eyes sent pure trust straight into his heart.

"Oh, hello," Timothy said to his baby. Isaac smiled the biggest smile Timothy had ever seen from him. His smiles so far had been rare, but this was a giant, drooly grin. His eyes turned into crescents, just like Isabel's when she smiled. Timothy leaned over and kissed his son on the forehead, then picked him up so he could sit with the small soft head nestled between his neck and his collarbone. He knew in that moment that he would never give his baby away to let other people raise him. Outside, the train beat the same rhythm, the sun fell quickly through the sky, the trees stabbed their arms upward. Timothy hummed a song to his son and watched it all.

Prema was looking out the window. He noticed that she had a loose eyelash on her cheek, resting on the top of her cheekbone. She had bangs that were cut to rest just above one eyebrow, but they slanted across her forehead at an angle, showing more of her forehead above the other eyebrow. It made her look inquisitive. Timothy was suddenly very certain that she had a tattoo hidden somewhere under her clothes. He wondered whether she would wear a swimsuit in Goa and whether he would see her in it—but he cut his thoughts away from that. The red ball of sun was dropping behind the horizon. She looked up to find him looking at her. He said something off the top of his head.

"This is your country in a way that it will never be mine."

She was quiet for a moment, looking back at him.

"I have family here, if that's what you mean," she said.

"I mean more than that. We're both foreigners, but I'm just a drifter. You have more than that."

She shifted in her seat, tapping a finger on the edge of her book. "To be honest, I thought it would be stronger, that I would feel more at home here," she said. "I am tied to this country, though, you're right. But I don't know how I'm tied to it. I don't know what it means."

She turned her head to look out the window again. The sun was nearly invisible now, there was only a red band.

"Where are we going in Goa?" she asked, looking at him again, her eyes on his.

Her eyes were beautiful, he realized again, but were the two of them going somewhere together? He hadn't thought that far.

"I don't know." His mind seemed incapable of planning anything other than Isaac's next feeding.

"I hear Arambol is nice. Seems to be a lot of music."

"Music is good."

"Maybe you'll play again," she said.

He felt hot and pulled his t-shirt away from his chest to try and get some air flowing. He hadn't thought this through! The two of them were going somewhere together like a couple. Isabel was knocking on the inside of his skull, wanting to know what was going on with Prema. But they'd only been talking, nothing had happened. The woman sitting next to Prema tapped her fingers on the edge of her steel tiffin, which she had pulled out to reveal a full Indian dinner for her and her husband—rice, dahl, and chapatti. Her tapping fingers clacked a contradiction to his thoughts. She looked at Timothy, and it seemed to him that she wasn't fooled a bit.

He was attracted to Prema and it hit him in the stomach like rounding the corner and bumping into a water buffalo. Was it the romance of the train striking again? It couldn't be romance, though. He loved Isabel. He hadn't had a friend in a long time, that was all. The dark night rushed by the fluorescent lights they occasionally saw blazing like fierce knives in the darkness.

When Timothy woke in the morning, Isaac was still asleep, curled into the hollow of his stomach, his arms flung up beside his head. There was dried formula in the corner of his mouth from the middle-of-the-night feeding. It was early—the benches were still all made into beds and he didn't yet hear the chai *wallah*. Beneath the rumbling floor he could hear the click of the tracks. All of his companions in this big moving container were hunched into sleeping mounds, soft and vulnerable. The young guys across the way were transformed into small boys with tucked mouths and scrunched eyes. Timothy eased out of the small bunk with the bed in place over him, and leaned over to see where they were through the open window.

The landscape was different. The train rolled through jungle peppered with coconut and banana trees. Flowering vines climbed larger trees, falling over as they strained to reach the sun. Cool air rushed in through the bars and Timothy bent to tuck the blanket a little more tightly around Isaac. The baby was sleeping so deeply that Timothy's fingers arranging the blankets didn't disturb him. Timothy rubbed at his face and looked in the mirror. He took the elastic out of his hair and shook it back, smoothing it back to the nape of his neck again, fixing the elastic around it twice. Isaac's mouth was open and slack, his eyes moving under his eyelids. Timothy decided to walk to the end of the train car, to stand at the door for a few minutes before the baby woke up.

Walking through rows of sleeping people felt like wading through water. They were trapped in their unconscious states and he alone was free. He walked quietly, out of habit, used to being silent around a sleeping infant. He reached the door and sat, letting the fresh breeze rush into his face, gulping big breaths of it, leaning out, turning into the gust of wind that soared past the train. The air felt fresh but damp—jungle air. He could see the long blue body of the train curving ahead. They were in low hills and a bright ray of sun reached him where he sat with his right hand gripping the bar. The sun bothered the dust particles, dancing between them, refusing to leave them alone.

He felt the pull to get back to Isaac pressing on his mind, but the quiet moment was like a miracle to his tired mind. The train crossed a bridge and a waterfall flashed into sight. Timothy let out a puff of breath. The white frothy water threw itself onto boulders, giving itself up.

Isabel couldn't have known how hard it would be, or she wouldn't have gone. The thought skidded loudly into his peaceful moment and his world tipped once again. He reached out suddenly and punched the wall, hard, hurting his hand, swearing softly. What had they been thinking? Why didn't she go to the hospital? Why didn't he make her?

Back in the compartment, Isaac was awake and Prema was holding him. She cooed into his face and he smiled back at her. Timothy caught his breath, a strange feeling in his stomach. He stooped and took Isaac from her, then sat next to her on the bench to apologize for snatching the baby out of her hands. He saw that her hair was sticking up at the back of her head and looked down at Isaac. He nuzzled at the crook of the baby's neck, and Isaac laughed out loud. They both sat smiling at the baby for a quiet moment. Prema was the first to speak, just as Timothy bent to tickle Isaac with his lips again.

"How's it going?" Prema asked.

Timothy pulled his face out of Isaac's neck. He thought of how to answer. Nothing seemed like it made any sense.

"Not so great this morning."

Prema reached up to smooth her hair, missing the part that was sticking up. The rising sun was turning everything in the compartment to gold, including Prema's skin, which was a warm cinnamon color and seemed almost to sparkle.

"Do you want to talk about it?" she asked.

"Not really." He paused, keeping his eyes on his baby's eyes. Isaac let out a stream of vowels and reached his hand out to claw at Timothy's face. The sleeping people on the train had begun to wake, one by one, like statues brought to life. The chai *wallah's* calls filled the car. "Chai, chai! *Garam* chai!" The beds changed to seats, the day began.

CHAPTER 14

In Goa they climbed off the train. The air was thick and hot, like soup, the fresh breeze from the morning in the hills long gone. They had reached Margao, which people seemed to pronounce "Madgao." As soon as Timothy's feet touched the ground outside the train station, the taxi drivers were beside him, asking him where he was going. Timothy turned away slightly and tightened the knot on his baby carrier. He swung his backpack on his back and picked up Isaac's bag with one hand. The packs were heavy. Timothy wished he could lighten the load, but nothing was expendable, not the bottles, not the journal, not the carved elephant or Isabel's French Bible.

Prema stood talking to the taxi drivers. Timothy noticed that the birds above them were incredibly loud. They shouted from the trees, demanding notice, so he craned his head to see them. He had never been good at spotting birds, and today was no different. He saw coconuts in heavy bunches in the tall palms, that was all.

"Beach? Which beach?" the taxi drivers near him wanted to know. Some were talking about Calangute, others insisted on taking them to Palolem.

Prema was about a hundred feet away, in earnest conversation with the taxi drivers who stood around her in a circle.

"Which beach?" he asked as he caught up to her. As the words left his mouth, he realized how intimate the question might seem to her and the taxi drivers. Something in his chest seemed to stretch and release painfully, like an elastic band. He felt confused. Was he part of a couple now? Surely not. Prema turned her full attention on him and smiled. He backed up a step.

"Didn't we say Arambol?" she asked.

There it was again, that word, "we." This was moving too fast. Timothy needed to think, to get someone's advice about whether this sort of thing was okay for people who were Just Friends, or whether he was treading into territory he had no desire to explore. (Not no desire, just no desire that he wanted to act on.) But the taxi drivers pressed in around them, sweat poured from his forehead, and his backpack was about to nail him to the ground. This was not the time. He forced his shoulders to relax.

"You made it sound nice," he said.

"So let's go!" she said, her smile flashing in her face, while Timothy tried to calm his anxious stomach. She turned and began negotiating with the drivers in Hindi. Timothy unstrapped his big backpack and swung it off his shoulders, setting it on the ground. He wiped sweat away from his back with his shirt bunched in his hand. The humidity was unbelievable; it was like the air was filled with water. Any more and they'd be swimming.

Goan taxi drivers seemed to keep their distance more than Varanasi taxi drivers. They spoke a language amongst themselves that wasn't Hindi. It sounded very different from Hindi, almost tonal, dipping and diving. The consonants were soft and tripped off their tongues, more rising and falling in the vowels. By the time all of them were in the taxi, the driver had tried to convince them to go to Calangute three more times. All Timothy wanted was for him to stop talking and start driving, so the wind would stir the air in the car and dry the sweat from his face and hair.

"Arambol," Prema said firmly. She had one elbow on the windowsill and was fanning air toward her face with her cupped hand. They both sat in the back of the small white van of the same make as taxis all over India.

"Not season for Arambol," the driver muttered, irritated. He pulled at his khaki-colored jacket, tugging it off and swinging the van out of the parking lot in one smooth motion. Timothy breathed a sigh of relief at the air coming in the windows. It felt fresher when they were in motion, actually drying the sweat from his forehead.

"Do you think he's right?" Timothy asked Prema in a low voice.

"I think it's early. It's probably still fairly empty. But it'll be fine."

Timothy nodded and relaxed against the back of the seat. Busy with Isaac, Timothy had missed most of the view of Goa flashing past the train windows, but now he saw that they were driving through brilliant green rice paddies. Water buffalos stood in the fields with large white egrets perched between their shoulder blades or hopping around them. In the distance a storm cloud gathered weight. Timothy watched it, frowning, wondering whether it would hold off until he could find a place to stay.

Prema sat texting on her phone.

"You are from?" said the driver in English from the front.

"Canada," Prema said, without looking up.

"You had your baby here?"

Timothy realized with a shock that the driver was looking at Prema in the rearview mirror. She paused in her texting, waiting for him to answer before realizing the question was directed at her.

"Oh!" She turned a very bright red. "This is not my baby, Ji." She switched to Hindi and spoke for a few moments before turning back to her phone. The man made sounds of understanding and sucked at his teeth, shaking his head. He looked at Timothy in the rearview mirror. Timothy's frown seemed to be enough to convince him not to probe any farther. How could this stupid man assume that Prema was Isaac's mother? To Timothy, the invisible shadow of

Isabel was still so real, he had imagined that she would have been visible to anyone passing by. And with deep dread it occurred to him that many people they had met had assumed the same thing, that Prema and Timothy were wife and husband, spending their days sightseeing in India. The truth was so far from this wrong assumption that he almost couldn't take the thought. He felt heat in his cheeks and forehead, a flush that put stars behind his eyelids as he closed his eyes briefly to keep the gaze of the taxi driver off him.

He opened them again, feeling sick, avoiding Prema's eyes. The rice paddies on either side of the road were wide and very, very green, but there were billboards lined up for miles, covered in ads for sunglasses and fancy toilets, which reached as high as the coconut trees that bordered the paddies. He regretted all of it, the travel, the friendship. They were not a couple. He felt an urge to speak it out. *There can be nothing between us.* But when he glanced at her she was gazing out the window and didn't seem to notice his turmoil.

Isaac tossed his head in his sleep and Timothy jiggled the carrier up and down, hoping to keep him asleep until they arrived. He didn't want to have to stop and fix a bottle. He felt a rush of weariness so real he could have lay down in a rice paddy and slept, just floated away. He watched the water buffalo and their little friend egrets.

"Look Isaac," he whispered, Isaac's eyes shut tightly in sleep. "Birdies."

"I think I'm going to like it here," Prema said. The van wound through villages, smoke filling the air, not the sweet smelling smoke of cow dung, but the burning of the trash piles with plastic bubbling into the air. Timothy put a scarf lightly over Isaac's face to shield him from the smoke.

Prema leaned over and lowered her voice. "Notice how um, fancy, this taxi is?" she asked.

Timothy couldn't help laughing as he looked around. The roof and dashboard were covered with fake fur and there were no less than five Queen of Heaven figures stuck on the dashboard, each of them lighting up, some flashing different colors.

"Wow," he said. "It's like extreme car makeover, Catholic style."

She started to laugh and couldn't stop. He watched her as tears leaked out of the corners of her eyes and she wiped them away.

"I'm sorry," she said, gasping. "I must be really, really tired."

Timothy smiled. "I think we both are." He wished he had come here with Isabel before she died. She had lived in Goa for many years, but she told Timothy she was tired of it, that it wasn't Indian enough for her, that it was too social. "And I'm so tired of being social," she had said. "I only want to be with you." He had eaten it up.

Now he saw what she meant. It looked almost like another country, another country with a very strong Indian influence, like how he imagined Nepal or Sri Lanka would look.

They turned onto a bumpy little road and curved through palm groves. Beside him, Prema wasn't in a fit of laughter anymore, but small eruptions of giggles forced their way out of her every few minutes. She muttered "Sorry," each time. Timothy felt his shoulders relaxing. One thing was certain, it wasn't possible for him to stay trapped in his own sad, torturous mood when he was with her.

They passed cows lying grouped on the road like stones, dogs rummaging in boxes dumped in the bushes, ladies walking along the road with their saris draped in a style Timothy hadn't seen before, tied between their legs like the *dhotis* the men wore in Rajasthan. It was certainly India, but like an alternate reality of India.

He had once told Isabel that he would be done with India soon. She laughed at him. Threw her head back like she was in a movie and laughed a big teeth, full-throated belly laugh. Timothy had never liked being laughed at. He didn't like it then, though her laugh was one of the most beautiful things about her.

"What?" he said, feeling irritated.

"You will never be done with this place," she said. "India, she will haunt you for all of your life."

He had thought it was funny, ridiculous even, when she said it. Now this statement struck him as eerie and true. He couldn't explain to his mother why he was here on his own with his motherless baby, he couldn't even explain it to himself. Somehow he was caught in India's web. Something was tying him to this part of the world. Maybe Goa would be softer with him than the rest of India had been. Maybe she would release him.

Isabel had said she hadn't planned on coming back after her first time here, but India pulled her. She couldn't forget the massive, heat-stroked country.

"It sounds like a crazy woman to say this, but it is true." She had shrugged, accepting her bonds.

Timothy needed to finish things here so thoroughly that he would never have to come back again. It was too much, he and Isaac were being pieced around the world. Now part of them lay in France, with Isabel. He closed his eyes.

He opened them again. The van had stopped. Prema was looking at him, waiting.

"Sorry?" he said.

"I asked you if you know where you're going," she said.

"Oh. No."

"I'm headed to the cliffs. Do you want to go there?"

He was still caught up in his thoughts about France and Isabel lying lifeless in some grave there. He looked at Prema and asserted to himself again, *We are not a couple.* It had been fun to spend time with her, but he needed to go his own way.

"No, no actually, I'll look around here."

He pulled some money out of his pocket and gave it to her for half the taxi fare. He started to open the door, then turned to look at her. She sat back against the seat, eyes on him, red *dupatta* now balled up on her lap. Her hands lay very still on her legs. Bright sunlight poured through the window and her face was shiny with sweat.

"I'm sorry, Prema. I'm—I have to be alone."

"It's okay! I didn't expect that we would be next door neighbors here or anything." She laughed, running her hands through her hair again. It seemed to be a habit. He saw the frown between her eyes, noticed that she looked away and didn't look back at him.

"I'm sure I'll see you around, eh?" he said.

"Sure. Call me if you need anything. See you around. Take care."

His bags were heavy as he loaded them onto his back once again. The taxi drove away and left him standing outside the fence of an enormous white church. He realized that he knew nothing about where he should go. Prema had her guidebook— she had been studying it, she probably had ideas about good food to eat, things to do. He hadn't been paying attention.

After searching for a few hours, he ended up staying in a house not too far from the beach. It was a little place, something they could afford, with one room and a tiny kitchen. He and Isaac didn't need much space. His apartment was connected to the main house, with the family who owned all of it living in the back, fitting many more people into a space only twice as large as his. There was a bathroom outside, on the side of the house. By far his nicest digs so far, with a balcony, and trees in the small garden in front of the house. He settled his baby, feeding and then putting him to sleep, and walked onto his new balcony, taking a deep breath, watching the clouds, which still looked like rain. He didn't know how the landscape could get any greener, everything seemed to be growing something, but just in case, he straightened his back and prepared for the deluge.

CHAPTER 15

Prema turned off her shower and dried off with the not-very-effective towel that had been supplied with her room. She pulled a red sundress over her still damp skin and brushed her teeth while looking at herself in the mirror. She had bought the dress from a man selling clothes on the cliffs with his two daughters, who were both adept saleswomen at the ages of nine and ten. "It is looking very nice with your skin," the younger one had said as Prema held the dress against herself in the tiny mirror. She grinned at the girl and bought three dresses. A sundress over a bathing suit had quickly become her uniform during the week she had spent here.

She spat in the sink and washed the toothpaste down the drain, taking a sip of bottled water to rinse her mouth out. When she checked her teeth, she could see the tiny chip on her left incisor, there since she had fallen while skateboarding (or trying to skateboard) when she was sixteen. She brushed her wet hair, put some eyeliner on, and shrugged at the mirror. Alrighty then. She was headed for church. Mass, rather. She grabbed a *dupatta* from her chair, to wrap around her shoulders for modesty in the church.

She walked out her front door and took a deep breath. Her little room overlooked the dark craggy rocks just in front of the cliffs on the north side of Arambol beach. She loved the sharpness of the rocks in the early mornings and the sea that flowed and roiled around them. She said hello to the father of the family she rented her room from and picked her way down the hill to the path that would lead her into the village and to her rented scooter. She smelled fires and incense, the salty air and chai. She reached the main path and smiled at the Nepali bakery workers where she usually drank chai in the morning.

"Not having any today," she said. "I'm going to church!"

The young guys in the shop smiled at her.

The one with his long hair back in a ponytail asked, "Do you want your croissant?"

She paused. "Ahh. You got me. Okay, I'll eat it as I walk." It was a bad habit, eating a chocolate croissant every morning, but Prema figured she was making up for it with all the beach walking she was doing. He started to put it in a bag for her and she shook her head quickly. "No bag."

There was trash everywhere in this paradise, just like every place she had been in India. Somehow the beauty and wildness of the place made it seem even more tragic. Walking over the river to her bike, parked on the road, she saw trash choking the little stream, waiting for a large gush of water that would carry it to the ocean. She wanted to set herself up as a blockade, keep any more people from throwing trash in the stream, but it wasn't possible. She didn't know how to fight it. Prema put the last of the Nepali version of a croissant, which was delicious, in her mouth and reached into her bag for her scooter key. She felt a pang of sadness. These came at odd times. She wouldn't have thought that Timothy could have got to her so much in such a short time, but somehow thoughts of him were etched into all sorts of little things and she wished they could have continued being friends. She pulled the key out of her purse and hopped on the bike, a large automatic scooter. She drove it carefully up the street, wobbling a bit. She had been practicing, wanting to get good enough at driving it that she would be able to explore the jungles and villages on her own. She was still on her quest to find some spirituality that she could embrace, even more now that Timothy was gone. Or not gone, but ah, it was all confusing. Should she call him? He had said he needed to be alone. Did that mean he had dismissed her from his life for good? Did he even have to ability to be a friend to anyone right now? She knew what her college friends would tell her; that he was messed up and grieving and she should steer clear. Her need to search for connection with God was clear and sharp in her mind, though, and she liked challenges. She smiled as she thought of the Mass ahead of her. Surely she would find something of God in a church in India.

But really, she thought later, sitting on a hard pew in the little church, someone must be able to come up with lighting better than this. The church had looked beautiful and ornate on the outside, but inside it felt institutional, partially because of the fluorescent lighting, bright and unforgiving as well as the pews, like something you would find in a park that hadn't been taken care of very well. They were halfway through the two-hour service, and Prema was lost. She didn't understand a word of the Konkani and didn't know what they were doing, with the standing and sitting and holding things in the air. Whatever she was looking for, this was not it. She stifled a yawn and distracted herself by looking at the brightly colored, sparkly saris many of the women were wearing. Her favorite, she decided, was a purple silk sari worn by an old woman in the front pew. It had a print of turquoise paisley, very nice.

When the service was finally over, she chatted for a minute with a curious group of women who reached out to feel her earrings and the ring in her lip, then squeezed through the crowd and almost ran for her bike. She hopped on and started it, turning out of the road and onto an unfamiliar one. She felt a bit wobbly but gained confidence as she went, the air in her face wiping all the fustiness of the service away. The trees overhead sang of God, she thought. She smelled flowers somewhere, the sun flashed through the trees, there were birds. She breathed a deep breath of clean air and laughed out loud with joy, shrugging off her disappointment in the church service.

She passed Portuguese-style houses with their slanted roofs covered in clay tiles. Some had columns in front, with wide porches and seats built right into stone. Some were trimmed with intricate designs and painted with brightly colored paint. Some melted back into the jungle, black with mold, covered with vines.

From her guidebook Prema knew that Goa had been colonized by the Portuguese and had become independent only in 1960. The feeling here was so different from the rest of the country, and she missed the *lungis* and thickly populated streets of the north, but she felt light and free here, almost as if she had come to a country where she had no roots to define her or tie her down. The opposite of seething Varanasi, Goa was verdant with its ever-present jungle and the lightness of the sea that held no bodies, no ancient city, nothing but fish.

After an hour or so of driving around the jungle roads, she came back to Arambol. She parked the bike and walked down to the beach to find something to eat. It was indeed early for the season in Arambol. The rains were still coming each night and many of the beach shacks weren't completed yet, so there were only a few to choose from. There were some travelers but only a few, really. The Nepali guys at the bakery had assured her that there would be thousands before long.

"Thousands?" she asked, skeptical. It didn't seem possible, with so few travelers here now. Just yesterday, a man with long, bright red hair had driven past, hair streaming behind him. Prema had reached her hand out to stop him and ask him a question, but he was gone.

"Just wait. They are coming soon. Next week maybe."

She had raised her eyebrows at him. She'd believe it when she saw it.

She walked into the beach shack restaurant she had adopted as her own, vaguely noticing that someone sat at one of the tables. She wished Timothy was with her as she looked at the menu, thinking they could have shared something, some Indian food. She still hadn't seen him, she had no idea where he had taken a room and she didn't want to call him first. He'd been clear about what he wanted, he could call her if he wanted to be friends. She decided to get *aloo paratha*, flat bread stuffed with spiced potatoes.

A beach dog sashayed over to her and settled at her feet with a *thwap*. She pulled her foot out from under him and spoke to him, "Really?"

At the next table, someone laughed. She looked up. It was a boy with short black hair and crinkled eyes, no shirt, holding a guitar.

"Right there on your feet, is he?" he said.

"Yes! As though there aren't miles of empty sand on this beach."

"You've got the best spot. Or the best spot is the one with you in it."

Prema looked at him sharply, but he didn't seem to be hitting on her. He shaped his hands into chords on the neck of his guitar and strummed a few notes, singing to himself. Prema ordered her food and watched him.

"Where are you from?" she asked.

"England. You?"

"Canada."

"But you're Indian, right?" he asked.

This was the most common question she had heard from travelers since she'd been traveling in India."

"My parents are from Punjab." If the boy was from India he would have expressed surprise that she was Punjabi, saying that she was so dark she looked like she was from the South, to which she would reply that she liked to play in the sun. But he didn't know the ins and outs of skin color and the propriety of walking under an umbrella if you wanted to keep your skin as pale as a high caste Indian woman, so he of course didn't say any of this, he just kept strumming his guitar and singing to himself.

"Do you play anything?" he asked her. "I've been looking for someone to jam with."

"Me? No." Unbidden, the image of Timothy and his silent flute, abandoned since Isabel, came into her mind. "I have a friend who is a musician. You should play with him."

"Boyfriend?" his eyebrows were up, his face quizzical.

"Nnnoooo."

"You don't sound so sure."

"Oh, I'm sure. He's definitely not my boyfriend."

"But you wouldn't mind if he was."

Prema had been leaning over to take a bite of *paratha* but at this she brought her chin up sharply.

"What?"

"I'm good at reading people," the boy with the dark hair said. "Everyone says so." He smiled again, and Prema didn't know what to think of him. "What does your friend play?" he asked.

"Flute. But I don't know if you can really call him my friend. He's going through stuff right now and we haven't been in touch." She shook her head, staring at her *paratha*.

"Oh, you've got it bad." He grinned at her.

Prema thought it was clear she would either laugh at this ridiculous person or cry, so she laughed. She had met strange and wonderful people this week, and conversations with travelers often took swift turns into depths of relationship or spirituality that would be unthinkable in Canada. It was one of the things she loved about the travelers she had met; they were lonely, so they cut through small talk quickly, heading straight for the heart of things.

"He also doesn't play flute anymore. But I'm taking a break from having it bad," she said. "I'm going back to my quest."

The boy stood up and brought his guitar over to her table, sitting with a thud, much the same way the dog had. Which had its head lying on Prema's foot again, she realized.

"Now you have to tell me," he said. "What's your quest? Oh, wait, never mind." He held out his hand. "I'm Linus, and yes, I know you Americans—excuse me, Canadians—can only think of that cartoon kid with the blanket when you hear the name Linus, but my mum loved the name. Who're you?"

"Hi, Linus," Prema said, smiling at him. "I'm Prema."

She found herself telling Linus all about her search for God, her quest to find a way of relating to him in India. At first Linus told her about all the different gurus she could locate in Arambol or in South India—he had been in Goa during the last season as well, so he knew a lot about what there was on offer, and yes, there really were thousands of people he said—but when she said she wasn't so much looking to change her religion as to find a way to practice her own in a more Indian way, he slapped his head.

"Well, of course you're not!" he said. "Of course! And yes. How could I have forgotten?" He smiled at her and she noticed he had a gap between his two front teeth, and that he had very long eyelashes, almost as long as Timothy's.

"What?"

"The Jesus people. They're a sort of tribe, there are a few of them. They sing on the beach in the mornings. Sometimes with flowers."

"Wait, what are you talking about?" she was laughing. She couldn't help it, he was so animated and funny. She found herself thinking that she really should try to get him and Timothy together, that he could help Timothy to have a little more fun.

"There are these Jesus people who live here," he said. "I don't know if it's exactly what you're looking for, they're not from India. But they sing on the beach and they make things, food and pretty flowers and things, pictures in the sand. You know."

"I'm so confused."

"I'm not describing it very well. I can bring you to them on the beach if you want. I've steered clear of them myself, they're a bit scary, not because they're scary but because they're not, right? I don't have a quest for religion, only for music, but they're really nice."

"All right," Prema said.

"I'll introduce you once they arrive. They should be here soon, but I haven't seen them yet. And then you can introduce me to your friend who doesn't play the flute anymore."

Prema felt oddly happy, as though with Linus telling her that she could introduce him to Timothy, it guaranteed that she would see him again. She reached down beside her foot and scratched the beach dog under his chin.

CHAPTER 16

About two weeks after he arrived in Goa, Timothy left his house early in the morning to look for dolphins. A traveler in Varanasi had told Timothy things about Goa that made him think dolphins would come right out of the water to kiss him. Timothy could imagine the feel of a dolphin's skin under his hand, how it would be rubbery and wet. Friendly.

It was very early when they started walking to the beach. The air was cool and wet. A storm had swept through the night before and the rain had flown into Timothy's little room. He had to hop out of bed and close the windows, but still it trickled in. The house had a tiled roof, with some broken tiles, and old windows. When morning came, the landlady brought a few towels and mopped the floor.

The sun was out as Timothy reached the long, straight beach. The sand was packed and wet, strewn with bits of old net and some leaves. Some distance to the north, rocks were pointing at the sky, clustered together with a string of buildings clinging to the side of a cliff. Prema had said she would be staying there. She'd be waking now, maybe, like him. He put the thought, the regret, aside.

He scanned the water, hoping to be able to point dolphins out to Isaac. He looked and looked, but didn't see anything except boats tussling in the rough surf, boats like the ones that were pushed up onto the beach, small fishing boats. He walked the beach's edge with his baby, hoping for a sight of something— another person, a dolphin, a restaurant.

They found a restaurant, at least, after walking for ten minutes or so. It was a beach shack, a squat building made of wood and woven coconut fronds, open on three sides. A large blue tarp was rolled up on the overhang of the roof. Timothy supposed this was rolled down when the rain came. Three straggly-looking foreigners sat at plastic tables, far from one another. Another man argued with the Indian man who stood behind the counter, but it sounded like friendly arguing, as though they knew one another well. Timothy sat at one of the tables, lowering himself slowly into the chair. Isaac had fallen asleep on the walk and Timothy would love to sit and have some coffee while his son slept. The transition from walking to sitting was tricky when keeping a baby asleep. If he would stay sleeping now, he should be okay for a while, unless shouting people or barking dogs turned up. Timothy eyed the beach dogs warily.

The man behind the counter called for someone and a waiter made his way from the kitchen to Timothy's table, taking his time, a slightly annoyed look on his face.

"Do you have coffee?" Timothy asked.

"Milk coffee." Milk coffee meant Nescafé.

"One milk coffee please. And a muesli with fruit and curd."

"One milk coffee one fruit muesli curd," the waiter repeated, looking off over Timothy's shoulder. "Okay." He walked back to the kitchen, calling out Timothy's order as he went.

The morning was going well, Timothy thought, feeling tentative with optimism. He wasn't too overwhelmed, no thoughts of the endless future without Isabel. He was gambling on the curd being good. There was nothing like overly fermented yogurt to take the shine off a morning.

At the next table a man was watching him. He was heavily tattooed, with short tufty hair. He was wearing only a lungi that was folded in half so it rested above his knees. Timothy had a sinking feeling. He knew this man. It was the guy he had met in Dharamkhot, the one who pontificated about the perfection of Isabel's death at her memorial. Timothy remembered he lived half the year in Goa and half the year up north, the way many travelers in India did.

The man spoke to Timothy first.

"Just arrive?" he asked.

"Oh, about a week and a half ago."

"Shocked?"

"Shocked? No, should I be?"

"Oh, you know. Some blokes show up not knowing that it'll be so wet here still. They get disappointed, pout a bit, head back to mummy."

Timothy thought his accent sounded Scottish.

"I knew it would be pretty empty," Timothy said. "We haven't exactly been anywhere in India 'in season' yet."

The man squinted at Timothy. His eyebrows were thick and black, his eyes green and intense, like an assault, beneath them. His hair was thinning, graying a bit. "Haven't we met before?" he asked.

Timothy's coffee arrived. He reached out and spooned some sugar into it. It was thick and milky. Did he want to let Craig know that he recognized him from the memorial service, that Timothy had been the one who had yelled "Bullshit!" in the middle of Craig's very long speech? Timothy wished he could just disappear. Or die. One or the other.

Craig made a quick motion, like a double take, at the bundle on Timothy's chest.

"No, I know who you are, you're that kid! Isabel's man!"

Timothy felt as if Craig had just punched him in the stomach. His mouth was full of the coffee and he thought he would throw up or choke if he tried to swallow it. He turned and coughed his mouthful of coffee into the sand at his feet.

"And you're Craig-the-universe-is-perfect-Scottish-ex-boyfriend," he said, his voice hard now, angry.

Craig stared at him for a minute, his eyebrows way up, forcing his forehead into a mass of lines.

"Yes, I remember you now. Bullshit kid."

Timothy didn't respond. He turned his head slightly to the side so he didn't have to look at Craig. Isabel had told him that she spent years being the girlfriend of too many men, one after the other. Craig was somewhere in the middle of those years, and he hadn't treated Isabel very well. Right before she met Timothy, Isabel had taken a three-year break from men.

"I was broken in half, though. I wasn't very nice to them, either," she told Timothy, talking about the boyfriends. She sat on a chair next to their bed in Rajasthan, looking miserable, as though to tell him these things she needed to get farther away from him. As though air could make any distance between them. They were in Rajasthan in the time that could be considered a honeymoon, soon after the desert wedding. Timothy didn't want to know about the other men Isabel had been with, but she felt that she needed to tell him, making a thing of it, sitting down properly in a chair with her hands folded. The names burned his ears, but he reached through the air between them and pulled her next to him on the bed. She was so small, like a bird.

Timothy felt hatred for Craig boiling up inside him. He spooned some more sugar into his coffee, hoping he could make it taste better. Craig rubbed at his forearm, then leaned back, pulled a bag of tobacco from a leather pouch slung around his waist, and started to roll a cigarette. Timothy took small sips of his coffee.

"I'm sorry," Craig said after he lit his cigarette and took a drag. "I don't remember your name."

"Timothy."

"Timothy, Isabel's guy."

"Do you mind?"

"What?"

"You're being so flippant."

"Oh, kid. When you get to be my age you'll see it. Life's a real bitch sometimes, so you have to look for the perfection, the way things fall into place, all of it is wonderful. Life knocks you down, you get up and laugh."

He was unbelievable, Timothy thought.

"I married Isabel, you know," Timothy said. "She told me everything." The drinking, the soupy spiritual words, the other women.

"She did?" Craig stared at him. He sat forward in his chair and pulled a piece of tobacco off his upper lip. Mid forties certainly, but very fit. Timothy was skinny and young with muscles that you could imagine if you squinted hard enough, just like his father. No, no, they were there, but he would never bulk up like Craig.

"Well, bloody hell. We only dated for three months or so. Before that we were friends for years." He leaned back again, took a long drag of his stumpy little cigarette. "To tell the truth, I never knew Isabel to get into a long go of it with a bloke. She must have thought a lot of you."

Timothy hated this. He hated sitting here having a trite conversation about the woman he had loved. He hated talking about her because it was so much less than being with her. He felt too depressed to keep the conversation going—to ask all the scripted questions about Craig's life and background and how long he'd been here. He didn't want to go deeper into his life with Isabel.

The waiter strolled past and stood looking out at the sea with one hand on the back of a nearby chair. Timothy tried to get his attention.

"Can I get some milk?" he asked.

The waiter appeared not to hear him and began walking in the other direction, so Timothy raised his voice. "Hello!" The waiter looked over at him.

"Milk please!" Isaac startled and cried at his loud voice. Timothy could have kicked himself. He pulled at the knots on the carrier to loosen it and pulled the baby out. The waiter brought the fruit muesli curd and forgot the milk for Timothy's lost cause of a cup of coffee, but it didn't matter because now Timothy needed to get the bottle out of the bag and feed Isaac before he did anything else.

He was fumbling one-handed with the zipper on his backpack with a crying, squirming Isaac in his other hand, when someone came out of nowhere and reached for Isaac. Timothy looked up, startled, and saw Prema standing beside him. She took Isaac and held him while Timothy used both hands to get the zipper unstuck. When he had the bottle in his hand, she passed the baby back, smiling at Timothy.

"Mind if I sit?" she asked.

He shook his head. She didn't have Indian clothes on, now. She was wearing a knee-length skirt and a spaghetti strap tank top.

"Who's this, then?" Craig asked, as Prema pulled a chair out and made it stable in the sand.

"I'm Prema," she said, shooting Timothy a look, like *who's he?*

"Prema, Craig. Craig, Prema," Timothy muttered. Isaac had his bottle and was quiet. Timothy watched the baby's eyelashes drift closed. He always closed his eyes when he ate. *What kind of guy talks to a grieving person like that?* Timothy hated Craig with more heat than he had felt for anything in months.

"Where are you from, Craig?" Prema asked.

"Edinburgh, and you?"

"Vancouver."

"Canadian, eh?" He smirked at his joke. "My girlfriend is from Quebec."

Timothy sat up. "Does she speak French?"

"Of course."

"Is she here? Could she teach me?" If he could read the journal, so much would be different. He could have her words, something of her. He could read it to Isaac at night, just before they fell asleep.

"That's a tall order, that," Craig said, laughing. "What do you want to learn French for? Looking for another French lady?"

Timothy downed the rest of his terrible Nescafé. Of course it was a stupid thing to ask. Ridiculous. Worthy of ridicule.

"No reason," he said. He looked at Prema. "Craig is an ex-boyfriend of Isabel's," he said. Craig whistled a few notes at a dog nearby. Prema held Timothy's eyes for a minute, then looked back down at her menu.

Timothy shifted Isaac so he was in one of his arms with the bottle, and used his other arm to put a spoonful of muesli and yogurt in his mouth. The yogurt wasn't bad but the muesli was soggy and the fruit salad was kind of banana heavy. He was sure that Craig was the rudest person he had ever met. The table was wobbly in the sand and when he put his arm down hard to rescue the bottle, which was slipping, the table tipped and Prema caught his muesli bowl as it skittered to the edge. Timothy kept his eyes on the ugly plastic salt shaker that sat in the middle of the table, grime in all its cracks. Tears were knocking at the door but Timothy couldn't let this guy see him cry. Timothy knew his type, a real bloky bloke. He'd mock Timothy the moment his back was turned.

"I don't see why it's a tall order," Prema said with her soft voice, emerging from behind the menu. She raised one hand and hailed a waiter, pushing her sunglasses back so they rested on her head. When she swiveled to get the waiter's attention, Timothy saw that he had been right, she did have a tattoo. It was right there on her shoulder, a small bird with wings spread, the tips of its feathers brushing her spine.

"You don't?" Craig asked.

"No." She shrugged and turned back to him. The waiter was busy. "People learn languages every day. I bet this waiter knows three or four languages. Bhaiya!" The waiter finally walked to her and she spoke to him in Hindi. He answered her. When he walked away, she turned to them. "Four. He speaks

Hindi, Marathi, Konkani, and Kannada. Five if you count the little bit of English he knows."

Timothy just looked at her, his mouth open. "How is that possible?" he asked.

"He's from Mangalore, in Karnataka, where they speak Kannada. But in Mangalore they also speak Konkani, which is why it's easy for him to move here—where they speak Konkani—and he learned Hindi in school. What else? Oh, he worked in Mumbai as a houseboy since he was ten. That's where he learned Marathi and practiced his Hindi."

"You found all that out by talking to him just then?"

"Yes, as fast as I just told you." She smiled at him. "India has anywhere from five hundred to over a thousand languages, depending on which surveys you believe. All Indian people know how to speak more than one language, even those who only go to school until they're ten, like that guy. That's why Timothy can easily learn French, if he wants to," she said to Craig. "Language isn't magic. You just need to practice a bit."

The waiter brought her toast with butter on the side, a banana, and a cup of chai, and she nodded to thank him. What was it, bringing these tears that were so urgently crowding behind his eyes now? The relief at seeing Prema? The gentle way she did everything from buttering her toast to contradicting Craig? The harsh descent into grief after a relatively good morning? The thought of the waiter as a ten-year-old servant to a rich family, sleeping on the floor alone? He looked down at Isaac and felt protectiveness and pity twist his stomach. He tried distraction, shoveling another spoonful of banana and muesli into his mouth, chewing desperately. He felt so weak in front of tanned tattoos and muscles over there at the next table.

Prema put a hand on Timothy's arm and he lost it. He put his free hand over his face and sobbed, covered in oats and yogurt, flecks of food in Isaac's hair. Every night alone, every hour that he hadn't been able to sleep because he was cradling their son, every look of Isabel's that he would never see again, it all came out onto the red plastic table that was so unsteady on the wet sand. Craig stood up and came near. He put a hand on Timothy's shoulder, heavily, so that it felt like he was pushing Timothy into the ground. He would go down deep, they could bury him there, Isabel could do it, this time she could be the one. *Why did you leave me in a world full of strangers?* he wanted to ask her. *After all the work we did, knowing each other so hard?*

This was far from the dolphins he had hoped to see; this table was no sleek body; there was no motion in the sea, no beautiful rubbery faces. He tried to calm down, but the squeaking sobs he was coughing out didn't slow or come to a stop. He took a deep breath and went through Bach's flute concerto in C in his head, and when that seemed to work, through the lyrics of the song "Let Down" by Radiohead, from the OK Computer album. 15/9 timing, which was incredible. He was gaining control of himself. Isaac watched him with big eyes, his bottle nipple half out of his mouth, and when Timothy looked at him, he smiled into Timothy's eyes. At his shoulder, Timothy heard Craig take in a raspy breath. Isaac's face was so much like Isabel's, his eyes the small slivers of moon which he smiled, her black angled eyebrows. Timothy glanced up at Craig and saw something hit him. Craig understood something he didn't get before, back twenty minutes ago when he was offering flat platitudes.

"How old are you, man?" Craig asked quietly.

"Twenty-four," Timothy said, testing his voice.

"Well, shit."

Prema took her hand away from Timothy's wrist, and he immediately missed its weight. He felt like she had been holding him together and where her hand had been felt cold and without substance. She took a bite of toast and chewed it, looking at the ocean. Isaac kicked his foot back and forth, the bottle back in his mouth, eyes closed again. Craig retrieved the cigarette papers and tobacco from his table and sank into the third chair at Timothy's table. It leaned wildly when it took his weight, but didn't tip over. He scooped a small pile of tobacco out of the pouch and onto a piece of paper.

"Isabel's mother didn't want him?" he asked.

"I want him," Timothy said, feeling the heat of anger in his chest. "But no, she didn't. She's very old."

"Wow. A big change, that. Single dad suddenly, at your age."

Timothy couldn't tell whether Craig was trying to be sympathetic or rude. He looked at Craig's scalp through his salty thinning hair as Craig bent over his cigarette, licking the paper to seal it. He placed the cigarette in his mouth and lit it. Prema absently tapped on the table near Timothy's wrist, a drum rhythm that was slightly offbeat.

"Yeah," Timothy said.

He met Prema's eyes and thought of their train journey. Life would be so simple if they had never needed to get off. If life was only journeys and no arrivals. Prema stopped tapping and leaned on her elbows, lacing her fingers under her chin. Craig shifted in his chair, looking uncomfortable. Timothy could see that he was putting the pieces together, coming up with his slow equation, the truth of what Timothy had here, of how quickly a life could change. He didn't know what to say, perhaps, he didn't know how to say he was sorry for joking about it, being flippant.

Or maybe the chair was just uncomfortable.

"Juliette and I would love to help out in any way we can," he said.

Timothy found that hard to believe, seeing that Juliette, who must be the girlfriend from Québec, couldn't know that he existed. But he appreciated the sentiment. Sort of.

"Here," Craig said. "I'll give you my number." He took a pen from Prema and scratched his number onto a napkin that he plucked from the ugly plastic napkin holder. He handed it to Timothy, who looked at the number as if it meant something and nodded. Craig stood, looked out at the ocean for a few moments, then gave a small wave, handed some bills to the restaurant proprietor, and sauntered off. Timothy watched him walk away down the beach until he was very small. Far off, toward the cliffs, he stopped and did a few sun salutations.

Prema buttered her second piece of toast. Isaac finished with his bottle and Timothy set it on the table. He lifted the baby to burp him, and Isaac nestled his head into the space between Timothy's shoulder and his neck. The baby was so soft and warm in Timothy's arms. Something light and warm moved into Timothy's chest. His son calmed him more than Bach's flute concerto in C had, which was saying a lot.

When Timothy had scored a burp out of Isaac and finished what he could of his soggy breakfast, he stood and paid his bill. Prema had been silent since Craig left. She stared off at the sea with a dreamy look on her face, writing in the little notebook she had with her. Now she looked at Timothy.

"I'm staying just over there," Timothy said, pointing. "In a pink house with a tiled roof, right beside the chapel. You can't miss it. If you ever want to hang out."

She pulled on one of her long feather earrings with one graceful brown hand, and smiled.

"Yeah," she said. "I'll see you around."

Timothy turned to go. He turned back just before he walked out from under the awning of the restaurant, onto the open sand.

"Thanks," he said.

She didn't ask for what.

CHAPTER 17

Isaac was a week past four months before Timothy realized he had reached another month-birthday. Isaac at four months was really different. It seemed that he had decided he liked living in the world. He smiled and kicked when Timothy came around the corner from the kitchen into the bigger room. The kitchen was tiny and terrible to cook in, but Timothy was glad to have a fridge to store cucumbers and watermelon. Their life started to take on a new rhythm. They woke at dawn. If it was raining, Timothy cleaned. Everyone had been telling him that the rains were unbelievably long this year, that in November it should be sunny already, that soon the sun would come and dry everything, that the skies wouldn't be so dark anymore, that his dreadlocks would dry out and stop smelling moldy. He wasn't sure he believed it. It seemed impossible that it would ever be sunny for an entire day, let alone a stretch of days with blue sky beyond everything, beyond even the sea. It rained. This was life now. So Timothy cleaned. He fed Isaac his bottle in the morning and got down on his hands and knees to scrub at the corners of the floor, which looked like they hadn't been washed for a long time. He used a toothbrush and a packet of laundry detergent he had bought for this purpose, and he had finished the line of grout along the base of the whole front wall. It looked fantastic.

"Cleanliness is next to godliness," he told Isaac, who was lying on his back on a blanket beside him. "Except that I never really understood how that was true. There are many things closer to godliness than being clean, but we should both try to be cleaner, anyway. Especially you, because you still poo everywhere." Timothy was still using a mix of cloth and disposable diapers, hauling the dirty cloth diapers out to the laundry lady down the street when the bucket was full.

The baby watched the ceiling fan whirl, kicking his small legs, which were getting chubbier by the day. When Timothy spoke, Isaac's eyes got wider and he kicked harder. The blanket moved along the smooth tile as he kicked, scooting him slowly across the floor, until he kicked himself right under the bed, where he was surprised at the sudden dark. He started fussing, and Timothy hauled him back out by pulling on the blanket, sliding him across the floor toward the windows and the light. Timothy hummed to calm the baby down, which usually worked so that he went back to watching the fan. This time he didn't stop fussing. It was time to walk around with him until he got sleepy enough that he would just nod off on the bed. Timothy walked and hummed, walked and hummed, and when he lay the baby on the bed, Isaac's eyes drifted shut and stayed shut.

"Good boy," Timothy whispered, and went back to cleaning.

There was a specific technique to cleaning out old cracks. You needed to coax the dirt out, you couldn't just rush in there and scrub it. Go too quickly and you ran the risk of pushing the dirt farther in, past the help of even a toothbrush. There were a lot of people in the world who didn't know how to clean properly. Timothy was lucky to be the son of his mother, who taught him all he knew. She would be proud of him if she saw the way he was taking care of this room. The clothes and bottles may have been a bit messy, but this edge of floor was sparkling.

It was the corners that were the hardest.

Sometimes the rain stopped and the sun even came out. Then Timothy and Isaac burst out of the house and walked to the beach, making a long loop along the beach and up into the village, to the *puri bhaji* place for breakfast and then back around to home. This week there had been four half-sunny days. It was close to the end of October. Timothy's landlady made a sucking noise against the roof of her mouth and shook her head.

"Too much rain this year," she said.

Last week there were four days in a row when it rained all day long. He cleaned the floor with the toothbrush, paged through Isabel's journal. No one had come by. Not even Prema. After his cry on the beach, Timothy felt a lot like soggy newspaper. He was glad to be alone, cleaning.

Isaac had been putting on weight and felt heavy in the baby carrier now, a large stone that kicked and even babbled. Every day something new. *Every day is a wonder,* Timothy reminded himself as he cleaned the floor or washed bottles or stuffed Isaac in the baby carrier. That's what his mother used to say. He hadn't talked much yet with the family who owned his house, though he could always hear their voices in the rooms adjoining his, like birds in the walls and just as incomprehensible. They smiled at each other in the mornings. He had the journal, his toothbrush, his baby, and the birds in the walls; this was his life now.

He worked on the edge that was on the other side of the door. He had been glancing at the sky through the window for a while, wondering if the sun was going to come out. It seemed possible, which would mean escape from the room, but Isaac was asleep on the bed and Timothy wanted him to finish his nap before they went out. Last night had been rough, with Isaac awake for hours, eyes wide open, kicking on the bed beside Timothy. "Just go to sleep," Timothy had said to him. He wasn't even fussing, only kicking, kicking, kicking, until Timothy thought he would go crazy.

When Timothy heard a knock, he jumped to his feet because the door was unlocked and he could be squeezed behind it if it opened suddenly. He pulled it open quietly and saw Maria, his landlady, and then two steps behind her, Prema. His stomach did a funny little flutter.

Both women stared at Timothy and the black toothbrush he held in his hand.

He put his finger to his lips. "I'm cleaning," he said, his voice nearly a whisper. Maria walked in with Prema just behind her. They looked at the single clean line stretched across the front of the house, like a line of white tape. Maria looked at him. Prema looked at him. Prema started to speak, but Timothy ushered her out of the house and onto the porch.

He sank onto a plastic chair, suddenly exhausted. He waved at the red concrete benches that were built into the little porch.

"Where is Baba's mother?" Maria asked.

Timothy stared at her. "What?"

"Dharamsala?" Maria asked.

"No, Auntie Ji," Prema said. "She died in Dharamsala." She repeated it in Hindi and mimed dying by acting like she was sleeping on her clasped hands. Understanding washed over Maria's face. She looked horrified, clicking her tongue on the roof of her mouth and crossing herself.

"I was thinking she will coming soon."

"No," Timothy said. He leaned over and held his head in his hands. They smelled like laundry detergent and mold.

"I am taking care of Baba," Maria said. "You go."

Timothy didn't understand.

"I was just about to say the same thing," Prema said, looking up at him and smiling. "That toothbrush tells me you need to get out."

He shook his head and looked at his feet.

"Now, Timothy. You should go."

"Yes," Maria said. "You are eating?"

Now that she mentioned it, no. Timothy shook his head because he hadn't been eating much. Bites here and there and yesterday he ate a whole bunch of bananas. He ate when it was sunny and they could sit somewhere long enough to eat. He looked at his wrists, pale and bony. He glanced up at Prema and saw her looking back at him with her dark eyes, her black hair falling just in front of her face. She smoothed it out of the way.

"Go," she said. "Auntie and I can watch him together," for confirmation looking at Maria, who nodded. "I know how to put a bottle together, remember?"

Fifteen minutes later Timothy walked down the damp dirt path, smoking a cigarette, feeling light and empty without a baby solidly tied to the front of him, without tiny arms and legs swinging or kicking. He had his phone and a stomach that roared with hunger and anxiety, so the first thing he did was walk to the little restaurant by the coconut shop that had opened just the week before. It was a long walk, but the beach shacks were far too expensive for him. If he ate out at all, he ate here, or sometimes up at the village.

Good smells greeted him as he walked inside the shop. He put his cigarette out and threw it in a trash pile. His stomach roared louder, loud enough for people to hear if it had been silent in the shop. Thankfully, a table full of Goan men were talking and laughing and his loud stomach wasn't noticeable. He ducked under the roof and sat at one of the tables, facing out into the coconut grove. There was a pile of young coconuts just next to the restaurant, waiting to be opened and the water drunk with a straw. The owner of the restaurant, a man named Sagar, stepped out of the sun and into the restaurant.

"Where is the baba?" he asked. Timothy had learned when he came to Goa that Goans said "baby" for girl and "baba" for boy. "Baby or baba?" was a question he heard a lot when he was out walking with Isaac.

"Sleeping," Timothy told him, waving his hand in the direction of his house. He ordered *puri bhaji* and waited as the man walked slowly back into the kitchen to get the food. A little kid hopped out of the kitchen and over to

Timothy's table. He moved a chair beside Timothy and climbed onto it, sitting down with his legs sticking straight out in front of him. Timothy smiled and ruffled the kid's hair.

Sagar brought out the plate of *puri bhaji*. The *puri* was deep fried flat bread, puffed from heat until it was almost as round as a ball, served with potato coconut curry. Timothy dug in. *Puri* was a very satisfying food to eat. Every time Timothy ordered it, it came to his table, golden, round, and steaming. He tore into it, devoured it. But there it was the next time he came for breakfast: perfect and mouth-watering again.

The sky was doing something where it was half storm cloud and half hyper-realistic color and brightness. As Timothy dipped the bread in the curry and put it in his mouth, his eyes were pulled back to the sky again and again. It reminded him of skies at home, the sun setting over the ocean, turning driftwood and stones to a deep orange. On the beach at home he wouldn't be sitting next to a massive pile of coconuts, though. He wouldn't drive back into the jungle on his scooter, see the green spilling over, verdant and flowering. Black mold and vines covering everything until the whole world seemed to be wet and alive, almost creeping along. Too alive for comfort.

It was hard for him to swallow for a moment, as he thought of his forested coast, of the sting of cold wind on his face and the brightness of the sun. He kept his eyes on the sky and took a sip of water. Swallowed. He thought of snow on fields, the crunch of it under his feet. It didn't snow all that often on the island, but when it did, you'd better believe they were out in it, his cousins running over to his house to collect Sarah and him as fast as their feet (or when they were older, the snowmobile) would carry them. He wiped sweat from his upper lip and his cheeks and chin as the chillies in the *bhaji* went to work on his throat and sweat glands. It was hot now that the sun was out. He was glad for the sun, despite the heat. He needed the sun to clear the clouds away and dry their laundry, to dry a little of the wetness that seemed to cling to the walls of his house.

Two people approached from the beach side of the coconut grove. Timothy recognized Craig from his shirtless saunter and bright *lungi* before his face became clear. He was walking with a willowy girl. Timothy asked Sagar for another plate of *puri* to mop up the rest of his *bhaji*, and sat back to watch Craig and the girl as they got nearer. He guessed that the beautiful girl was Juliette. She looked twenty years younger than Craig, roughly the same age as Timothy. They spotted him and approached with smiles, like people coming close to a dog they were uncertain of.

"Morning to you," Craig said as the two of them reached Timothy and stood at the restaurant's entrance.

"Good morning."

"You're looking remarkably alone," Craig said. Juliette flashed a quick look at him and he added, "The baby sleeping, eh?"

Timothy felt the familiar pain in his sternum. Pity shone from Juliette's face, clear as glass.

"My friend is looking after Isaac," he said.

"Your friend?"

"My landlady," Timothy said, amending his story swiftly. He didn't want to get into the story of Prema with Craig. He stretched his hand out to the girl. "You must be Juliette. I'm Timothy."

She leaned forward and shook his hand. He saw that she had tiny circles tattooed above her eyebrows, following their shape. She was as beautiful as if she were from another planet. Timothy looked back and forth between Craig and Juliette. They were both tall, looming over him in his chair, and deeply tanned. She had straight, light brown hair that fell to her shoulder blades. She was dressed in a skirt and tank top. No bra. Timothy looked away. After North India it was shocking, seeing so much skin, seeing a girl's shoulders and legs. Even Prema had started wearing sleeveless dresses in Goa. Juliette had more tattoos lacing up her legs and on her arms. Was he staring? He didn't mean to be staring. The two of them looked chock full of life, it was brimming out of them; they were golden like the *puri*, verdant like the jungle. He looked down at his own pale, bony wrist as he pulled his hand back.

"It is nice to meet you, Timothy," Juliette said. Her accent was French, but it wasn't like Isabel's soft Parisian accent. Juliette's voice was stronger, the vowels were wider. Her accent sounded like the French channel he watched on TV in his childhood, thinking that the words would eventually arrange themselves in his brain in a way that he could understand. He could sometimes pick out a few of the words he was learning in his French classes at school. Some he remembered now. *Oeuf. Poulet. Fantastic! Je suis désolé. Voulez vous repetér s'il vous plait.*

"Do you want to join me?" Timothy asked them. The two of them were standing in full sunlight, which Timothy knew was just barely tolerable. They looked at each other and spoke without saying any words. *Do you want to?* she was saying. Timothy could see it, and the tiny shrug Craig gave in return. He was surprised to find that he wanted them to stay. "I can't sit long," he said in a rush. "Have to get back to Isaac. But we could have a chai."

"I can't see why not," Craig said. "What do you say, darlin'?"

"*Oui*, I'll have some chai," Juliette said, pulling a chair out.

After some scraping of plastic chairs on the concrete floor, and some rearranging, they were seated. When the two of them weren't as tall or shining in the sunlight, they looked more normal, as any sweaty human might. Okay, Craig looked like any sweaty human; Juliette still looked like a particularly beautiful alien. But Timothy was relieved. He rubbed his hand over his face. His beard had grown, filling out more than it ever had before. He sat up a little straighter and found that he was staring at Juliette again, trying to follow the pattern of circles above her eyes. They weren't black, he found, but dark brown, just a little darker than her skin. He turned away, embarrassed, and called to Sagar for chai.

"You should take a swim while you're out here," Craig said. "Nothing like a good swim in the morning."

"Isn't it dangerous at this time of year?" Timothy asked. People had told him not to go in.

"Nah, not now. Should be fine. It's nearly November, for God's sake. I can't believe it's been raining this long!" He shook his head.

Timothy had noticed that expats in India got frustrated when the weather did unexpected things. They had learned to trust in the faithfulness of Indian seasons. Hot, monsoon, cool, and repeat. It shouldn't change. At home on the Island, they didn't have anything so regular to trust in. The winter could be cold or mild; the summer could be warm, or it could be rainy and cold.

The cups of chai arrived, sweet and thick in tiny glasses that burned your fingers unless you picked them up exactly at the rim. Craig blew on his chai, then went on.

"Just don't go out too far. Today it looks calm." His Scottish accent was strong. When he pronounced *calm*, it rhymed with *ham*. "You'll like it now, when the beach is empty. Next week you won't even know this place, all the foreigners will come pouring in. It'll be packed in no time at all." He shook his head gloomily. "Just have a look at the water, why don't you, when you get down there."

"He must be careful of undercurrents," Juliette said. "You can't see them. He won't be able to see them, Craig, because they're under the water."

"That's right, Julie. She's a smart little lady, this one," Craig told Timothy, laughing and patting Juliette's head. She smacked him on the upper arm, and the sound was sharp, with some power behind it.

"Because you told him to have a look," she said. She seemed upset.

Timothy tried to think of what his sister, Sarah, would say, or do even, if someone called her a smart little lady. He smiled at the thought.

"What's the smile for, Timmy? Usually you're looking so glum."

The smile slid off of Timothy's face.

"Usually? We've only talked once," he said.

"Ah, but I've seen you hither and thither. Passing by on the beach with your lad strapped on your chest, carrying him like a cross. I've never seen anyone who needs to lighten up so much."

"Thanks," Timothy said. He swiped his last piece of *puri* in his *bhaji*, a little harder than necessary, and tossed it in his mouth. He took a napkin and wiped his hands, chewed and swallowed, picked up his chai to take a sip.

"I was thinking about my sister," he said.

"Oh yeah? Is she pretty? Available?" He winked at Timothy and then yelped as Juliette pinched the skin of his forearm between her fingers. "I'm only taking the mickey, darlin', only kidding."

Timothy chose not to answer. "I wish she would come visit."

"Yeah and why not? You should ask her."

"I guess I thought she would know I want her here, with everything that's happened."

"Never assume anything. That's what my dad always said."

A flock of crows swooped into a clump of coconut trees in the grove, fluttering and squawking as if they were crazy things. They sat and insulted the neighborhood for a while before launching off in a bird wind. Juliette ordered a second chai and when it arrived she took a sip and yelped. She had burned her tongue and now Craig had to take a look at it to make sure it was all right. They went on like this for a while, with *poor Julie's* and kisses, until Timothy decided it was time for him to go.

"I'm gonna head out," he said. He nodded at the two of them and walked to the doorway to pay Sagar.

"We need a real get-together, mate, cheer you up," Craig called to him. "I'll get people to my house, we'll do it next week, when more people come rolling in. We'll have a jam."

"Yeah?" Timothy said. He put his change into his waist belt.

"Where can we do it?" Juliette asked.

"We could do it at our place, love, what do you think? We've got the room." Craig turned to Timothy. "Gorgeous little place in the jungle on the Pernem road." He tipped his chair back and Timothy watched it bend alarmingly. Craig looked pleased at his idea, rubbing one of his hands through his hair. He patted his bare stomach, which showed not even a whiff of a paunch. "That's it, then. You live in the little pink house next to the juice place, right? I'll come by once we settle a date. Try to get a babysitter and we can have a good time. It'll be the cheering up Timothy party."

Put like that, it sounded horrific. A party in general didn't sound good or bad, but if everyone was going to be looking at him to see if he was perking up the whole time? *Sure, fine, great*, he said. Juliette's hands were wrapped around her chai like bows on a gift, so lovely. Timothy had been staring at her too many times, but he knew it was Isabel he wanted.

CHAPTER 18

Timothy paid and left. The path was packed and dark orange, made of dirt the color of one of his sister's conté crayons. The heat seemed to fight him, trying to keep him away from the water, but he pushed through it, trudging off the path and over the dunes until he was spit out on the beach, lightheaded from heat and freedom. He waved at a familiar fisherman who stood pulling fish out of his net and throwing them into a large basket.

"Baba?" the man asked.

"With Maria," Timothy said. The fisherman was Timothy's neighbor and knew Maria. Timothy thought they were related somehow, somebody being married to someone else's brother or sister, he wasn't sure. The fisherman nodded and smiled. The people who lived around Timothy seemed so gentle and happy, not pushy like Craig.

Timothy remembered Craig's words about him carrying his cross, looking unhappy. He gave his arms an experimental swing and straightened his back, marching to the water. Cheerful walking. He swung his arms higher, took big strides. Not far from him, two young Goan women stood beside a fishing boat, watching him and laughing. Timothy stopped with the cheerful walking and walked his normal way down to the edge of the water. The sea stretched in front of Timothy, spreading out from the long beach and moving into infinity. The sun pushed against some massive storm clouds that sat like heavy old men in the distance. It looked like a losing battle. He saw a handful of fishermen pushing a boat back onto the beach, moving it along wooden beams that were slick with oil. One man ran the beams from front to back as the boat moved onto the sand. At another boat, a cluster of people took fish out of their nets, tossing them into baskets. As a woman tossed one into the basket, it caught the light, flashing white and silver like a mirror in the sun.

The sea swept out to the horizon in swathes of teal, dark blue, and grey. He thought about what Juliette had said, all the swirling that went on beneath the surface. But all around, the morning was bright and clear, and the only people out here were working hard. He owed it to the brief sunshine to enjoy this water. He took his shirt and pants off, stood in his boxers for a moment, then ran straight in.

At first the water surprised him with its warmth, and then, with its kindness. He waded beyond the surf and let the water surround him. He kicked back and floated on the surface, his pale stomach and chest glowing in the sun. Small waves splashed over his face so that he had to close his eyes and mouth to keep from swallowing the sea and all that was in it. He floated like that for a while, then opened his eyes and saw that he had drifted farther than he meant to. He turned and swam back to shore. There was no undercurrent that day. The waves were small but strong. He bobbed around for a while, letting himself be tossed and scrubbed by the sandy floor.

The sea felt like a person, like a welcoming friend, like a woman. It felt like the nicest conversation he had had in months. Out of nowhere, he thought of Prema, her hair at her neck, her brown eyes on him, one hand up at her mouth when she laughed. He dove down and tried to sit at the bottom, but the waves were coming quickly and he was knocked around and ended up with water in his nose. He surfaced, coughing up salty water.

The family around the boat was stashing their net away. One woman put the large basket of fish on her head and swayed up the beach, heading for home. Timothy stood and waded out of the water. He collapsed on the sand, lay his face on his arms. The sun was hot on his back immediately. He felt clean and tired. He rolled over, stretched out and lay there with his eyes closed for a long moment, letting the sun dry him. Then he felt the first raindrops.

He jumped up. "What the—?" He hopped into his pants. The clouds had knit together quickly and he was pelted with thousands of raindrops. They plunged out of the sky and toward him, divine from the clouds. There was a flash and a loud crack as lightning struck. He carried his shirt in one hand, flip flops in the other, and sprinted toward home. Laughing.

Prema met him at the door as he stepped onto the porch, dripping. Timothy smiled at her, still laughing a little, breathless.

"Hi," he said.

"Hey," Prema said. "Wow. You need to get stuck in the rain more often." She looked behind her, where Maria and her daughters sat on the floor in Timothy's room, playing with Isaac, who was cradled in one of the girl's laps.

"We're all smitten," Prema said. "He's got us eating out of the palm of his hand."

Timothy smiled and wiped his feet the best he could. He scuttled to his backpack like a beach crab, to dig out dry clothes. He stepped into his bathroom and shivered through a cold shower, then dressed in pants and an old t-shirt. This time when he entered the room he made a beeline for Isaac, scooping him out of Maria's daughter's lap. The baby was kicking and smiling, and his eyes grew wide and he smiled bigger when he caught sight of Timothy. Timothy hugged him close and rubbed his nose on his baby's nose.

"Hi, little bear," he said. "I missed you." He turned to Maria and Prema. "It was okay?" he asked.

"Yes, okay! No problem, no problem," Maria said. The daughters nodded in agreement. They were around eight or nine, Timothy thought. Prema leaned against the wall with her hands behind her, watching Timothy with Isaac.

"Were you all here together?" he asked.

"I was here on my own for a bit, then about a half hour ago they came over to play with him. He's adorable, Timothy. Such a sweetie."

"He is, isn't he? How long was I gone?" He sank to the floor to sit with Maria and the girls. They took turns trying to catch Isaac's attention, smiling and laughing at him. He gurgled and cooed back up at them. In the dark room the baby was as bright as the sun.

"Two hours," Prema said. He had noticed earlier that she was wearing shorts. She had several leather anklets tied on one ankle and a silver jangly one, which was brilliant against her brown skin, on the other.

"Two hours? I didn't realize it was so long," he said. "I'm sorry, thank you—"

She interrupted him with a hand on his arm. "Don't mention it. I wish I had offered to help before. You look so much better." She smiled and he could see she meant it. His shoulders lowered a little.

After Maria and the girls left, Prema walked over to sit on the edge of the bed.

"Why don't I come back tomorrow?" she asked. "I can watch him for you for a while."

He didn't know what to say. In some ways it seemed like a very bad idea, but he didn't want to hurt her feelings.

"You don't have to do that," he said.

"I know I don't *have* to," she said. "But I'm not doing all that much right now." She shrugged. "I don't know, I'm glad to help."

He thought about it for a few moments. *The water, the morning and the sea.* "Well, sure then."

"Okay," she said, and she stood up and walked to where her bag sat, at the end of the bed. She picked it up, her movements graceful, the flash of a fish in the light. "I'll see you tomorrow then. I'm meeting someone now."

"Meeting someone?" Timothy felt a small lurch in his stomach.

"Yeah, this guy named Linus. You should meet him sometime. I told him about you. He's a musician."

Timothy shrugged and saw her to the door. He couldn't see how he could ever find the time or the heart to play music again. "That sounds nice," he said, just to be kind.

He called his mother to ask her to come to India and bring Sarah. The connection they got was okay; not great, not bad, but it was cheaper for him to call her on his Indian SIM card than it was for her to call him, and from time to time she sent him money for calls. He sat on the porch with his phone while rain poured off the awning in sheets, onto the garden below. The world was a rain world, water coming down so hard it was leaping back to the sky from the ground. He told his mother about his tiny house, about the kitchen and bathroom and the rain.

"What do you do all day?" she asked.

"Make bottles. Change diapers. Clean." He thought of his black toothbrush. "I've been getting a lot of cleaning done, actually."

"It doesn't sound like much of a life, Timmy," she said, and he had trouble breathing for a minute. It had taken every bit of strength he had to make this much of a life, to make the rhythm his days had fallen into. All around, the rain pounded. A mosquito buzzed close to his ear and he moved one arm like a windmill, trying to shoo it away.

"You're a mother, do you like the question 'what do you do all day?'" he asked.

"No, I guess I don't," she said.

"Okay, then."

"But that's beside the point. You're in such a different situation. I have your dad, his work, the farm. Our house."

"Yup! You're right, Mom! I have none of those things. Thanks for the reminder."

She was quiet, and then spoke again. "But you do have those things. They're all right here."

She wanted him to come back. To be a son in a large family. His throat felt tighter. She wanted him to fit right back into it all. He wasn't only a son anymore, though. He was a husband. A father. A widower. He couldn't slip into his old life as if nothing had happened.

"Come to India, Mom." He fully expected her to say no.

"Well, we've been thinking about it."

"Really?" he was stunned.

"Sarah and I," his mother continued. "Her semester's done next month. We'll have some time, but it's a lot of money, and I always imagined traveling in Europe, never India. But... well, I'm not promising anything."

"I'm shocked."

"Sarah said you would be. It's not that strange."

"Yes, it is that strange."

"You're there, doing whatever it is that you're doing, and we should see you and Isaac. If you won't come home, that is."

"Not yet."

"To be honest, this feels like a tantrum, and if it is, it's the biggest one you've ever thrown, honey." Her voice was soft and she spoke as though she was joking, but he could hear her voice thicken, like there were tears just underneath.

He picked at a piece of peeling paint on the concrete porch. It had all been painted a dark red at some point, but he could see straight through to the green underneath. He felt stung.

"The fact that you would even say that shows why I need to stay here for now."

His life with Isabel would disappear if he left now; it would be as if she had never existed. If he didn't learn how to be a father, he could imagine his mother simply acting as though Isaac was her son. Isaac could turn into Timothy's little brother. The two of them would be reabsorbed into his family, he saw it all clearly. He'd go to work in his dad's shop, let Mom take care of Isaac, live in a place where he had no memories with the wife he'd loved. He'd be left with a quickly fading picture of what he was before; his wife, his almost family. He shuddered.

He didn't want to talk about it anymore, so he told her about Isaac.

"He lies on his back and sings to the lights. I put him on a blanket and the floor is kind of slippery, so when he kicks, he slides himself along or turns in circles. The other day he ended up under the bed." Timothy had been building a small pile of paint shavings from the peeling paint on the porch, now he made a divot in the center with his finger. "And he gets really excited and crazy if you stand over him when he's lying on his back. He kicks and kicks and his eyes get really wide."

"Oh, I remember that stage," she said, and sighed. "That's so cute. Those last pictures you sent were so beautiful."

What else? Timothy wanted to have more for her. "He's really smiley now. Lately it looks more and more like real smiling, rather than opening his mouth wide. I got a picture today. I'll send it to you when I get to an Internet café."

"Is he babbling?"

"He just started."

"What sounds does he make?"

The wind had picked up, and a large coconut frond fell suddenly from a tall tree in front of the house. It flew for several feet before landing, heavy end first. Timothy couldn't help thinking that one of them could kill you.

"Dada. He says Dadadadadada. He says it all day long."

After he hung up with his mother, Timothy lit a cigarette and watched the rain tear up the garden, the wind whip the coconut trees around. The lines Timothy had drawn in his life were becoming blurred. No longer a husband,

CHAPTER 19

Prema started taking care of Isaac for a little while every day, so Timothy could get out and swim. She justified it in her mind by calling it a tithe. Ninety percent hanging out on the beach, ten percent helping out. She was at loose ends, and she loved it. She ran on the beach in the early mornings, stopping to talk to the fishermen pulling fish out of their nets after the early morning catch. She swept her small room on the cliffs, read a little, washed her hair and dried it in the sun. She walked along the beach, all the way to Timothy's house, and every morning she felt a little shiver of excitement, knowing she would see him again. She tried not to dig into these feelings too much. He was newly widowed, for heaven's sake. But she felt that helping the two of them was part of her quest, also. She wanted to learn the spirituality of care, and holding the chubby baby, walking him to sleep, kept her rooted in her body, in the tangible nature of love. It taught her something new about God.

Isaac had become a star in their part of the village. Timothy told Prema he couldn't walk anywhere with the baby without being accosted by elderly women with saris tucked up and tied between their legs, wearing large black glasses on their faces. Maybe there was only one woman, he said, but she he was a father, son, brother. Mother. The garden had become a lake. held the phone in his hand and it felt substance-less, so light it cou been air.

seemed to be everywhere, cackling and pinching Isaac's cheeks, talking and talking in Konkani, a language Timothy didn't understand.

One day Prema was with them, the three of them walking to the *puri bhaji* place for breakfast. Prema had woken early and hadn't been able to shake the thought that something was wrong. She took her morning run, but this time ran all the way to Timothy's house, only to find him sitting on the porch feeding a bottle to a happy baby. Isaac pulled away from the bottle when he saw her and smiled a huge smile. She leaned in and kissed his round cheek, getting close enough to Timothy as she did that she could smell the toothpaste on his breath. Her face felt hot and she backed away.

They decided to go to the *puri bhaji* place together, or the PBP as Timothy called it. "You could just as easily call it the *thali* place," Prema had once told him. "They serve that too."

"It's just what it's called in my head. I don't make these rules," Timothy told her.

"What, the rules of your head? Then who does?"

"The guy who names things in my head."

"Aahh," Prema said, and laughed. "I see."

The three of them curved around on the small pathway from the house, heading out to the main road, Prema in the lead, Timothy and Isaac just behind. Timothy was singing a song about *puri bhaji* to Isaac and Prema realized that this was the first time she had heard Timothy sing, and that he had a beautiful voice. Around the bend, in the tight squeeze just before they left the maze of buildings and popped out onto the big road, she saw Maria's husband's mother. She was stooped, with a sari tied in the Maharastran way, looped between her legs, and large black glasses on her face, just the way Timothy had described. She beelined for them, talking a mile a minute, reaching her hands out toward Timothy and the baby snuggled on his chest.

"This must be Isaac's admirer," Prema said to Timothy quietly. He nodded. "You do realize she lives at your house, don't you? She's Patrick's mother."

"*That's* why I see her so often. Do you understand what she's saying?" Timothy asked.

Prema stopped to listen. The old auntie put one hand on Prema's shoulder and squeezed. She was speaking Konkani, and so far Prema had only learned a very little. It was nothing like Hindi or Punjabi, but the auntie was sprinkling some Hindi words in. Prema couldn't quite catch what the auntie was saying, but she knew it was something about Timothy, about what a good man he was, good father. She leaned in and caught the Hindi word for wedding. Her face suddenly became very hot.

"I don't understand," she said, lying. "Sorry."

She stood back and watched the old auntie pinch Isaac's face. Had it really been what she thought? Isaac was remarkably well-mannered. He watched the auntie with his deep eyes. He smiled at her and cooed her a love song.

"Auntie Ji," Prema said. "We are only friends, there won't be a wedding." She spoke Hindi. The old lady didn't reply, but she looked at Prema as if to say *You expect me to believe that?*

At the PBP Timothy didn't even order; the owner brought him *puri* and *bhaji* right away. He brought some for Prema too, and she shrugged and reached for a piece of *puri*, fresh from the oil. She preferred fruit in the morning, but today the smell of the curry was making her mouth water. Timothy ordered a milk coffee and asked Prema what she wanted to drink. She asked for a chai.

"How are things?" she asked, when they were about halfway through the pile of *puri*. She was letting the chai cool a bit, but Timothy had already gulped most of his coffee back.

"Things are ... things." Timothy said.

She waited. She knew he had more to say. She watched him, the bones of his face. He had high cheekbones, and the most beautiful, deep set, blue eyes. Dark black eyelashes. He had some healthy color now, from spending more time outside, but he was still too thin, she thought, as he moved and she could see his shoulder blades jutting out underneath his shirt.

"I'm angry a lot," he said. "I mean, I should say, things are good, especially these mornings you're giving me. Have I thanked you for that, by the way?"

"Many, many times." She had to force him out the door sometimes, he was so reluctant to impose on her.

"It helps so much. But sometimes the baby wakes up at 3:00 in the morning and he won't go back to sleep. I have so much rage in me then, not at him, you know? Just at... this. All of it, the world, Isabel, death. My head feels like it will bust."

Prema knew that anything she said would be stupid. She sat in silence for a while, willing herself to just listen, to only absorb, to try to take a little of his hurt by letting it into her. She reached out and touched Isaac's cheek and then she was talking without meaning to.

"You should try running," Prema said. Timothy looked at her, surprised.

"Running?"

She nodded. "In the mornings, before you swim. Run, then maybe you'll be too tired for anger."

He looked off toward the beach. Isaac cooed at Prema and she reached out and took him from Timothy. He let the baby go absently. "Running."

Prema settled Isaac into her arms and felt the solid weight of him. He immediately started chewing on her wrist. She moved her bracelet out of the way so he didn't try to eat it, and let him slobber all over her hand and arm.

"Yeah," Timothy said. "Maybe I'll try that. So... the nights are hard. But mornings are better. I wake up and Isaac is lying beside me, kicking, sometimes staring at my face. I'm thinking about my swim, and some chai. I think, maybe I'll eat a whole pineapple today, maybe I'll finally see a dolphin. And I get up."

Prema waited for more, but he seemed to be done. She felt a deep sadness, though she couldn't say why. Then she realized. He hadn't said anything about getting to see her. He couldn't know that it was the thought of him that had her waking in the morning, staring off into the water churning around the cliffs with a smile on her face.

"So what about this party?" she asked after a pause. "Are you going?"

"Oh. Is that tonight? Aw, I really don't like parties."

"I don't think you'll hear the end of it if you don't go."

"You're right. Craig will never stop talking about it." He leaned forward and smiled at Isaac, who wriggled and babbled a stream of vowels when he looked into Timothy's eyes. Anyone could see that the baby thought the world revolved around his father.

"You come with me," Timothy said. "I don't want to show up alone. I'll get Maria to watch the baby."

"I would love to go," Prema said. "But I don't know if I was invited."

"It's a cheer-up-Timothy party, for goodness' sake. You'll be the only one there who will cheer me up."

Prema felt the sadness lift and a warm glow surround her. As Timothy ordered two drinking coconuts, Prema realized she felt almost as though she could fly.

That night they barely made it out of Timothy's little house. Prema worried that she looked too dressed up, but it was Timothy who took forever to get ready. He opened the door when she arrived at his house, still wearing shorts without a shirt, Isaac kicking and crying on the bed.

"You look nice," he said, sounding shocked, with a slightly dazed look on his face.

"Thanks."

"I like the bindi on you."

"Thanks," she said again.

As he turned back into the house, explaining that he was running late, she followed him, clinking and jingling as she walked. Her clothes were simple, really, just a long black skirt and a lace and leather vest over a tank top. But she had layered bangles up to her elbows and had at least three anklets on each foot. Dark eyeliner around her eyes, a row of bindi in the center of her forehead, brass plugs in her stretched earlobes. She was hiding her anxiety with jewelry, whispering to her bangles, to help herself calm down.

She plucked Isaac from the bed and sat with him. He stopped crying and grabbed at her arms. This time it was impossible to keep her bangles from him, so she let him chew on one made of polished wood. Timothy raced around, fixing bottles and finally calling out to Maria that he was ready to leave. Maria came through the doorway and took Isaac, murmuring to him in Konkani as she tucked him into her arms. Timothy and Prema walked out the door then, and Prema sighed in the moonlight and the breeze that was cooling things off, but Timothy ran back to give Maria last minute instructions three times, until Isaac was tired and crying and they left in a rush. Finally.

Timothy had rented Maria's husband's bike for the night. Before they climbed on, he pulled out Craig's scribbled instructions on how to get to his house, and Timothy and Prema bent their heads over the piece of paper, peering at it under a streetlight. Timothy's hands were sweaty. He smoothed them down his pants and handed the piece of paper to Prema. He looked back at the house.

"I should go back. I just want to hold him."

"Never hear the end of it, remember?"

"Right. And I've paid for the bike."

"Right."

After the eleventh try, the kickstart worked and the two of them were wheeling along the dark road, driving up out of the beach area and into the village. Prema saw all the tiny Indian shops lit up, the sweet shop, the chemist, the general stores, the juice store, and then they were on a dark, fragrant road, the road to Pernem. Craig's house was supposedly somewhere along this road. Prema thought that this ride was the best thing this week. She smelled the sweet grassy smell of cow dung burning, breathed in the scent of some kind of flowers. They passed homes and slowed down to see if any of them were

Craig's. Prema looked into the rooms with lights on. All the homes she saw were almost bare, like the ones around her room on the cliffs and the rooms around Timothy's house near the beach, with only a table or a couple of plastic chairs, sometimes a heavy wooden sofa with velvet cushions. At one house an old man sat on a concrete seat built into the porch, staring out toward the road, his two hands resting on a cane. Other people sat on the floor in the room behind him, just beyond the doorway, eating. They trailed their hands in their food, brought small bites to their mouths. Timothy slowed down to look. Prema let out a big sigh.

"I love to look in people's houses when their lights are on at night. But it makes me sad."

"It is a sad thing. A sad happy thing."

"I want to join them," Prema went on. "I want to invite myself in, sit down and take a plate of fish curry and rice."

"You should," said Timothy, deadpan. She laughed, imagining it.

He slowed down next to another house. Prema loved that he liked to do this too. They watched a teenaged girl play with a toddler, and pull the kid back to her by his shirt again and again, as he tried to get away. The little boy could barely breathe, he was laughing so hard. He pulled hard, finally breaking away as she lost her grip. He fell and started crying, and the girl scolded him, lightly slapping his cheeks and shushing him. Timothy drove the bike back into the dark jungle.

These home lights were not for them. The jungle certainly didn't belong to them. They wouldn't last long in a jungle like this. The large red ants that Prema called scorpion ants left a sting the size of a small hill, and here there was no cover from them. In Prema's room it sometimes felt like Man vs. Ants (Woman vs. Ants), but to be in the jungle, well, that was something else. It seemed deceptively friendly as Timothy and Prema drove through it. As they rushed past large spaces of deep black jungle, the air from inside reached out to them, carrying a sweet smell. Prema wanted to lean in, unpack her bags, move there. Maybe she could learn to manage it.

They paused beside a street light to look at the map again.

"I think we drove too far," Prema said.

"I was enjoying the drive too much," Timothy said. "Could we be any later for this party?"

"We could be. We could show up tomorrow."

"Maybe we should just call it a night and show up tomorrow. Sounds good to me."

Their eyes met over the map and suddenly Prema couldn't breathe. Timothy frowned and looked back at the map. He cleared his throat.

"If we're really over here," he said, his finger on a dot on the map, "we need to go all the way back to this crooked line."

"That stick figure is his house?"

"Yes. That very happy stick figure."

"Deliriously happy." Words bubbled out of the smiley face. *You're there!* Prema couldn't work up the same level of enthusiasm for the party, but she did love being with Timothy. She felt a little embarrassed about how much she loved it, actually. Hopefully it wasn't too obvious. Back on the bike, Timothy made a U turn and pulled the accelerator so they could retrace their route.

When they reached the house, it was lit up with strings of white lights, like a Christmas tree. It looked beautiful, and looking at it, Prema felt her heart rise up. "We can go inside this one," she said.

Timothy nodded. "Not just for looking this time."

Prema heard a shout. "I think we've been spotted," she said.

"Tim!" Craig came out the front door and walked down the path through the garden to stand beside them. "You made it!"

"I did," Timothy said. "Thanks for the map."

"Listen, no problem. Anything to cheer you up, mate." He glanced over at the scooter on the road. "Is that what you drove? What are you toddling around on one of those for? You should get one of these! Get them for a song here." He waved his hand toward his Enfield motorcycle. It was an old model, a Bullet, with a brand new paint job. Prema could see the look on Timothy's face as he gazed at it. The metal gleamed. It was beautiful.

"Never learned," Timothy said. "And I don't have money to buy an Enfield. I don't even have a song, whatever that translates to in real money."

"Ah, you can learn to drive in no time," Craig said. "I'll teach you."

They walked toward the house with Craig's hand clamped on Timothy's shoulder. Timothy looked at Prema with his eyebrows raised in that way he had, and Prema could barely keep herself from laughing.

"Careful," Craig said. "This path can be lethally slippery after it rains."

The lights on the house were drawing all the bugs out of the jungle. Thousands careened into the bulb, into the wall, reckless and clumsy. Craig's place was one of the old Portuguese houses, with a clay tiled roof, a large porch with seats sculpted right into it, and red concrete floors. Both the outside and the rooms inside were decorated with twinkle lights. Paper stars hung from the rafters. People sat along the walls on mattresses that had Indian bedsheets spread on them. It was lovely, the effect somewhat dampened by the low table that was covered with ashtrays and packs of cigarettes, a half drunk bottle of Coke, and a couple of empty bottles of rum.

Prema smiled at a few people when she made eye contact with them. She saw a couple that she knew from the beach—they always practiced yoga when she ran in the mornings. She gave them a little wave, then glanced at Timothy, who had his hands clenched into fists. Craig wasn't making introductions, he was kissing Juliette in the doorway to the kitchen. Prema squatted down beside the low table and turned to the girl who was closest to her. She had really short hair with a little sheaf of dreadlocks jutting from the crown of her head and trailing down to her waist. She was very deftly rolling a joint and she looked up to give Prema a quick smile.

"I'm Prema," Prema said. "And this is Timothy."

"Ella," the girl said, offering her face for a kiss. Prema kissed her on each cheek and received little kisses in the air in return. Ella turned back to her work and licked her cigarette paper to seal it.

"Where are you from?" Timothy asked, settling onto one of the mattresses. He stretched his wrists in circles, curled his hands around his ankles. Prema sat down as well, cross-legged, tucking her legs under her.

"From the universe," Ella said. She leaned back on the pillows behind her and lit her joint, drawing smoke into her lungs and closing her eyes. "From everywhere. Really, what is this obsession with place? I am from the earth, that is enough." She opened her eyes and smiled.

Prema looked at Timothy, but he was staring at his hands. It would have seemed rude to get up and walk away, but Prema thought this girl had killed Timothy's attempt at conversation as violently as if she had plunged a knife into it. Prema opened her mouth to say something, but just then the man beside Ella leaned over and plucked the joint out of Ella's hand. He offered it to Prema, who shook her head no. Timothy did the same, when the man held it in his direction.

"She's from Spain," the man said. "I am from Spain also, but this one hasn't learned her manners yet."

He put the joint to his lips and the end flared red as he sucked on it, hard. He kept the smoke trapped in his chest for a long stretch of time before he exhaled. He was a lot older than Ella, with curling gray hair and a magnificent black beard, trimmed close to his face. He tapped his steel cup of rum and Coke with a long finger.

"Do you want a drink?" he asked. "There is no ice, but the Coke is cool."

"No thanks," Prema said, just as Timothy said, "Sure."

"Just Coke," Timothy added. "No rum."

He took a cigarette from one of the packs on the table. Prema arranged her legs more carefully under her. She would have liked to have something to do with her hands as well, but she couldn't stand Coke and she wasn't a smoker.

"I hope this is okay," Timothy said in a low voice. "Taking a cigarette. I mean, I'm assuming a lot. I'm assuming it's okay, and that even if it's okay, that I'm the kind of person it would be okay for."

"You're exactly the kind of person that it's okay for," Prema said.

"Right. This isn't easy." The skin on the sides of his eyes arranged into lovely lines when he smiled at her. Prema could imagine him old. He would look practically the same, but the lines would reach a little farther each year, his eyes would be more deep set, their clear blue more radiant in his face.

"But I'm a lost person, nothing is easy for me anymore."

Prema felt a deep pain in her chest. "You're not lost," she said. "You're sitting right here."

He fumbled when he lit the cigarette. He dropped it, unlit, picked it up and put it back into his mouth. His hands shook as he flicked the lighter starter. She looked away.

The Spanish man eased past her with a steel tumbler and handed it to Timothy.

"I'm Marco, by the way," he said, holding his hand out to her. "And you're Prema, I know."

"And I'm Timothy," Timothy said. "Thanks for the Coke."

"You can thank me after you taste it. I think the steel makes it taste horrible, but he has no glasses."

"Craig has no glasses," Timothy said to Prema, in his low voice. "That's a point for me."

"You're competing over glasses?"

"Over everything. So far he has a nice house, a beautiful girlfriend who is still alive, and an Enfield. But he doesn't have glasses for his guests."

"Neither do you."

"Ouch, traitor," Timothy said, putting his hand to his heart and giving her a pained look. He took a sip and grimaced. "I think Marco forgot to make this a plain Coke."

"Rum?"

"Lots of it." He took another sip. "Small sips. I should be all right."

Ella and Marco leaned back on their pillows, speaking quietly to one another in Spanish. Their language was fluid, dripping and flowing. Marco turned to Prema and told her it was his mother's birthday. When Prema talked to Marco, she could feel his accent pulling hers into the same lyricism. She couldn't help it. Timothy smoked his cigarette in silence and then lit another one. He didn't seem to want to enter the conversation.

"I thought you were cutting back," she whispered to him.

"This is like a war zone," he whispered back. "The normal rules don't apply."

Craig wandered into the room.

"What? No music?" he said. "Where's Linus? Where's the guitar man?"

He walked away without waiting for an answer. Prema heard him outside, calling, "Linus?"

"Linus is here?" she asked the room at large. "You're finally going to get to meet Linus," she told Timothy.

"Cool," he said.

"Do you play anything?" Prema asked Marco.

"Guitar," he said, shrugging. "A little, like everyone. And you?"

"I don't play. Timothy plays flute, though."

Marco raised his eyebrows.

"Craig!" he called. "You have a flute player in here!"

"Oh, but I didn't bring it," Timothy said. He shot Prema a glare. Marco refused to listen and shouted for Craig again. Prema laughed. She had never seen Timothy so flustered.

Craig popped his head back into the room. "You've been holding out on us, Timothy," he said. He disappeared into the far part of the house again. Prema could hear him walking through the house.

"Juliette! Where did we put those flutes?"

"I haven't played in months," Timothy said, making a little chopping motion with his hand. He lowered his voice again, so only Prema could hear. "The last time I played was when Isabel was in labor. You know, my flute used to be like a part of my arm, but now Isaac is. I don't think I can play now."

Prema wasn't laughing now. She was worried.

"Sorry, I didn't know it was so difficult for you," she said.

"You don't know much about me," he said. He sat for a moment, then straightened and shifted so there was more space between them.

She looked at him, a little taken aback, but calm. "That's true," she said.

He looked at her, but couldn't keep eye contact. His eyes skittered away.

"Craig looks for a flute for you," Marco said from where he sat beside Ella. "He will find one and you will play again!"

He didn't seem to feel the ripples between Prema and Timothy, the disappointment oozing off her.

"I hope so," she said. "Excuse me."

She stood in the small space and lifted her arms up for a little stretch. She smiled at Marco, then walked out of the room and farther back into the house. She looked for a bathroom; she looked for any other place to be. She wasn't hurt, she told herself sternly. He was.

CHAPTER 20

Timothy knew why he was being a jerk. He couldn't help the feeling of happiness he got when Prema walked into a room, but he could control how comfortable they both got with it. Watching her go, though, he realized he really didn't want to hurt her, he only wanted to hold himself back. It would be hard not to notice her, he told himself. It didn't mean anything. He felt like a cheater. He had been a widower for four months. It was just a guy thing, he told himself. Of course he noticed a pretty girl like Prema.

He took another sip of rum and Coke. As soon as it was in his mouth, he remembered that he didn't want to drink it, but he couldn't put the cup down. It held an occupied space in his hand, it was something he was *doing*. He thought of his silver flute and his wooden flute. Both had traveled long distances in his backpack with the small wooden elephant. When he and Isabel were in Varanasi together, he had taken a few lessons in Indian classical music, learning to play the *bansuri*, the wooden flute that was so haunting. He and his teacher had climbed onto a cycle rickshaw together and wheeled through the streets to find him the same flute that now sat, unplayed, in the backpack. They had tapped and probed each one until his teacher finally nodded approval and said, "This one," over a mouthful of *paan*. A new wand. A new piece of protection against a life without music, a life he now found himself in.

Craig turned up now, a cheap *bansuri* in his hand.

"Knew I'd find this somewhere," he said. "Have a go, will you?"

The candles in the alcoves in the walls flickered as people drifted into the room and tumbled onto the mattresses, called by some force. Possibly Craig had rounded up an audience for Timothy, in his aggressive good-hearted way. To cheer him up.

Prema was sitting across the way with Marco, who had brought her back. Timothy had to look through rum bottles on the low table to see her face. Marco bent down to say something to her and Timothy felt a small twisting in his gut. She was sitting over there because of him. Because he was rude. Because he didn't want to like her too much. It was too late. He already liked her too much.

He put down the drink and ran his right hand down the flute. It was poorly made. His flute teacher in Varanasi wouldn't have given it a second glance. It was a flute that would be hawked on the street by a flute seller playing the theme song from *Titanic*. "Flute, sir? Hundred rupees only."

He blew across the mouthpiece, experimenting. It was no piece of art, but it would make music. Of a sort.

He thought of one of the *ragas* he had learned during those weeks of classes in Varanasi. Days of sitting in the home of his teacher. Nights with Isabel. A *raga* was an Indian scale, played with room for embellishment, if one advanced into the music world enough to embellish. The raga he chose was a night raga. Suitable for grief, for the time when the sun went down.

He closed his eyes and played. The sound spooled out of the end of the flute and flowed around the room. He played and played. At first all was quiet, like everyone had stopped breathing, even, but as time passed, people began talking again, picking up where they had left off. He kept playing. He was vaguely aware of motion, of people standing and walking out of the room or walking into the room, people passing, the brief breeze of motion. He kept playing. He switched from the night raga to some folk music. He played Joni Mitchell and Tracy Chapman. He stuck with folk music, with easy stuff. The flute wasn't up to the Western classical music he knew so well.

At an awkward party thrown to cheer him up and somehow shock him out of his grief, he had found something he could do. He kept playing. He played until his mouth and his throat muscles began to ache, and he played some more. Finally, when he realized he had nothing left to play, he stopped.

He opened his eyes and put the flute carefully in his lap. He rubbed his hands along his pants, felt how numb his fingers were, and opened and closed his hands a few times, stretching. Ella was asleep on the cushions beside Timothy. Marco sat in a corner speaking to a girl with a shaved head. The candles were very low, guttering in their alcoves. Prema still sat across from Timothy. She smiled and pressed her hand to her heart to show that she had heard him. Timothy smiled back at her. Next to Prema, a young guy sat with a guitar in his lap, staring at Timothy. As soon as Timothy made eye contact, the boy smiled.

"Didn't want to interrupt," he said. "The way you were playing, I thought even a few notes played along would disturb."

"Oh." Timothy felt embarrassed and didn't know what to say. *Sorry* felt called for, but he didn't feel like saying it. He felt jolted back to an unpleasant place, resurfacing in this room. Smells of incense, cigarettes, someone's spilled rum.

"I'm Linus," the boy said, standing with his guitar clutched in one hand. He walked over to shake hands with Timothy. Marco had left his corner and was sitting with Prema again. Her mouth was stretched into a wide smile and she had her hand at her neck. He was saying something to her as he sat beside her, a little too close. Maybe it was just the Spanish way, Timothy thought. In any case, he was finding it hard to focus on Linus.

"I'm Timothy," he said, bringing himself back, shaking hands with Linus.

"I know. I've heard."

"Do you want to play together?" Linus asked.

"Maybe I'll take a break for a minute."

"Oh. Sure, mate, take your time." He sat and looked at Timothy. His hair was so thick and even and short that it looked like a brush on his head. He was young, maybe even younger than Timothy. From England, by his accent, but he didn't look ethnically English.

"Where are you from?" Timothy asked, before remembering how loaded the question could be. He glanced at Ella, sleeping, then at Marco, who seemed to be drifting nearer to Prema. He pulled his attention back to Linus with effort.

"England," Linus said. "But my mum's from Chile." He pronounced it like a Spanish speaker would. *Cheelay.* "Crazy, huh? Worlds apart. My dad moved there in his twenties and fell in love."

"Crazy."

"And you're Canadian, like Prema."

Linus said it as a statement, so Timothy only nodded. Linus moved his fingers around the neck of the guitar, fingering different chords, and began a complicated strum. It was amazing from the first moment he touched the strings. He moved into the song in earnest, the sound filling the room. His face was so animated, in constant motion, Timothy had already noticed, when he was talking and smiling, and now, playing. Ella stirred in her sleep, but didn't wake up. Linus stopped strumming and started picking the melody of what sounded like a fast Middle Eastern folk song, but Timothy couldn't place it, he had never heard it before. He closed his eyes. It sounded like a dream, like a village full of dancing people.

He wanted to pick up the flute, but he had truly overdone it already and the muscles in his face were like putty. He reached for his drink and took another huge gulp of tepid rum and Coke. The music was bringing an ache to the back of his eyes. He stood and shook himself. His cup was empty and he looked at it for a moment. Did he really drink it all? He put it on the table and stepped over Linus's knee, stumbling a bit, to get out of the enclave of mattresses. He knew Prema was watching him, that her eyes were on him, but he didn't look at her.

He left the room and walked through the house. He touched walls as he went, picked up small decorations and put them back again. In one room a single potted plant sat on a table and a crucifix was propped on an altar on the wall. Beside the cross was a picture of Mary. It was a nice one. She wasn't like the glittering Queen of Heaven, almost alien in features. This was a Mary you might get to know.

"What's up?" Timothy asked her. He touched the cross and felt pulled toward it. He fought the urge to kneel.

The suffering of the plastic Jesus looked the way Timothy felt when he couldn't sleep at night. He thought of Isabel again, and the mysteries he would never know about her. What had she really thought of him, of the baby growing in her belly? He should have known it already, know that she had loved them, that she had wanted to stay. But it was twisted in his brain, somehow. Looped and crossed over. It looked now as though she hadn't been able to wait to get away, that she didn't want them anymore, that she cast them aside.

She was dragged, he reminded himself. If she had any power, she would have been kicking and screaming.

"Timothy!"

Craig came into the room at precisely the wrong moment.

"So you've found our shrine. Wow, we really can't get you to party, can we? Shall we say a Mass?"

"Why do you have a shrine?"

"All the Goan Catholics have them in their homes. You can't take them down. It means automatic hell or something. Don't you have one?"

Come to think of it, he did. It was tiny and high on the wall. Just a shelf with a couple of figurines. He hadn't really thought of it as a shrine. He shrugged.

"I should go soon, man," he said, rubbing at his neck. "Thanks so much for the invite."

"Hell, the whole thing was for you. To cheer you up. But it looks like we failed."

Timothy's shoulders were so tense they felt like they could crack. He didn't want to have to appear "cheered up" to show that the party hadn't been a failure. His head felt cloudy and he realized he was tipsy. He couldn't drive. Tipsy, for God's sake, with a baby waiting for him at home.

"Juliette!" Craig called. He slipped into the next room. "Hey, come say 'bye' to Tim."

She followed Craig back into the room where Timothy still stood staring at the shrine, feather earrings swinging around her shoulders. Her eyes looked slightly stoned, but very kind.

"You are going so early!" she said.

"I know, I have to get back to Isaac. My landlady's babysitting. I'm probably the only parent here," he said. "So of course I have to be the first to leave." He wanted to say something to make Juliette feel better. Her eyes looked sad at the prospect of him leaving. He was trying not to look at her waist. She wore a little vest with nothing but a bra underneath, and her waist was there, bare skin winking in his peripheral vision. He looked for a minute, then cut his eyes back to the crucifix.

She laughed. "You are not the only parent here!" Her laugh sounded like bells.

"I'm not?"

"Of course not." She elbowed Craig. "How many children do you have?"

Craig flushed and shrugged. "Two."

"Maybe half the mans here have children hidden away somewhere, Timothy. But they leave them behind."

"Juliette." Craig looked upset now.

"It's true, darling! How many diapers did you clean?"

"That's not... You've had too many drinks."

"Maybe I have," she said. She swept her hand through the air, grandly, like she was about to take a bow. "But it is true. You are, how do you say— rare, Timothy. Like a money from a long time ago. A coin. I think you can count the diapers Craig has cleaned on one hand."

"Who else has kids?" Timothy wanted to know if what she said was true.

"Marco, for sure... and maybe..."

"Juliette. Enough. Stop parading our sordid mistakes for our young friend."

"Kids are mistakes?" Timothy couldn't help himself.

"They are if you didn't want them," Craig said, and his eyes were hard. "Hey. I gave it a go. Wasn't the best dad, that's all."

"Awwww. I bet you were great," Juliette said. Her eyes looked liquid, like tears might spill out. "Craig, let's have a baby."

Craig gave Timothy a wide-eyed look, like *look what you did*, but then Juliette was kissing him and Timothy crept away. He walked through the living room, nodding at people as he left. He felt light and springy somehow, though he didn't know why. A tight band that had been around his chest was loosening.

Linus caught up to him in the hallway.

"We need to play together. If you want. When can we do it?"

Timothy felt even happier at the thought of hearing more of Linus's music.

"Maybe some night? I'm always at my house. Do you know where I live?"

"No. But I know Arambol well. Just draw me a map."

Timothy did, holding a flyer for a party advertised in 2012, three years before, against the wall, sketching a map in pencil.

"How long has Craig had this house?" he asked.

"Five years, he said. He comes back every season." Linus dusted some wall plaster from his shoulder after it crumbled away from Timothy's writing spot on the wall.

"Sorry about that," Timothy said. "Here's the map, anyway."

Linus peered at it for a second. "Looks about right. Oh yes, I know where that is. A mate of mine stayed there last year. Pink house?" Timothy couldn't get over how happy a person Linus seemed to be. He was overflowing with energy, standing on his toes, like a kid.

"Pink house. I have my real flutes, too. Better than what I was playing on tonight."

They wrapped it up with nods and claps on the back. Both of them were smiling, happy to have someone to play music with, and Timothy felt the effect of the alcohol making everything a little happier, shinier. Prema was suddenly there beside Linus. Timothy felt his face getting hot. He watched Linus and Prema talking easily together and remembered that they knew each other already, that Prema had wanted to introduce them. He turned and took a few steps toward the door, toward the garden. He was going to have to ask Prema to drive. He hoped she was up for it.

"See you later, Linus," he heard Prema say behind him.

She followed Timothy through the door and onto the porch. They stood there for a minute, then Timothy walked into the garden to look at the sky, studded with stars. The air was so humid that it felt as though he was breathing underwater. Like he'd been dunked in a bucket, then wrapped in cotton. He lifted his hair to give the back of his neck some air. Prema walked to stand beside him.

"You seem ... troubled," she said.

"Troubled? That's nothing different." He looked at her, but she was tilting her head back to look at the sky. Her throat was like the throat of a jungle bird, dark and soft.

"Like you're annoyed at me."

He didn't say anything.

"Remember our only friends thing, right? I'm not offering anything else. I only thought we could be good friends. We seemed to understand each other."

"We did. It's not that I don't want to be friends."

"Then what is it?"

"It's nothing. I don't know."

"How can you not know?"

How can you not know? She sounded like Isabel. Like his sister, Sarah. *How can you not know what you're thinking? Normal people know what they're thinking. They're these things called thoughts. They run through your brain and as they run, you look at them to see what they're made of.*

Not me, he thought. *I don't.*

"You have to trust me," he said. "There's a lot going on in me, but I can't talk about it. I don't even know how. But I'm not mad at you. You didn't do anything wrong."

He kept looking at her while he spoke. She didn't seem to be hiding anything, standing there in the blue outer rings of the porch light. He was probably the only one in this scenario who was hiding something. That strong, sour betrayal of friendship. Attraction.

"We can be friends. Of course," he said. He didn't mean it. He didn't want to be friends for the same reason he wanted to be friends. Because every time he was around her he felt like he was cheating on Isabel.

You could have had me for my whole life, Isabel. I would have stayed with you forever.

"Good," she said, and she finally looked at him.

"As a friend, can I ask you for a hand?" he asked.

"Sure, what do you need?"

"Can you be the driver on the way back home? I accidentally drank a cup of rum and Coke and I shouldn't have."

"How can you accidentally drink a rum and Coke?"

"I can. Trust me."

"Of course I can drive. I've been practicing."

She smiled. Her eyes were so brilliant in her face.

"You don't know how to drive a scooter?"

"No I do, but I've never driven with a man on the back before. I can try."

Timothy thought of Yoda. *There is only do or do not, there is no try.* A quote which was certainly applicable to driving a scooter in the jungle. He felt so fuzzy. How many shots had Marco put into his drink? Three? Four?

They walked out to the bike, Prema's bangles jingling gently as she followed him on the path. When they reached the bike she climbed on and put her legs on the ground on either side. She gripped the handlebars until her knuckles turned white and stood out brightly against her long brown hands. She released a handlebar and tucked her hair behind her ears.

"Ready for me to get on?" Timothy asked.

"Yep."

He climbed on, but she wasn't really ready and the bike rocked precariously on the road's shoulder.

"Whooops!" Prema planted her legs more firmly on the road.

"That's good," Timothy said. "Because now I'm on." She laughed. "At least I'm a skinny man," he said.

"A skinny manly man," she said.

"Really? You think I'm a skinny manly man?" he said. "Even when I'm carrying a baby?"

"Especially then." She said, starting the bike easily, as though it had never given him trouble.

"How did you do that?"

"Magic hands."

He smiled. She was just too perfect. This was such a danger zone. He slid as far back against the back of the bike as he could without flipping over backwards. He wanted no accidental touching.

She pulled off, moving forward slowly into the darkness of the jungle. At first they wobbled like drunk unicyclists, but she gained confidence in the new weight of the bike quickly and soon she was whipping along. She was laughing and talking away, but he couldn't really hear her because the night stole her words and carried them away on a warm, humid wind. The breath from the jungle cooled him. He was at a fever pitch, filled with hunger and jealousy, relief and horror at the way his heart was yearning toward Prema. He really didn't know a thing about her. But there was something singing in him, something slightly shameful, but healing, which had nothing to do with Prema.

Craig had children.

He left them. He didn't stay. Timothy didn't hate Craig anymore. His hatred had fizzed out completely, leaving him empty and unsatisfied. But also, strangely hopeful. Because whatever he had done wrong as a parent, however horrible it was that he hadn't protected Isabel enough, he had stayed with Isaac.

When Prema pulled up at his house, he waited until she had her balance, then hopped off the bike. She turned it off and searched for the kickstand. He helped her find it and she climbed off the bike and turned to him.

"Thanks," he said. She swung her bag over her shoulder, watching him, smoothing her hair away from her face. Her bangles were musical on her wrists.

"It's nothing a friend wouldn't do," she said. Her voice was light. "Call me if you need anything, and I'll come over in the next couple days to watch Isaac for a while." She was walking away talking over her shoulder. She gave him one last smile and disappeared around the corner, heading into the small alleyway that led to the main road. Timothy folded his hands under his armpits and walked into his house.

The red floor glowed in the light from the bathroom, spilling into the darkened room. He saw Isaac asleep on the bed, arms flung up beside him, Maria asleep on a straw mat on the floor with her daughter curled up beside her. It was the eight-year-old, Valanka. Maria opened her eyes, stood and smiled, sleepily. She pulled her daughter to her feet and rolled the mat up quickly.

"Everything okay?" Timothy asked, barely whispering.

"Okay, yes, okay Tim. No problem."

They backed out the door, going around the house to their rooms in the back. They would roll the mat back out on the floor and sleep on it in there, the whole family stretched out together like kittens.

Timothy walked to look at Isaac, knowing he would be tired in the morning. It was after 1:00 am, much later than he usually went to sleep, but he didn't turn off the bathroom light right away. Instead, he dug through the backpack for some clean clothes, and took a quick shower, wrapping his dreadlocks around his head to keep them dry. The water was warm from sitting in the tank during the day. He rubbed soap on his hands, his stomach, his arms, everywhere. He washed and the warm water made him sleepy and took the sticky layer off.

When he settled on the bed beside Isaac he felt like a baby himself.

Craig had kids and left them.

"I'll never leave you," Timothy whispered. Isaac sighed a tiny sigh and turned his head toward Timothy in his sleep, so that his face was the last thing Timothy saw before he drifted off.

CHAPTER 21

Isaac grew rounder and more smiley and the rains waned and then stopped. Timothy found himself in a new life rhythm and was surprised that it was good. Prema came many mornings to watch Isaac while Timothy left to swim or take a walk on the beach. The beach filled with other travelers so quickly that Timothy sometimes wondered if it was the same beach as the empty place he had moved into. He still hadn't seen any dolphins. The sun turned the waves to slate and green and gold as it fell toward the sea in the late afternoon.

Isaac put on weight, learned to sit, and began laughing, mostly when Timothy looked at him suddenly and said "Boo!" The gurgle of his laugh was so joyous that Timothy felt even more warmth slipping into the hurt places inside him. One month went by, and then two. With each month-birthday they moved into more normality and less moments of panic over no clean diapers or running out of formula, or that one time when the open formula tin went skidding across the floor and exploded everywhere, but they also slipped farther away from Isabel as she moved into the more distant past. Timothy could feel her shadow growing lighter until he was afraid that soon he wouldn't remember her at all. The idea was painful and he grabbed onto it, because the pain meant he wasn't forgetting her. He kept her photo in his wallet and slipped it out often to look at it, but though he was glad to have her face in his mind, he couldn't remember the exact tone of her voice or hear the cadence of her Parisian accent.

He thought often of Prema, even when she wasn't around. They kept a lot of physical distance between them these days, but there were still moments when the warm smell of her head—rose shampoo and something that was her sun-warmed skin—slipped up to him and he remembered the night on the scooter after Craig's party, how he had stared at the small of her back and had wanted to touch it, how he hadn't touched it.

Sometimes the deep sadness returned and threatened to bring him back into darkness. He curled up on the hill of rocks that he called a bed. He lay staring into nothing, Isaac sleeping or kicking beside him. He tried to rouse himself to call Prema or Linus or go to Maria's, but often he couldn't get himself out of a lying position.

When Maria discovered that Timothy didn't eat much after Isaac went to sleep in the evenings, she invited him to eat fish curry rice with their family, and that became part of his daily ritual too, one that he could count on even on the darkest days. Sometimes Prema or Linus joined them and Timothy thought of Sunita and Gopal, and how he was playing family with a different family now. When he brought this up to Prema, she looked at him for a while and then said, "Yeah, but isn't that how you do everything? You play like you know how to do something for a while and then you eventually you're doing it, not playing at it anymore." He had never thought of it like that. He had obviously never felt that way about learning to play flute—that had been more like climbing a mountain with each of the steps on the bottom of the mountain feeling miles apart and gradually reaching to top to find he was able to sprint on the ridge of the mountain. But it was pretty close to how he felt about being a father—as if he was playing at it, wearing a dad shirt, pretending to be somebody's father. If Prema was right, maybe one day he would wake up and find that he really was a father.

He was always surprised by Prema. Every time she popped her head into his doorway he was stunned by how beautiful she was, having gotten used to how normal everything else looked in comparison. Dark skin is the best skin, he would find himself thinking, watching how her color made her eyes shine or her white teeth flash when she laughed, and then he would feel immediately guilty, thinking of Isabel's pale skin and shadowed eyes. Prema had laughed at the look on his face when a couple from Delhi had commented on how dark she was one night in a restaurant, advising her to wear a hat. When they were done with their small talk the couple moved on, leaving Timothy staring at their backs, stunned.

"What was *that*?" he asked.

"They don't like dark skin here," she said. "Haven't you noticed? The darker you are, the lower in caste you are, so they don't understand why I don't take better precautions against darkness."

"Well, you're perfect the way you are," he said, and he busied himself with his food so he didn't have to look at her.

Now that she had brought it up, he did notice it, especially during dinner, on the ever-blaring TV in Maria's house. The commercials that advertised skin-whitening cream always featured a sad, lonely girl with a dark face becoming popular and captivating as she used the lotion and transformed into a light-skinned girl. Once, when he and Prema were eating the very spicy fish curry and fried fish with Maria and Patrick, he commented on it.

"That ad would *not* fly in Canada," he said.

She smiled. "No. But there's a lot here that wouldn't fly in Canada."

Which was true, Timothy knew, but he couldn't exactly remember what wouldn't be okay in Canada. He found it harder and harder to remember what life was like there. He knew the overt comments on skin color would be frowned on. And there were little things about the way life was done—slaughtering pigs in the street, religious signs on public buses (Jesus Saves

Buses! Krishna Tours!), but especially the littering. Seeing people threw trash in the street still grated on him whenever he witnessed it, since he had grown up believing that littering was a mortal sin.

But as much as he was surprised by Prema and her warmth and friendship, he was even more surprised by how close he was growing to Linus. They had found each other on the beach shortly after Craig's party and had been playing music ever since. There was an initial bit of awkwardness when Linus discovered that in fact Timothy was "the" Timothy he had heard about, the one with the baby and the dead wife. Somehow Linus had missed it, happily oblivious to anything in the world that wasn't music related.

"You have a baby in a pouch!" he'd proclaimed happily when he caught up to Timothy that first morning. "Like a mama kangaroo." Crows circled over the coconut trees as Linus told Timothy his life story. He was twenty-five and had been traveling in India, Thailand, Nepal, and Europe for three years. Before he started traveling, he had been a pre-med student, living in Manchester with his family. He loved music and his mom's cooking. He didn't know how to tell his parents that he didn't want to study medicine anymore. He had a few panic attacks three years before and headed out of the country for a break. His parents wanted him to move off-campus and back in with them, but he was terrified of the idea.

"I would have gained twenty kilos," he said. "You don't know Latin American mothers— she would never have stopped feeding me and I would have gotten stuck playing video games and eating. Besides, at the end of the day, music is all I want. Well, music and... the whole world, there's that too."

They were standing at the sea by then, a short distance away from each other, with Isaac asleep in the baby carrier on Timothy's chest. The waves were breaking gently with a little lift and then a tiny crash. Not much, just enough to froth and make sighing sounds in the air all along the shore.

"Your go now," Linus said. Timothy took a deep breath.

"My story is a lot like yours, actually. I'm twenty-four, from Canada." Linus was drawing a lopsided circle in the sand with his toe, but he glanced up and nodded when Timothy stopped talking. Timothy continued. "I left home two years ago. Quit school. Or 'took a break,' like you, as my parents still choose to see it. They weren't happy, but I needed to find something meaningful. Something, anything. I traveled through Thailand, Laos, and Cambodia before coming to India, and when I got here, I met the most amazing woman,"—he was frustrated to find his voice was breaking—"the very first week. We got married on a whim. Happiest year of my life. She died, though. She died during childbirth. You've met Isaac. He's our son." He kicked at the sand.

Linus had paused in the midst of a third lopsided circle he had drawn with his toe. He stared at Timothy with wide eyes and straightened slowly.

"So sorry, mate. I didn't know."

"I thought Craig would've told you."

"Didn't say a word." Linus rubbed his hand over his chin and moved to stand closer to Timothy. He put one hand on Timothy's shoulder and gave a hesitant squeeze. "Maybe I heard something, rumors somewhere about a guy with a kid. But I didn't know the guy was you."

"It's me," Timothy said. Isaac woke up and started to fuss. Timothy began pulling him out of the carrier, hands under his damp little armpits. The smell of formula and baby sweat gusted up to his face. "It's us."

"Wow."

They stood side by side for a minute, both watching the waves.

"What was your major?" Linus asked.

Timothy watched Isaac as he tried to get used to the bright sunlight after the relative dark of the carrier. The baby blinked and scrunched his face. Timothy lifted him closer to kiss him.

"Music," Timothy said.

Then there was the first day he had swum with Isaac. The poor kid had a persistent heat rash and seemed miserable with it. Timothy remembered stories his mother had told about sea water helping rashes, and so he brought Isaac into the water with him after taking his clothes and diaper off.

"Ready, kiddo?" he had asked.

Isaac had looked at him and said "Eaugh eh ah."

"You're an incredible swimming baby, Isaac. Just like those videos Mama and I watched when you were in her belly. Of those Russian swimming babies."

Timothy walked into the water with his son for the very first time. He held him tucked against his body, and jumped over the tiny waves to get a smile from Isaac, who looked startled. Timothy plowed on ahead to just beyond the breakers. He didn't go too deep—just until they were out of the waves. Isaac's eyes widened as his legs went under the water. His lip trembled and he looked like he would cry, but he mastered it. The rims of his eyes were pink.

Timothy jiggled him up and down, singing, "Little Isaac, in the water, little Isaac in the water." He had no tune, it was just a sing-song rhyme. Isaac watched Timothy's eyes, and he must have found something good there, because he smiled. A big smile, a huge one. Timothy kept going with his sing song. "Little Isaac in the water, little Isaac in the water. My little Russian swimming baby."

The water collected them, cooled them, and warmed them simultaneously. Isaac's gummy grin and slippery little dolphin body against Timothy's moved into the empty spaces in his chest. He felt something that was almost like pain, but it wasn't the pain of losing. It was belonging.

CHAPTER 22

Linus started showing up at Timothy's house often, and the two of them played music on the tiny porch, first the songs they both knew, and then Linus taught Timothy some folk and gypsy music, while Timothy taught Linus some Bach on the guitar. Linus was surprised to find that Timothy could play guitar, but Timothy shrugged it off.

"I learned most things in school. One of my professors felt that we wouldn't be as proficient as we could be at our instruments if we didn't have a wider range. I learned piano and some trumpet as well as a little drum kit and djembe. But I like flute best."

Sunset would find Timothy and Linus walking out to the sea along with many other people from Arambol, which had filled with travelers until Timothy was almost overwhelmed. There were other traveler babies, but they all had mothers. Sometimes Prema met them at the water, wearing a *lungi* like a sarong if she had been for a swim, or a dress if she hadn't. She often plucked Isaac straight from Timothy's arms and then he played music with Linus and other musicians while the sun went down, plopping into the sea like a giant, glowing orange. They lingered until Isaac's restlessness propelled them back to

Timothy's house, or to a nearby restaurant, or sometimes he parted from them there and walked home with Isaac alone, often to eat fish curry rice with Maria's family.

His life had contracted into something simple, small and bare, but happy. There were no treats the way he had been accustomed to having treats. No movies coming out or new albums that he had been waiting for. He felt disconnected from that old world, as though he was floating in an Indian sea. Somewhere movies were still being made, new albums were still coming out, but he was sealed off. He was lost to the old world and it was lost to him. It was hard to believe that he had used those other things to get up in the morning—coffee at his favorite bustling coffee shop, the chance that his most beautiful professor would be wearing her purple shirt that day, a video game that a friend wanted to try out. There were other reasons he woke up now. The stillness as he watched his sleeping baby. Isaac. Chai with Sunita, back in the bad days when he could barely face getting out of bed. Now, music with Linus, the brilliance of Prema's smile. And because it was what people did, whether they had a reason or not. Every morning his neighbors, the villagers, woke up and brushed their teeth outside in the morning light. They fished, swept their yards and the dirt on the lanes in front of their homes. They made the fires that burned under the giant rice pots. It was what people did.

He and Prema went out for breakfast once or twice a week. One morning he told her that he was sometimes afraid of what he felt for his baby. Starbursts of love would explode quickly and without warning, and it was love that felt like longing, that felt like pain.

"My mom says it's normal, though," he told Prema, watching as she pushed her bangles nearly up to her elbows, one by one. He took a sip of chai. It was early and the light was still shining directly into the waves, making them a brilliant blue-green. Soon the sun would be overhead and the water would be a steely grey again.

"You talked to her recently?"

"We Skyped for the first time last night. I went to the Internet café near the falafel place."

"Wow, you never Skyped before?" Her hands were so graceful around her cup of chai. Timothy knew her well enough now to know that when she gestured, her hands were fluid and looked almost as if they would bend backward. The backs of her hands were a dark brown like mahogany, while her palms were lighter, more like pine.

"We tried a few times, but the connection was so bad that she couldn't see Isaac at all and everything kept freezing up. We both got so frustrated that we didn't try again until yesterday. Then I asked her about the sad love feeling, whether it was because of Isabel. She told me it was called parent love, that it felt like pity or longing sometimes, that it's what keeps us with them."

"How did the call go?" Prema asked.

"It was okay. We argued a bit—she wants me to come home."

Money was getting tight for Timothy and he was ready to dip into the money his mom's mother had left him—money he shouldn't touch until he was ready to build a house or start a business. If he spent any of his Granny savings, it would be the biggest rule his family had ever seen him break, the biggest no-no he had committed. Except, perhaps, for marrying a girl they hadn't met, two months after he had met her, without telling them.

"Was Isaac with you?"

"Yeah, that was amazing."

The sight of his mother had been almost too much to take. He realized he had been shutting them off—pretending away the existence of his family so that he wouldn't be sad about missing them. His mother had been wearing a Mexican-style smock with embroidery scattered across the front of it, a shirt she'd had for twenty years. Timothy remembered being a small boy and chasing the birds around her shirt with his fingers, pretending they were racing. There were silver streaks in his mother's brown hair, tucked behind her ears, and people had always said he had her eyes, the brilliant blue of them. Eyes and forehead from his mother, hair and jaw from his father.

"Where's the baby?" Timothy's mother had said the minute she came into focus. Timothy smiled and inched the baby out of the carrier, turning him around to face the computer. Isaac immediately reached for the keyboard.

"Look, Isaac!" Timothy said. "It's Grandma!"

Isaac didn't know where to look. He turned and looked up at Timothy, then grabbed for his beard. He kicked suddenly and the computer mouse went flying. Timothy caught it and put it back on the desk. He stood Isaac on his legs. Timothy's mother had her hand pressed to her mouth.

"Hi, Isaac," she said, pulling her hand away from her face. "Hi, Lovely." Her eyes were pink.

Isaac heard his name and looked around, but he couldn't seem to place the voice with the picture on the computer.

"Look there!" Timothy said, putting his hand on the monitor. "There she is."

Isaac looked at the wobbly, out-of-focus woman on the screen and then looked up at Timothy again.

"He's so beautiful, Timmy. He looks like you did when you were a baby." Tears slowly ran down her cheeks and she dashed them away with her fingers, smiling at the screen, though her smile kept falling in on itself. Timothy felt terrible—he hadn't tried nearly hard enough to make this call.

"You think so?" he asked. "I can only see Isabel in him."

"Oh, he looks like you as a baby. But look at that black hair!"

"That's Isabel all the way," Timothy said, looking down at Isaac's head. The baby looked up into his face again, listening intently. "What do you think? Do you look like me?" Timothy asked him.

"I'm so glad I'm finally seeing him. But I'm missing so much of his life! I miss you Timmy. I wish you would come home."

He could see bits of his childhood house behind his mother on the screen, and it made him a bit dizzy. That place was so far away from where he was now, physically and in the things he understood, the life he led now.

"Sarah! You have to see Isaac! Come here!" his mother called. She played with the rings on her right hand, a gesture Timothy had seen her make a thousand times. She was like a new person to him, after his absence. He felt like he could see her as a real person and not just his mother.

"Have you gone to the beach lately?" he asked.

"No, it's winter here, dear. No, wait, your dad and I did go for a walk last week, twice actually."

Timothy smiled. "Since when does the weather keep you away from the beach? Where is Dad, anyway?"

Before she could answer, Sarah was there, perching on the chair that their mother was sitting on, pushing to get her to move over and make room.

"Oh, he's beautiful!" she said as their mom made muttering sounds and moved over.

Timothy looked at his son again and saw him through the eyes of a grandmother and auntie, the way his cheeks had filled out, his whole little body so round and cuddly. He pulled the baby closer to his face and kissed the place between his neck and his shoulder. Isaac let out a peal of startled laughter and there was a scuffle on the screen in front of Timothy. Sarah had fallen off the chair when Isaac laughed, and she was sitting on the floor while Timothy's mother was in a fit of giggles, wiping tears away from her eyes.

Timothy's face felt stretched by smiling, more smiling than he had done in months.

"Okay," his mom said. "We're pulling it together over here. Go get a chair," she told Sarah. "We're a bit wound up from the wonder of seeing the two of you," she told Timothy as Sarah walked away and emerged from the side of the screen carrying a chair. Their faces looked hungry as they stared at Isaac.

"Are you still taking pictures?" his mom asked.

"Yes, nearly every day."

"You don't post them."

"I have them on my phone, but it's hard for me to get a strong Internet connection."

"Well, send me some."

Sarah smiled. "Did she tell you our news?"

"Not yet," Timothy's mom said quickly.

"News?" Timothy said, looking back and forth between them. He sat up a little straighter. "Wait, where *is* everyone?" He hadn't seen either of his younger brothers or his father and at this time of night they really should be home.

"Away on a church retreat," his mother said. "We didn't go because we had details to figure—"

"We bought our tickets!" Sarah shrieked. "We're coming to Goa next month!"

They both grinned like cats. Timothy felt stunned. Above him, the fan spun and spun, whipping the air. He hadn't believed they would actually come, despite all his invitations. He couldn't tell what he was feeling.

"You don't seem excited," Sarah said, her voice flat.

Timothy began to fold Isaac back into the carrier, averting his eyes from his mother and sister. He needed a minute away from their eyes to get used to this crazy idea, but he didn't have a minute. He jiggled Isaac to keep him happy, making his chair squeak. The girl at the computer next to him gave him a look. He ignored her as Isaac's eyes began to drift shut.

"I'm excited," he said. "It's just hard for me to know how I feel about anything anymore. And I don't want you to hate it here."

"All the more reason for us to come," his mother said. "You need someone other than you to think along with you. Besides, babies are family affairs. It's not normal to parent a baby completely alone."

Timothy thought of Prema and Maria and Linus, but he knew that what his mother said was true.

"I'm excited," he said again, knowing that he wasn't convincing anybody by saying it three times in a stiff voice. Sarah stared down at the floor. Timothy looked at his mother and saw that she was looking back at him with soft eyes.

She had questions for him about vaccinations and what clothes they should bring and what else they should have with them, all sorts of things that he had no answers for. Clothes? Vaccinations?

"We could bring some clothes for Isaac," his mother said.

That made sense. He latched onto that. He checked on Isaac. He was asleep, like an angel, his little bow lips slack and open. Timothy stroked his forehead with a finger and Isaac's eyes moved back and forth under his eyelids.

"Yes, please. Isaac really needs clothes. We have hardly anything that fits him anymore."

Sarah and his mother exchanged a glance. Timothy closed his eyes and felt so tired that he could barely open them again.

"I need to get home," he said. "But I have an idea. My friend Prema is from Canada and she's got it together more than I do. I'll ask her what she think about what you should bring, if she can make a list."

His mother smiled. "Good idea, honey. You look like you really should get more rest."

Sarah looked up and he saw that she had tears in her eyes.

"I don't know what made you think I don't want you to come," Timothy said. "I love you so much, I've been dreaming of this... It's just..."

"No, I get it," Sarah said. "I think it's just that you seem so different, like you're drifting away from us..." She broke down and cried. Timothy's mother put her arms around her and Sarah cried into her neck. Timothy's stomach was full of pain. He pushed the red button on the screen while they weren't looking, and logged out of Skype. Hopefully they would assume there had been a power cut.

He got out of his chair slowly and paid the man behind the counter with a few crumpled ten rupee notes. The man made a face over one of the notes that was lightly torn in the middle, and Timothy exchanged it for another, bouncing Isaac all the while to keep him sleeping. The night was brilliant with stars when he opened the door and stepped out of the building. He walked home under them, the silhouettes of coconut trees like feathers against the sky.

He told Prema a lot of it as they sat together at the table, drinking sweet milky chai in the hot part of the afternoon. He told her about how excited his mom was, how they were both coming to see the baby. He didn't tell her about Sarah's tears, or how worried he felt about the visit, but he thought she maybe knew anyway, because she grabbed his wrist with her soft hand.

"It's going to be amazing, Timothy. We'll make it amazing."

And he watched the wind in the coconut fronds and let himself believe her.

PART 3

CHAPTER 23

Prema liked to sing, especially in the morning. She often stood on the steps of her porch and sang to the cliffs below her, the water breaking in white sheafs of spray around the dark rocks that rose out of the sea. She mostly sang old folk music, though sometimes she broke into musicals like *Annie* or *The Sound of Music*. And occasionally, (very occasionally) she would sing a few Bollywood songs. Her family, the Goan family who rented a room out to her, had grown used to this, all the different songs. Uncle Ji, the old grandfather of the family, often poked his head around the porch columns to see her there, bare feet planted on the floor, arms outstretched to the salty air. She smiled at him and continued singing. This morning she was singing church songs, something she hadn't done in a very long while. She sang the doxology in her highest voice, then did a few jumping jacks and some yoga and got ready for the day, eating a bowl of muesli with one hand, journaling with the other.

She was lonely. She admitted it, but only to herself. She would have liked to be with Timothy more, and she used these rituals to make her stay here, doing things, being things, before she began the long trek to his house, all the anticipation she held in her heart building with every step. It was too soon to go first thing in the morning when she first opened her eyes to the sun hitting the yellow paint on her wall, and the string of beads she had hung from the curtain rod. She watched them spin and flash and thought, "A couple hours. I'll wait a couple hours." So she sang and did jumping jacks. She curled her already curly eyelashes but didn't bother putting mascara on. She tucked her hair behind her ears and dumped her drawstring bag of jewelry on the bed to see what she wanted to wear. She settled on a string of coral beads and several thin silver bangles. She put her purple sundress on. It brushed the tops of her knees as she walked out the door. She drank a cup of chai with the old man and his daughter-in-law, waited for the one fried egg, roti, and banana that she ate with them as a second breakfast every morning. She picked up the little three-year-old and tickled his belly, said goodbye to the family and made her way down the side of the hill to the path that led across the face of the cliff and eventually down to the beach.

On Wednesday and Friday mornings it was easier to keep herself occupied. She was busy those mornings, singing on Wednesdays and meditating on Fridays. True to his promise, Linus had introduced her to the Jesus people, as he called, them, a group of mostly women and a couple of young guys who sang on the beach. Prema felt awkward with them at first, but she stuck to her quest and soon she felt that they were her people too. There were three German women and a young guy from Austria, as well as a smattering of Americans, one Italian, and one Indian woman. They lived together in a cluster of houses not far from Timothy and one of the women had offered to find her a house nearby, but Prema wanted to maintain distance, not from them, but from Timothy, so she stuck to her room on the cliffs and her little family with the three-year-old and the old uncle. She arrived early on the mornings they sang, so she could join them in drawing shapes on the sand and scattering flowers over top, or digging holes in the shape of a sunburst or flower. It seemed so natural to make the space beautiful before they offered their devotion, and this was what she had craved, this beauty! Sometimes when she sang with them, she imagined their voices all gathering into a huge, crystalline globe that floated into heaven and reached the heart of God. They meditated some days, too, speaking words of scripture very slowly or contemplating the sea, or just listening, and the stillness helped Prema maintain her balance when she was in danger of becoming completely off kilter over Timothy. His eyes had somehow captured her, his eyes and the way he smoothed Isaac's eyebrows, his hands on his flute or on Isaac in the bath. She was completely gone, frantically trying to keep her head and focus on her quest.

The sun was a little higher and Prema had a hat on to ward off the headaches that came when she was in the midday sun too long. The fishermen were at the boats, plucking fat fish from their nets and tossing them into baskets. The coconut trees stood in their line, fronds spiky against the sky, the pine trees beside them leaning from their years in the wind. The whole world was clean and shiny. It was the end of December and there was more and more music around, more gatherings on the beach and more impromptu jams in beach huts that were increasingly full. The season was in full swing and Prema found herself in the middle of it. She questioned herself sometimes: had she come to India to hang out with foreigners in Goa? It didn't seem right, somehow, but at the same time, her heart was fuller than it had ever been. Her mother merely sighed when she was on the phone with her. "You're in Goa?" she said, her voice rising in disgust. "You went all that way to party on the beach?"

"I'm not partying," Prema said. "Don't worry, Mummy."

"What are you doing if you are not partying?"

Prema thought of the music in Sanjay's restaurant last night, of Linus and Timothy building notes upon notes, a tower of music. She had envisioned the notes reaching around the fat moon that she watched from her cushions on the floor of the beach hut. The moon slung in the black sky with Venus close enough to look like its distant cousin, the silver pathway on the water, narrowing to the far horizon. She thought of the candles on the tables, of the smell of incense, of how utterly contented she had been, of how she sat up and, surprising even herself, sang a song that she had made up on the spot.

"Listening to music," she said. "I met some nice people, from Canada and England." What was it that the three of them had become? They were best friends, quickly, suddenly, with Linus the perfect buffer for whatever was happening between Prema and Timothy, the thing she knew he was not ready for, and maybe didn't even want at all. She remembered the way Linus opened his eyes when she started singing, the way he winked and smiled at her, diving back into his guitar to form a thick wave of music for her to soar on top of, the way Timothy watched her and played under and around her. The way they all jumped with delight when the song was finished, everyone clapping, the way she lay back down on her cushion, tears in her eyes from happiness.

She was nearly at the place on the shore where she should cut across the dunes, into the village to get to Timothy's house. She was aware that she was far too happy, that this couldn't last. Or was it possible that she hadn't known who she really was, all those months that she had felt so uncomfortable in her classes? Had she been wrong to choose philosophy and critical thinking? Was she an artist? Was this remaking her?

An empty milk bag was floating in the surf and Prema waded in after it, picking it up with her index finger and thumb and carrying it with her. She trekked up through the exhaustingly soft sand. Her dad had spoken with her on the phone after her mom.

"We only want you to be safe," he had said.

"Oh, I'm safe," she said. "I'm safer than usual, here. You should see this place sometime, Daddy, you really should. It's so different from the India you know."

She heard him sigh, and then he said, "Oh, the world is so big, so full of places to learn to love. I'm afraid to see any more, in case I'm left always wanting something that is far away."

"It seems wrong, somehow, to not learn to love something only because you don't want to be sad when you leave it," she had said.

But she wasn't sure that she had been right about that, as she approached the little house with the red tiled roof where Timothy lived, her heart beating a drum solo in her chest. It would calm down once she saw him, once she had been hanging out with him for a while, she knew this now. It was only the first few minutes, the first sight of his blue eyes, the first scent of him, the first smile he aimed in her direction.

As she got close she saw Linus sitting on the one chair on the porch. He was reading something on a sheet of paper and he finished just as she climbed the steps. He passed it back to Timothy, who was perched on the porch railing.

"That's a surprise, that is," he said. "Hi, Prema."

"Hi," she said, pulling her hat off and setting it on the porch railing beside Timothy. He smiled down at her.

"Do you want to read this?"

"What is it?" she asked, but she already had it in her hand, an email he had printed out.

Dear Timothy,

And... disaster strikes! The boys have chicken pox. Sarah, too, which is terrible because it's really rough on her. This was not what I was imagining back when I declined the vaccination, that when I was just about on my way to see you I'd be stuck at home with sick kids.

We got mostly reimbursed for one of the tickets, and they let us switch the other one. We really feel like someone should be there with you right now. Dad's coming.

Love you, don't forget to eat breakfast and get some vegetables in you sometimes.
Mom

"Wow," Prema said. She handed it back to him. He folded it into a little package and held it in his palm. She watched his hands, thinking, *I can't, but* not knowing how to finish the statement, because what was it that she couldn't do? Stay? Leave him? Stand there watching him? She cut off the thought and walked to the garbage can on the porch to throw away her milk bag beach litter.

She quietly let herself into Timothy's room and plucked a knife and two spoons out of the dish drainer. The dish drainer was only a colander, but it didn't matter—he never used the colander because he never cooked. He made bottles and tea and that was about it. Prema knew he could make a killer cup of tea, she'd had more than a few of them. She crept out of the house again, managing to not wake the baby, who was sleeping soundly on the inside corner of the bed. She sat on the porch railing beside Timothy, pulling a papaya from her bag and slicing it in half. She scooped the seeds out and tipped them into the trash as well.

"Here," she said, handing one of the halves of the papaya and a spoon to Timothy. "It's not a vegetable, but it's close enough."

He took a bite, made a face of pleasure. She had a talent for picking a perfect papaya that she was inordinately proud of. "I'm surprised that you found two spoons in there," he said.

Linus was fishing through his bag now.

"I would offer one to you, but I know you don't like them," Prema said to him. "What are you looking for?"

"They taste like vomit," Linus said. "I'm looking for spare rupees. I just really don't want to make a trip to the ATM today. Hey—there's a show tonight. I completely forgot about it, look at that."

He held up a tattered piece of paper.

"What kind of music?" Prema put another spoonful of papaya into her mouth. Timothy tapped his spoon against his cheek, sitting back against a column with his feet on the railing, elbows on his knees. The air was dry and cool, the sun bright in the garden. Prema could understand why people said Goa was paradise. She watched as Timothy took another bite of papaya, then ate a spoonful herself.

"Sufi music, looks like," Linus said, squinting at the piece of paper. "It's a bit muddled now."

"Give me that," Prema said, hopping off the railing and pulling it out of his hand. "Linus! This show happened last Friday." She smacked him with the piece of paper before giving it back to him.

Timothy laughed.

"Right you are," Linus said. "So where's the flyer for tonight? Sod it, I really wanted to go to that show."

"I went," Prema said, sitting down again. "It was okay."

"Just okay?" Timothy asked.

"Just okay." She scraped the papaya really close to the rind, then folded the empty skin up like a present and tossed it into the garbage can. She brought her legs up in front of her so she was balanced on the wide, marble railing with her feet together and her knees up under her chin. "I don't know, the sound wasn't good at all. I could tell the band was good."

"That's the problem here—" Linus said.

"The sound," Timothy finished for him.

They had done one show together, and although Prema had praised them to the high heavens, Timothy and Linus insisted that it was "just okay," thanks to the sound system crackling like popping corn for the full two hours.

"But back to the other thing... before Linus so rudely interrupted us..." she shot a look in Linus's direction, "when is your dad coming?"

Timothy looked at the email for an answer. "He arrives in three days."

"That's crazy. And you got the email yesterday?"

"Yeah, well, my mom sent it a week ago, but I haven't been to the Internet place. I can't think of why she hasn't called me, except that maybe things are too crazy around there and she can't take a breath."

"There's the time difference thing too," Prema said.

"That too."

"My mom wants me to call her more, but I like my mornings peaceful and in the evenings I sometimes feel too exhausted to talk," she said.

"Yeah, but how much do you talk to her?"

"I don't know... twice a week?"

Timothy raised his eyebrows at Linus and bowed toward Prema. She pushed him away with her foot, laughing.

"My mother should be so lucky to have a child who calls her that often," Linus said. He was still rifling through his bag. He paused and looked closer at something in his hand. "A fiver! I found a five-hundred-rupee bill!"

"Why don't you broadcast that to everyone in the village?" Prema said. "My aunties would be horrified by the way you treat your money."

"I'm just glad that I don't have to take the scooter to the ATM. It's not running so well."

"Why don't you trade it in?"

"Too much bother."

"Wait, what's wrong with the Arambol ATM?" Prema asked.

"It's down for repair. For a week now, and anyway, the line is always so long there and I always end up drinking more sugar cane juice than I want to because the bells clank on the juicer and they *call* me. They call me." He shook his head, kissed the rupee bill, and put it in his pocket.

"What do you and your mom talk about, when you call home?" Timothy asked Prema.

"She does most of the talking. She tells me about the weather and what my brother and sister are up to, what my dad is up to, what new things she's bought. Then she tells me not to drink the water and we talk for a while about how bad the food must be in Goa and how long I'm going to stay here with these dirty hippies. I tell her I'm a dirty hippie and she cries about it for a minute or so and reminds me of my life back home and I tell her that I'm in love with India and then she cries again."

"Do you ever think you'd just stay?" Timothy asked.

"Here? No. No, I'm Canadian, through and through. And this is not really India, is it? I'm enjoying this strange international community freedom that we have. Has your dad ever traveled out of Canada?"

He smiled. "You really know how to keep talking about what you want to know," he said, teasing her. Her skin got hot and she put the back of one hand against her cheek.

"Only to the States," he said. "He traveled all around down there before he and my mom got married, but recently he's only gone to the other islands, the ones on the American side. He's taken ferry rides or driven to Seattle."

"Wow," Linus said. "He's in for a treat."

Prema had to agree. India was another universe. She tried to envision another, older Timothy bumping around Goa.

"Yup," Timothy said. He shook his head. "I was ready for Sarah and my mom. But this is something else completely." He looked down at his half-eaten papaya. "You're sure you don't want any papaya, Linus?"

"Sure as sure. Don't like it. Papaya is the world's most evangelized, bad-tasting fruit, besides, perhaps, durian," Linus said. He had pulled his guitar into his lap and was fingering the strings gently. "When's the little guy going to wake up?"

"How would I know that?" said Timothy, shrugging. He ate the rest of the papaya in a couple bites and threw the skin into the garbage like Prema. "But I don't really know if I'll be able to play, even after he wakes up. I have to feed him and stuff."

"I can feed him," Prema said. "If you make the bottle."

He only looked at her, until she looked away.

"Thanks, Prema," Linus said, accepting for Timothy. Timothy kept looking at Prema and when she glanced back at him he smiled. *Thanks*, he mouthed, not making any sound.

It was good timing. They heard the sounds of Isaac waking up in the room. Timothy swung his legs off the railing and walked inside. Prema followed him.

She wondered what his father would do when he first laid eyes on Isaac. She and Timothy looked at Isaac together. He kicked and babbled in the bed Timothy had made for him on the floor; a little fortress of mattresses and pillows.

"He's getting so big," Prema said. She bent down and touched his forehead, then poked him in the ribcage softly. "Hi Isaac boy!" she said. He laughed.

"That sound, oh man," she said, feeling something in her chest that was sharp and warm all at once.

"He's nearly six months old. I can barely believe it," Timothy said.

He lifted Isaac out of the bed, holding him under the arms so that his legs dangled and kicked around in the empty air. The room didn't smell very fresh. Prema opened a window and wandered over to the sink. She turned the water on. Turned it back off again.

"It must be hard," she said.

Timothy seemed to know what she meant. "It is."

On the porch Linus let his hands dance over the guitar strings. "Get out here, flute boy!" he called.

Timothy put a bottle together quickly and on the porch Prema sat on the ground and held Isaac in her arms to feed him. She let her head fall back so she could see the coconut fronds shining and dancing in the sky above the house. She listened to Timothy's wandering flute and Linus's dancing guitar and watched the brilliant blue sky, the gentle fronds waving, waving. In the distance eagles circled on a warm draft. She leaned in to look into the baby's eyes, deep brown pools that reflected all of it back to her, the house, the sky, the porch with all of them on it.

When the day was leaning into the evening, and Linus left to go wherever it was he went most evenings, Prema and Timothy ate fish curry rice with Maria and her family. They walked the few steps to the door to Maria's house together, Isaac babbling at the sky as though he was telling it some important truth.

Prema ducked into Patrick and Maria's doorway and felt that pang of familiarity she always felt here, although the tiny rooms were a world away from her auntie's fancy house in Punjab. There was something about an Indian woman in her own house, no matter the difference in station or dress. Maria wore one of the short, just-below-the-knee length Goan Catholic dresses that Prema always thought made Goan women look like schoolgirls, her thin brown legs poking out from her hem. She knew her aunties or mother would die before showing their legs in public— it was one of the many things that signified who you were in this country where religion was so important, so public. In Goa you could tell at a glance whether someone was Hindu or Catholic by their necklaces, their anklets or lack of anklets, whether the skin on their legs was showing, whether they had bindi. In other parts of India you could tell where a woman was from by the colors of her bangles, how she wore her sari, the stripes of color after temple. Then there were of course men with their beards or clean chins, turbans for Sikhs, flat hats for Muslims, swords and long hair and paint on the forehead and statues in cars and signs on the walls and there wasn't anywhere you could go in this whole place where you wouldn't know where someone came from, what their parents (and perhaps they) believed in.

Prema thought about all of this as she walked into Maria's house and again came face to face with their shrine, a large plastic cross and a pale Jesus slung over it, bleeding pink blood. She shuddered and then looked curiously at it, wondering what it was like to live with something that was perpetually dying. She heard the prayers of her own house owners sometimes in the evenings, led by the mother of the house, the murmuring of call and response. She admired the devotion of the prayers, the constancy of them, and yet in that moment, standing before the shrine on the wall, she realized in some small way she had made a step in her quest, that in a way she was no longer searching. It had something to do with the peace she felt as she sang in the mornings with the

German women, and it had something to do with her dislike of plastic. She had made a small step. I am this, and I am not this. It made her feel proud, and she turned to beam at Timothy at the same time that Maria stepped forward and plucked Isaac right out of his arms, so that he missed her smile, but she felt the weight of it still in her heart, like a cascade of light that was solid, like gold or water or a stream of fishes.

"Come, come, come," Patrick said. "Sit, sit." He pointed at the only two chairs in the room.

Prema loved the way the people she knew in Goa repeated their words for emphasis in almost every sentence. "Good good, slowly slowly, yes yes yes." It made them seem impossibly enthusiastic. The room was small, a square with two doorways, one that Prema and Timothy still stood in, and one more that led to the kitchen, a lean-to off the house. The family lived in this one room, rolling out sleeping mats at night. The floor was laid with tiles with a scalloped brown pattern splashed across them. A TV stood proudly in the corner, draped with a tasseled throw. The house was spotless.

Maria passed Isaac to her oldest daughter and disappeared into the kitchen, her bare feet making hardly any noise on the floor. She returned with two plates of fish curry rice. They looked and smelled incredible. The plates were huge, with fish curry, a mound of rice, a bowl of some sort of vegetable dish, a piece of fried fish, and chapati. Prema looked at Timothy. She could almost see his mouth watering as Maria handed one plate to him. He made a sound of delight and Patrick and Maria laughed. They laughed all the time. They laughed when they talked about money, they laughed when they were embarrassed, they laughed when someone else was embarrassed. And they laughed when they were happy. Maria handed one plate to Prema.

"Are you going to eat?" Prema asked.

"After, after," Patrick said. They were going to sit and watch Timothy and Prema eat, like usual.

Prema and Timothy settled themselves on the floor and Prema scooped fish curry onto the rice with her hand, mixing it up so she could form the little rice package that she delivered to her mouth with her fingers. The first bite burned and Prema realized that maybe Maria hadn't known that they were coming and hadn't held back on the chilies.

"Do you have water?" she asked, with a bit of a gasp in her voice. Timothy turned to look at her and she saw that his eyes were streaming. Maria fetched an old Sprite bottle filled with water and poured it into two cups. "Boiled?" Prema asked, but she barely waited for Maria to nod before throwing the water into her mouth.

The rest of the meal was a beautiful ordeal. Under the glare of the fluorescent light and the watchful gaze of the crucified Christ and the Queen of Heaven, Timothy and Prema ate the most delicious, spiciest fish curry Prema had ever tasted. Maria and Patrick laughed as Timothy gulped water and wiped his nose between each bit.

"Chili?" Patrick asks.

"Yes, chili. Very spicy," Timothy said.

Prema painfully finished the wonderful, violent food. Maria and her daughters had been sitting with Isaac while she and Timothy ate, playing with the baby's feet, tickling his toes. He laughed and babbled at them in response. Prema waited for her lips to feel normal again. She wanted to go deeper with Maria and Patrick, to know more of what their lives were like, what their dreams were, but she didn't speak their language. So she and Timothy spoke their thanks into Maria's dark-fringed eyes and accepted her invitation to eat with them the next night.

"Chillies no," she said, and it was the sweetest thing, and Prema missed her own mother. They walked into the night air and Isaac once again starting talking to the sky.

CHAPTER 24

Timothy called Maria's brother, who was a taxi driver, when it was time to go to the airport to pick his father up. They left in the early morning before the sun was really even up, and drove in silence. Isaac slept on Timothy's lap; his face round, beautiful, and calm. Timothy hadn't left the tiny village of Arambol for over two months. He spent his days and nights in the small fishing village, only traveling as far as the beach, and a couple of times, the cliffs. He was amazed at the length of time it took to drive to the airport. The billboards felt violent to him—advertisement for products thrown in haphazard strokes across a mile of space in the sky. Beneath the billboards, water buffalo chewed their cuds, tall white egrets standing on their shoulders.

He waited a long time once they reached the airport. It took approximately one bottle and two diaper changes, because the plane was delayed. Finally, people began to enter the strange upstairs gallery that led to the stairs down to the baggage belts. He almost didn't see his father because his father was so much taller than he remembered and his eyes passed over him—nope, not that one—before skidding back to the most familiar face, looking back at him.

"Dad," he said.

"Timothy."

Timothy had Isaac in one arm, but his father slipped an arm under Isaac, another arm over Timothy's shoulder, and pulled them both close. He gripped them hard. When he pulled back, Timothy could see tears in his eyes. He felt himself welling up in response and took a shaky breath. It felt unreal that his father was standing in front of him. He stared into his dad's familiar face and felt the room whirl as his worlds crashed together.

"It's so good to see you," he said.

"Oh, I'm so glad to see you," his dad said. "And so glad to be off that plane. And..." he turned his head to look at Isaac, who stared back at him. Isaac offered a smile. Timothy's dad, put a finger under each lens of his glasses and wiped at the tears that had escaped. He smiled back at Isaac.

"May I?" he asked Timothy.

"Of course..."

Timothy's dad put his hands under Isaac's arms and brought him to one hip. Isaac grabbed at his glasses, and Timothy watched as his father captured the little hand and kissed it.

"Grandson," he said. "I'll have to get used to the sound of that."

"Let's look for your bags, Dad," Timothy said. "You must be exhausted."

"I could use a nap," his father said. "But I'm full of adrenaline right now. Look at your face." He reached his hand out and put it on Timothy's cheek. "I've missed you so much."

The bags, when they came, were brand new. Timothy admired them out loud, and his dad looked embarrassed.

"Your mom insisted I bring these ones that she just bought. I had perfectly good ones, but she said no one uses those old leather ones anymore."

Timothy knew exactly the suitcases his dad was referring to. They had an old brown and old red one packed together in the attic of his childhood home. Leather cracking, held together with fat zippers as well as two buckles each.

"Is this it?" he asked, looking from the two new suitcases to the luggage conveyor. Around them people plucked bags from the belt and hauled them onto carts. Tourists gazed at Lonely Planet guides or maps. A performer Timothy had met once pulled a bag from the belt and adjusted it on the ground. He was holding a set of juggling clubs and had a sitar strapped to his back. Timothy had seen him on the beach just a few days before. He played in different Indian cities and was probably arriving from a gig somewhere else.

"Yes, just the two. One is for me and one is full of stuff for you."

"Wow," Timothy said.

"Don't worry," his father said. "Most of it is edible. You won't have to tote it along with you."

They each took a suitcase and pulled it along the floor of the airport, heading for the door. They passed their customs tags to the officers and were lazily waved through. A sea of taxi drivers dressed in white met them as they stepped outside, holding signs. Timothy's dad blinked in the bright, hot sun. He bumped into Timothy when Timothy stopped suddenly to adjust the suitcase he was pulling. The taxi drivers ignored the two of them. They were there to pick up specific people, holding signs with names printed or scrawled on them. It was only when they got to the entrance of the parking lot that the stray taxi drivers, the hopefuls, clustered around them. They addressed David, measuring him, accurately, as the softer of the two.

"Taxi?"

"Oh, well, I don't know. Timothy? Do we need a taxi?"

"No, we have one already." Timothy scanned the parking lot for his driver. *Where did he get to?*

"No, no thank you," David said behind him. "Thank you, though."

"Where going? Arambol?"

"Where are we going, Timothy?"

"Arambol. We don't need a taxi, though." Timothy turned and addressed the driver. "We have one! Ask someone else!"

The driver grumbled and walked away slowly.

"Thank you!" David called after him.

Timothy caught sight of his driver as the driver unwound himself from a scooter that he had been sitting on and detached from a group of people. He gave a wave goodbye to the other drivers and turned it into a wave at Timothy.

"Ready, Dad?" Timothy asked. His dad was peeling off a long-sleeved shirt, leaving a T shirt underneath. For a second, Timothy saw the white of his stomach. He was still in great shape, probably from all the lifting he did in the shop, Timothy thought.

"Yeah, ready. It's hot here, eh?"

"It is."

They wheeled their suitcases toward the little van. Timothy had Isaac in one arm. The wheels bounced and whined against the rough ground. The sun was sharp at midday. But lately it had been beautiful and cool in the evenings, at night, in the mornings. Paradise. Timothy glanced at his dad to see if he was appreciating paradise. He looked a bit stunned.

The driver took Timothy's suitcase and hauled it into the back of the small van, but David tossed his in the back himself. They climbed into the taxi and Timothy's dad let his head drop against the short seat behind him.

"I guess I'm more tired than I thought," he said. "It's not normal that I have so much trouble crossing a parking lot."

"You must be exhausted. We'll get you to your room and you can sleep."

"No, no. Your mother told me I have to stay up until dark at least. Reset my clock."

"That's fine. It will practically be dark by the time we get there."

"Oh really? Far, eh?"

"A couple of hours."

Timothy settled Isaac on his lap so that he faced outward, tucked in between Timothy's arms. David looked startled.

"You don't have a safety seat for him?"

"No. Everything's different here."

David frowned at this and checked his watch. He looked out the window as they pulled out of the parking lot and into traffic. There was a traffic signal at the intersection leading into the airport and it was the only one Timothy had ever seen in Goa.

"What is that?" his dad asked, pointing.

"That's a water buffalo," Timothy said.

"Water buffalo? I haven't seen one in real life! Would you look at that? Incredible."

Timothy felt a surge of love for his dad.

"Why is there so much trash everywhere? You'd think people would take more care than this."

Timothy shrugged, moving quickly from love to irritation. Maybe Prema knew why. He was suddenly glad that she would be there. That she could answer some of these questions. That she was herself.

"No helmets," his dad muttered. On the highway helmets were required, but only for the driver, so the taxi careened around families of three or four on scooters or motorcycles, the drivers wearing helmets, the beautiful, black, braided hair of their wives bare.

Timothy watched his dad's face. Right now, because it was winter at home, his face was pale, and all his emotions were in full display, as he smiled or frowned over things he saw. Timothy had never realized how transparent his father was.

When they pulled up on the small road in front of Timothy's house, Maria was sweeping the porch. The garden looked beautiful with hibiscus and yellow climbing flowers in bloom. The sun was just past the golden hour and the sky was rosy.

"This is where we live," Timothy said, proudly, as they retrieved the luggage and paid the driver. His father turned to look at the little rooms with the big porch. They walked in under the small archway made of bamboo and a yellow flowering vine. Maria waved from the porch.

"Hello!" she said.

"Hello," Timothy's dad said.

"This is my father," Timothy said. "Dad, this is Maria. She's my landlady. With her family."

They all smiled at each other. Timothy slipped his shoes off and went through the doorway, into the one room that held him and Isaac. His dad paused on the porch to unlace his boots.

"Suppose I should get myself some of those," he said. He pointed his chin toward Timothy's *chappals*, which were falling apart, and only held together by string and tape. He frowned for a minute, looking at them, then looked at Timothy and raised his eyebrows. Timothy laughed.

"I guess I should get some new ones myself," he said.

"We'll get them together."

Isaac had fallen asleep in the car, but he was awake again and hungry. Once his father managed to get his boots off and walked into the room, Timothy handed the baby to him.

"He's wet," Timothy's dad said.

"I'm just going to get this bottle ready, then I'll change him. It helps to have something to feed him straight away."

Timothy's father looked around the room. He stood in his bare white feet, holding Isaac with both arms. Isaac fussed. He wasn't outright storming, but he whined and it seemed like it would soon turn into a full blown cry. Timothy sped up his bottle making. His father jiggled the baby in his arms.

"Hey, it's all right," he said. "Your dad's getting you something. It's coming along shortly."

"If you can get him to understand that, you're a genius and I'll pay you well."

His father laughed. Timothy had forgotten what a great laugh his dad had. He couldn't really believe that his dad was standing there, right there in his tiny room.

"So this is where you live?" he asked, looking all around, as though it was just now coming into focus.

Timothy nodded.

"Yes. We like it." His house in Canada was ten times the size of this room. But this house had taken him in. He finished up and retrieved Isaac, laying him on the bed for a quick change. Just a wipe and a new cloth diaper and the old one in the pail. He scooped his son to his chest and sat on the bed against the wall like usual. His father pulled Timothy's one red plastic chair closer.

He looked tired, Timothy thought. He could see the shadows under his dad's eyes.

"What are these walls made of?" his dad asked. He stood and puts a hand on one wall.

"It's this rock they have," Timothy said. "You'll see it in piles around here. Lots of holes in it, I think it's volcanic. They build with concrete sometimes too, but I think this is rock, because it's an old style house."

"Old style?"

"Yeah, the roof. The tiled roof is old style." They both looked up at the ceiling, which was laid with clay tiles, overlapping a simple system of thick and slender beams.

"They don't ever use wood for framing?"

"No. Never. People don't use a lot of wood here, Dad."

Timothy could see his dad running that through his head, trying to get his mind around it. He thought of the island in Canada where his dad had been born and raised, the sheer forests on it, the wood that seemed endless. All the branches leaning into the sea. Driftwood fires, the green, yellow and blue flames.

"They don't have the forests for it," Timothy went on. "We have our massive forests and thirty million people. India has forests, sure, but they have over a billion people."

His father wiped at the wall with his hand and sat back down in the plastic chair.

"No wood," he said. "I don't think I ever thought about the size of India in that way before."

Timothy had seen his father spend an entire day shaving a table to perfection. The thing he was known for, the thing his grandfather was known for, was intricate drawers within furniture. Tiny boxes that fit between other drawers. Wood for Timothy's father was love and smell and sun and sustenance.

"I can't imagine a life without wood," he said.

"Oh, but it's not that there's no wood," Timothy said. "It's just that they don't use it here in Goa to frame houses. There are houses made largely of wood in the Himalayas. Old houses. But it's true. Most new buildings are concrete."

"Ah. Well." Timothy's dad sat up a little straighter and slapped his thighs. "What's the plan for the rest of the day?"

Isaac was nearly finished with the bottle. One of the best things about him getting older was that he didn't fall asleep the way he used to. A feeding was just that, a feeding, not a wake-sleep-tickle-a-thon.

"This little guy's nearly done. Are you hungry?"

"Very."

"What do you feel like eating?"

"Oh, I don't know. I'm not from around here. Whatever you're having."

Timothy was overcome by a flash of uselessness. There was nothing that was going to make this visit any less awkward. It would be awkward ad infinitum. Just then there was a clatter of steps on the porch, a pause, and Prema stuck her head in the door. She had a flower tucked behind her ear.

"Hey! You're back!"

"Prema! Hey Dad, this is Prema. Prema, this is my dad."

His father stood to shake Prema's hand. "Hi there, you can call me David."

"Thanks, David. How was your flight?"

"Good, I think. I've never been on such a long one before. You must be the Canadian girl Timothy was telling me about."

Timothy felt himself blushing. He hid his face in Isaac's neck as he lifted him to his shoulder to burp him.

"Sure, that's probably me. I feel like we're the only two Canadians on this beach right now. Oh, but there's three of us now that you're here!"

"We were just talking about where we should go to eat."

There were squares of light on the wall, the same ones that showed up every day at this time as the sun got ready to set and hit the window just so. Prema looked at Timothy with her brown eyes, the tips of her black bangs curving against her forehead.

"Well, did you decide on anything? Are you settled in yet? Ready to go?" Prema asked.

"Settled in?" David looked around and wiped at his head with a handkerchief. "Right, Timothy, where am I going to sleep?"

"Oh! I completely forgot. I got you a room next door. This place seems a little cramped for the two of us, and Isaac is still waking up sometimes at night."

"Why don't you finish up with Isaac and I'll show him the room?" Prema asked.

"Thanks," David said. "That would be great." He stood up and they wandered out onto the porch. David popped his head back in.

"Do you mind if I borrow your thongs?"

"Sure, Dad."

Prema stuck her head in the door again and winked at Timothy. He laughed out loud. Canadians called flip-flops thongs, but on this beach they had already seen many of the other kind of thong. Timothy scooted off the bed and pulled Isaac toward him. Isaac opened his mouth in a wide smile. Timothy put his face in his son's neck and blew raspberries. Isaac shrieked with laughter. But he was dirty. Timothy looked for a clean shirt. He eyed the second suitcase, really hoping there was some clothing in there. He found a clean baby shirt for now, though it was dull with old dust and stains. He washed his own hands, splashed water on his face and neck and hair, then tied the baby carrier on.

He wondered what was taking Prema and his dad so long. The room he had reserved was just next door. It was a simple room, just a box with a window and a bed, really. There was an attached bathroom. It was cheap, clean. Nice owners. They were Maria's family, actually. But as he stood on the porch and looked over, he didn't see either his father or Prema.

He walked back into the room, hot now because Isaac was strapped to him. He washed the bottle and set it in the dish drainer, working around Isaac. He remembered that the other bottle, from the airport, was still in his backpack, so he washed that too. Still they weren't back. He was getting that hungry feeling in his stomach, impatient about waiting. He was nervous and twitchy, as though he had drunk too much coffee. He paced. Straightened the bed. Scooped up Isaac's old shirt and put it in the bucket of dirty clothes that Maria would pick up in the morning.

Where were they?

The thud of footsteps on the porch. Voices, laughing. Timothy met them at the door.

"What happened?" he asked.

"Your dad didn't like the room." Prema said. "We looked around a little more, found him a beach hut."

"It's nice, so nice. Smells like living things," his father said.

"Like coconut," Timothy said. "That's a kind of wood."

"A kind of plant," his dad said.

"That's what I mean," Timothy said. He jiggled Isaac in the carrier. He was annoyed at the change of plans. Now he would have to cancel with the family who owned the other room, and he thought he had prepared well, finding a place for his father to stay. He looked down at his baby, trying to rearrange his face. He looked up at Prema and she must have seen something in the way he looked.

"We talked to the family next door," she said. "They're fine with a change because someone else has been asking about the room."

"That's good," Timothy said. He was quiet again, stroking Isaac's forehead where his hair formed a peak.

"Well!" Prema said. She clapped her hands twice. "I think we should take your dad for fish curry rice."

"Sounds good. What is it?" Timothy's father asked.

David and Prema walked out of the house and through the arbor with yellow flowers that climbed and leaned from it. It took Timothy three tries to get the lock on his door to cooperate. He jammed the key in his waist belt pocket and joined them while Prema explained Goan food to his dad. They turned onto the path, then onto the road. Timothy waved at a few people he knew. His dad quizzed Prema on her upbringing and her precise location back in Canada.

"Oh," he said. "I have a friend who lives just a little way from there. I've probably been by your house many times."

"And now we meet here," Prema said.

"And now we meet here."

Timothy thought again of how kind Prema was. She was possibly the kindest person he had ever met. She was wearing a red dress that brushed the bottoms of her knees. He can see the tattoo on her right calf and he felt a longing sensation as they arrived at the fish curry rice place. All the details swarmed into each other as Timothy began to fall into a well of sadness. *I wouldn't be noticing her at all if you were still here Isabel*, he thinks. *I would have been true to you forever.*

Lines of Bob Marley's *Stir it Up*, reached him from the speakers at the restaurant across the street. *Little darling, stir it up.* Crows lighted on a pack of old bread that had been thrown onto a pile of trash. The fish curry rice came and Timothy's father dipped his fingers in for the first time.

CHAPTER 25

Prema couldn't really say, later, how she had gotten so involved with Timothy's dad and the sea turtles, or how she had been turned into a translator, a mediator, really, between the two sides: pro turtle and pro food. It started with a walk along the beach and continued with a motorbike ride. Timothy had been cleaning his room while Isaac slept. He pulled out the old toothbrush, which made it obvious to Prema that he needed time alone, though he didn't seem to know how to say it. She suggested that she and David look for Linus and go for a walk.

They found Linus on the steps to his beach hut, across the way from David's hut. He was playing his guitar. The man who ran the restaurant and beach huts that were called, inexplicably, Golden Watch, was hosing off a large plastic table not too far away. Linus smiled as Prema approached with David, but his fingers didn't stop moving on the neck of his guitar. She paused and waited for a while, thinking about musicians and how these boys could get so involved in what they were doing that they barely noticed time passing. She thought of Linus and Timothy, lost in their world of rising and falling notes, of Timothy's beautiful voice whenever he pulled the flute away from his face and sang a few lines of whatever song they were playing. She thought of David sitting on the porch with them, always with them these days, silently watching his son. And Timothy never quite leaving the world as a musician anymore, even when he played music, a part of him always watching out for his baby and his father. Prema imagined that he was just a boy, once, a boy a lot like Linus. She wondered what it would have been like if they had met in Vancouver, at university, she a philosophy student and he a music student. They would have been young and carefree together, he wouldn't have the heavy silent weight he seemed to carry everywhere. But maybe they wouldn't ever have sat on the beach singing while the sun set over the water. They wouldn't have watched Goan women wade in the surf, throwing tiny clams into a bucket. They wouldn't have Isaac. The thought made her breath catch. She was glad she met him exactly when she did. She didn't know where their relationship was headed at all. But she was glad she had found him, a heart friend.

Prema walked between David and Linus as they made a beeline for the cliffs. Linus hummed, bringing his hands up to his imaginary guitar in that way he had. David gazed off toward the sea. Prema wondered what he saw there. Did he miss his Canadian ocean? Prema missed Timothy, second-guessing her decision to leave him alone.

It was like this that they came across the first sea turtle any of them had ever seen in the wild, not knowing, as they approached, what they were even about to see. There was a small crowd of people gathered on the beach and as they walked toward it Prema wondered if someone was hurt or falling down drunk, but when they drew close they saw a sea turtle in the sand, slowly pulling itself along the beach, parallel to the water and heading slightly inland. Beside her, David gasped, and when Prema turned to look, he was stock still in the sand. His eyes were wide.

"I've never seen a sea turtle," he said. "She's so beautiful."

She was beautiful. Prema could see exactly what he meant. The turtle looked otherworldly, as though she had come from some distant place, much farther than this regular old sea in front of them. Linus had moved closer and was leaning over the turtle, looking into her face. One of the men standing nearby waved his hand in front of Linus's face. "Move back," he said. "You are too close." Prema noticed that some of the people standing around had the stance of bodyguards. They looked alert, ready for action. With a bad feeling in her stomach she noticed the Goan fishermen standing a little distance away, arms across their chests, watching the scene.

"What's going on?" she asked the nearest person.

"The fishermen," he told her. He was compact and muscly, with startling blue eyes and a strong Russian accent. He looked like a member of an Olympic swim team. "He want to eat her. Is laying her eggs and he want to eat her."

"Oh dear," Prema said.

"Why would they do that?" David asked. He looked horrified.

Prema opened her mouth to answer, but it was too late. Six young Goan men were approaching with ropes. She held her stomach with her hands and tried to figure out what to do. Next to her, the swimmer tensed up, his hands balling into fists.

"Because are asshole," he hissed, and the next thing she knew, he had charged at the Goan men and pushed one of them backwards. Fists started flailing all around and Linus was somehow caught up in the middle of it, hands over his head, trying to back away. Prema lost a flip-flop as she tried to get some distance. The sand was scorching hot under her foot. Suddenly she was angry. She saw David in the middle of the fight, holding his hands up in the air, trying to speak. She saw him get hit by a flailing wrist, a blow not meant for him, and she was angry.

She waded in.

"Stop!" she screamed, and oh it was a scream. A loud, Indian scream, somewhere from the depths of her the lungs she had inherited from her mother. "Stop now!"

She spoke to the people— the Russian man she met, all the others. "This is not your beach," she said. "You cannot tell them what to do—I know! I know, it's terrible, they shouldn't eat the turtle. But you are guests here in this country."

She wasn't done talking before they were shouting again. David and Linus were staring at her, shocked. Prema knew that they couldn't understand why she was taking the side of the people who wanted to eat the gorgeous animal. People had stopped hitting each other, but one man was being restrained by two other men, and one man was sitting in the sand, his head on his knees as he tried to stop the blood streaming from his nose. A man with a German accent and nothing on but a Speedo was shouting about the sea turtles being endangered.

"Turtles are protected on this beach!" he shouted.

"Go back to your country!" a fisherman yelled in his face. The atmosphere around the beach was seething with barely restrained violence. Prema felt a surge of hopelessness, knowing people would start hitting one another very soon, but then she saw four cops making their way through a beach shack, knocking tables aside, sticks in their hands. She turned to David and Linus.

"We need to leave. Now."

Linus nodded, but David looked over and saw the police. He shook his head.

"No," he said. "I want to see how this resolves."

Prema was not at all sure that he really wanted to do that, but she settled back on her heels and waited for the police to approach. A couple of foreigners were still talking very quickly and loudly, but the fishermen had calmed in the presence of the cops. They knew how the sticks were often put to use. The cops used their body posture to threaten and held their sticks in the most intimidating way possible. They looked around, perhaps for an instigator, someone to pin this on.

"What is the meaning of this?" one said. Another spoke in Konkani, and two or three fishermen began to speak at once in the Goan language, rapidly, angrily. The cop gestured and the Goan fishermen moved to the side a little, having their own discussion. The Russian man that Prema was talking with answered the cop who spoke English.

"A bastards want to eat the turtle," he said.

"But what is that to you?" the cop asked.

"Are protected," he said. "Yes? You have seen the nests in Morjim?"

"They have protected sites in Morjim," the cop said. "Not in Arambol." There was a ripple, a muttering of anger across the group of foreigners. "However, we will try to convince these men not to eat the turtle because it is not permitted to eat the sea turtles anywhere in Goa."

"Try to convince?" an American man asked. "Can't you enforce it?"

"Do one thing," the cop said, hitting the sand with his stick. It made little *thunking* sounds and a few grains of sand flew upward. "Walk away from this place. This is not your concern."

The group, which had grown, had to listen, though Prema could see that no one wanted to walk away from the turtle. The little group walked away and clustered not too far away.

"What will happen?" David asked.

"I don't think it's going to be good," Prema said. "They'll probably pay the police and then take her home and eat her."

David shook his head. They watched, silently, waiting. One of the police men, the youngest one, walked over to them after a few minutes.

"We will find a place for her to lay her eggs," he said.

"And then?" David asked.

"Don't worry about that," the officer said, making a dismissive gesture with one hand. "Just go on now."

Prema shared a glance with Linus. She was almost certain they had been paid off and the turtle would be eaten. Still, if the eggs were laid, maybe there was a fighting chance.

"I was surprised to hear about the protected nests in Morjim," Prema said.

"Do you think they're really doing it?"

"Let's go see," Linus said, looking up from where he was drawing a large picture of a sea turtle on the sand. He had been bending down with a tiny stick in his hand, drawing loops and circles until his turtle drawing enclosed them all. Prema with her white dress blowing in the strong wind that had picked up while they were arguing about the turtle, David in Hawaiian shirt and khaki shorts. The beach was flat and hard after the tide, covered in small clam shells, the tiniest things, only the size of a fingernail.

"Go see?" Prema echoed.

"Yes," David said. "That's what we ought to do. I want to, anyway. You?" he looked at Prema, asking her opinion, her permission. She hesitated, thinking of Timothy back in his little house. He might have been wondering about them. But she remembered that he had been on his own for a long time. It might have been good for him— all the quiet in the house making large circles for him to stretch in. But she was confused. She frowned at Linus a little. This walk wasn't supposed to be complicated— Linus was complicating things.

"How will we get there?" she asked.

"Drive," he said.

They walked to Linus and David's beach huts. Linus jammed on flip-flops and grabbed a *gumcha* from a pile of things on his porch.

"Do you have one of these?" he asked David, holding the strong cotton scarf out. "You're going to want one. It'll be incredibly hot and the sun will scorch you."

Prema glanced at the thinning dark blond hair on David's head. Meeting Timothy's father had her thinking of Timothy growing older, of the way his shoulders would look when he is forty.

"How would I use that?" David asked as Linus wrapped the cloth around his own head, his arms flailing. He emerged looking like a bandit. After a moment, Prema picked up the piece of cloth, limp in her hand, and wound it quickly around David's head.

"Thanks," he said. "How do I look?"

"Like a proper rickshaw *wallah*," Linus said, and Prema surprised herself by laughing.

"How are we getting there again?" David asked.

"On my bike," Linus said. He whistled a short song as they walked out to the road. His whistle was like a bird's, sharp and aching.

"All of us?" David asked. He stopped short in the road, looking at Prema for help.

"Only if you want to," she said. He looked so lost that she felt bad for him.

"No, you have to!" Linus said. "Don't worry, the locals do it all the time."

"Three on a scooter," David said, following Linus down the road as a taxi narrowly missed him. "I could never, ever have guessed I'd be doing this, but if it's the way here..." he trailed off as Linus stopped at his bike. He looked up and grinned at David.

"It's going to be cozy."

They drove with David in the middle. Prema may have been up for this, for the awkwardness and all the strange looks she would get—an Indian woman on a scooter with two foreign men—but she was *not* riding in the middle. And that left poor David in the middle, just a victim to this scheme which had started with the idea of a walk on the beach and had led to the three of them wheeling through the jungle on their way to Morjim, the sun hot overhead, Prema barely clinging to the back of the bike.

"Everybody scootch!" she said, after a large bump nearly threw her off. The men in front of her scootched obligingly, and she laughed again. Her laughter was loud in the jungle, and they pulled away from the dark trees and into the open sun, coming up quickly through red cliffs and into sight of the beach. There were egrets overhead, white birds flying in a tight formation, coming right for them. Prema felt a hot surge of joy. The loose end of David's *gumcha* whipped her in the face. The air coming from the pavement was hot and the sea in the distance was very, very bright.

CHAPTER 26

In Morjim they parked the bike and awkwardly climbed off, Prema making a few hops so she didn't fall. She ran her hands over her dress, trying to straighten out the wrinkles, and swung her arms, pulling one elbow over her head to stretch it out. Her hands hurt from clinging to the back of the bike a little too hard.

"I've never been here before," she said to Linus.

"I've only been here once," he said. "For a party at one of the clubs. I left early, though, it was such a weird scene. All Russian women, Indian men, and cocaine."

"Sounds terrible."

"It was."

They walked toward the space where they knew the sea to be, breaking onto a very different beach than the one they were used to in Arambol. This beach was curved and smaller, with large fancy clubs that looked shut down and empty in the middle of the day.

"So we just walk until we see a turtle?" Linus asked. "Is that our plan?"

"Sounds right to me," David said.

He still looked lost. Prema wished she could make things more normal for him. The sea was calm with slight, gentle waves crashing nearly at the shore. Two naked toddlers played in the surf near their mothers, Russian goddesses in bikinis. Prema slipped her *chappals* off and carried them by their straps, swinging them by her side.

"How did you end up at the club anyway?" she asked.

Linus glanced at her, then up away from the sea, toward the dunes, which were pushed far back on this beach.

"Oh, that's the one there," he said, pointing at a place with floating canvas roofs. "I was playing guitar at a restaurant and a guy asked me if I wanted to play at his club. He paid well. I played and then left."

"How come I didn't know about this?"

He smiled at her, dimples popping into view.

"Maybe you weren't paying attention to what I was doing," he said. He emphasizes the word "I." Prema's face felt hot. She hadn't known he was aware of how she felt about Timothy, but of course, he must have been. She glanced at David to see if he had caught Linus's teasing. He was looking at his feet, walking on her right, where the water met the sand. His feet left deep indentations in the sand, while she, walking where the sand was harder, left hardly a trace. He looked up at her for a moment, very seriously, no teasing in his face, until she looked back at Linus, her eyes pleading him not to go any farther with it.

"No seriously," he said. "I don't know why. I told Timothy about it, wondered if he wanted to come play with me, but he didn't want to have Maria come round to babysit. He was tired, I think."

"I would have babysat," Prema said, putting her feet down extra hard.

"Right, but he doesn't want to ask you all the time, you know."

"I don't know why, I've told him he can."

"Do you really not know why?" David asked.

There was a pause. She wondered what on earth he was going to say.

"Timothy is careful, you know," David said. "You may have the best intentions, but so does he, and he's very aware that Isaac is his son. He doesn't want to impose."

"He's caught, really," Linus said. "Between his need for help and not wanting to put anyone out."

"I just think it's so silly," Prema said. "Of course he needs help! He should just take it! Whatever we offer him!"

"I don't know," David said. "Men are like that, they don't like to need too much help with what they feel is their responsibility. And Timothy is a man."

Prema let out a short gust of air and wiped at the hair that was always falling in her eyes. She should just shave her head already, it was so annoying sometimes.

"Didn't matter anyways," Linus said, putting a hand on her elbow briefly. "It was a bloody terrible gig. Timothy would've hated it."

They walked in silence for a while, a quiet nearly complete because of the sand under their feet and the hushing sound of the sea. Prema thought of her reaction back there on the beach with fishermen on one side and travelers on the other. She knew why she had rushed to the defense of the fishermen, though she wondered if the others understood. These villagers had only their small village, the line of the shore, and the small distances they traveled in their small mango wood, or more recently, fiberglass boats. They didn't have the BBC; *An Inconvenient Truth*; *Guns, Germs, and Steel*. They didn't see the ocean in satellite vision, with infrared dots showing where turtles were the most in danger. They saw a turtle wander in and it looked like a special meal, one that didn't come their way very often. They ate from the sea and their nets weren't the ones capturing and drowning turtles for the sake of a few pounds of shrimp. Prema got mad just thinking about how people always thought they knew better than one another, and yet she knew she had the ability to measure all these things because of her Canadian education, which taught her not only about the earth and the plight of living things, but how to imagine a different world and to think about things differently, that taught that there were many solutions to the same problem. Prema thought of the children marching in rows and coloring in unison in the village schoolyard and knew they were locked in tradition and that India in general had a clear bias toward keeping things the same and not moving out of the accepted ways. Especially people in small villages that were only known because of their nice shores that fed fishermen and washed up the occasional turtle.

The turtle had been very beautiful, though, and this whole situation was a perfect example of why Prema didn't fit anywhere in the whole, wide world. Some people could root wholeheartedly for one way or the other, but Prema always had to try to understand every person's position, and usually could.

"Of course I could murder someone," she had said once in her anthropology class, prompting the rows of students in front of her to peer around at her. "Just give me the right circumstances, too much adrenaline, not enough nutrition, drugs, bad early parenting."

Of course she could eat a turtle, if she didn't know how beautiful they looked when they were swimming, how old they could get, how there were so few left in the seas. She would have been the small child dancing around when the fishermen came home with such a treat carried in an old sari between them. A bit like a child rejoices at a toy he gets in his Christmas stocking, not knowing the story of the overworked indentured woman who made it in Bangladesh. Prema was letting the racing mind thing happen again, and she sighed. David looked at her, but didn't say anything.

Linus saw the turtle nest first.

"What do you think of that?" he said, pointing into the distance with one long, brown arm. There was a bit of mesh fencing with a red and green sign, a plastic chair and an umbrella beside it. An older woman sat on the chair, reading.

They weren't too far from the club Linus had been talking about. Prema was shocked by the idea of turtles hatching so close to dancing and music. Wasn't that bad for them? She tried to think back to the nature shows she had seen.

"That looks like something," David said. "But they couldn't be so near to all of this..." he gestured to the buildings back from the beach, what looked like three large clubs that must have been bright and loud in the nighttime, when the turtles would be trying to get to the sea.

"They could be," Prema said, her stomach twisting.

The woman sat forward as they draw closer. She was Indian—clearly Goan, with her graying hair in the short-cropped style Prema had often seen on Goan women. She wore tortoise shell framed glasses and a knee-length skirt with a printed silk blouse. She had a book propped open in front of her, and carefully placed a bookmark in it as they approached.

"You have come to see the turtles?" she asked in English. She had a lovely cultured Goan accent. Prema smiled.

"Yes," Prema and David said in unison.

"We were told about the turtles here in Morjim after we came across a turtle in Arambol today," David continued.

"You spotted one in Arambol! How wonderful, it is not often that they nest there."

"Oh— it seemed that... well." David broke off.

"It looked like some villagers were trying to capture the turtle to eat it," Prema said.

"That's a shame," the woman said, sitting a little straighter, with her hands on her knees. "That's a true shame. That's why I've come out here today. Well, not that there are any villagers here to eat these eggs, but we cannot be too careful. I'm also hoping to catch sight of them hatching. I've been a turtle fan for years and have seen three hatchings. These little ones are ready to hatch in the next few days—the forestry workers moved their nest up here, you know? Farther up the beach and all, they were laid too close to the water. I'm retired, nothing else to do. So here I am, with my book. I only pray the turtles hatch soon. There is a party scheduled up there—" she gestured at the club, "this weekend and I don't know if the turtles will make it to the sea in all the madness. Ahh—" She reached into the plastic bag beside her. "Will you sign this petition to get this party shut down? We are trying to have all the parties finished for the remainder of the season. These people are having no respect for the turtles and all."

She pulled a wrinkled piece of paper out of her bag and seemed to finally take a breath. Prema's head felt hot from the bright sun. She stepped beneath the woman's umbrella and peered down at the nest. She couldn't see anything. The eggs were buried, but the sign beside them proclaimed the date they were laid.

"What's the petition for?" David asked, reaching for the piece of paper.

"It is meant to light a fire under the government and cause them to really pay attention to the laws they have already formed. Having these loud parties near the nests is against the law. And it is up to the government and the police to enforce the law."

Prema moved closer to David and looked at the list of names. There were about forty, all of them Hindu or Catholic names, the Hindu ones names like Nikil and Sahin, the Catholic ones like Rodriguez and Fernandez. Viman Naik had written his name and phone number in bright red pen, with six large exclamation points following. Prema took the pen from the woman and signed her name neatly, holding the paper against the woman's newspaper to make a hard surface. *Prema Singh*, she wrote, and added her Indian mobile number. David took the pen from her and added his own name, hesitating at the phone number.

"What's Timothy's number?" he asked.

Prema told him without thinking, listing off the numbers as easily as if she saw them written in the sand in front of her. She remembered when he first gave it to her as they stood at the chai *wallah* in Varanasi— how she memorized it on the walk home so that the paper could vanish, could evaporate from her tightly clenched hand, and she would still have it. David wrote down the numbers, then looked at her for a moment before handing the paper to Linus. Prema's face felt hot again. She had given a lot away with that quick recitation. She wondered what David thought of her. He always seemed to be weighing something when he looked at her. Measuring, the way she imagined he measured a space with his eyes, decided which cabinets would fit in a client's kitchen. She didn't know if she measured up to his hopes for his son. And how about Timothy, she thought suddenly, angry. How would Dr. Singh have felt about Timothy? She imagined her mother's voice saying, "It doesn't appear that he washes his hair, Prema. How will you put your face close to him? It is very important, how a man smells, he must take perfect care of himself."

What would Prema have told her in response? Would she have told her about the scent of lavender that rose off the top of Timothy's head when she leaned over to pluck Isaac out of his arms? Would she have dared to talk about the way he lay on his stomach on the floor in his room, Prema cross-legged on the bed, Timothy resting on his crossed arms, both of them watching as Isaac sat in his mound of pillows playing with an empty water bottle. The way Timothy's unprotected elbows and the long line of his back made her stomach swoop.

She sighed, thinking, *Neither of us, really, is any good for the other. But tell that to my heart. My heart! My whole self, really, my fingers and toes, my stomach with its daily roller coaster, my eyelids at night when I try to sleep and they play me movies of what he said, what he did.* She was angry while she watched Linus sign the paper. Nothing else meant much now, the ocean seemed empty without Timothy in it, playing with his boy. The coconut trees were dulled. How had this taken her over? *That's it*, she thought. *I'm done. No more of this craziness. I'm keeping my distance now.*

But later, after David had carefully given the woman with the petition Timothy's phone number with a promise that she would call if it seemed like hatching was imminent, and the three of them had trekked back across the sand to the motorbike, and somehow fit themselves on the small seat, Prema thought differently. She knew that she couldn't stay away, any more than she could fast from eating, an experiment in college during her Gandhi phase that had been a dismal failure. She knew it because as they drove with the sweet air reaching them from the jungle, scents of burning dung and incense as evening fell, as all of this crowded in on her, her strongest thought was what she would tell Timothy of the day, and how she wanted to see his face when he heard about it. How his eyebrows would rise as he heard about the police and his father demanding to stay and see what happened, how he would react to his father's idea of making flyers for the clubs, teaching them about the imminent hatching, asking people to boycott the parties. "First I'll canvass the clubs," David had said. "I'll try to make them see reason. Then, if that doesn't work, I'll stand outside and turn people away." Prema wanted to see Timothy's face, the astonishment that showed in his widened eyes, the way they crinkled when he laughed, the look he would send her way when they laughed together, using only their eyes.

There was no possibility that she would stay away.

CHAPTER 27

Isaac's first real food was a piece of potato from Timothy's *puri bhaji* plate, late one morning in December. Timothy had rubbed off the spicy parts and was feeding his son like a baby bird, pulling the potatoes off his plate and placing the little pieces into his baby's pink, open mouth. Linus was late, as usual. None of them kept a schedule, really, but Isaac wouldn't be happy forever, he would need to go back to the room and sleep soon, and Timothy wanted to talk to Linus.

There he was now, walking to the thali place with his guitar in his hands. He stopped for a minute and plucked a series of notes, then continued on, waving to some of the taxi drivers as he passed them. "*Deo boro dees due!*" Timothy heard him call. Good morning in Konkani. All the taxi drivers, the restaurant owners, the gypsy sellers knew Linus. People couldn't help loving him, with his new beard and his hair, now growing from his head in eight different directions as it grew longer.

"Timothy!" Linus called as he walked into the grungy little restaurant, a drinking coconut already in his hand. "Sorry, mate, I had a lie-in."

Timothy smiled. The things Linus said, completely seriously. He used words like *mollycoddle* and *persnickety*. Words that Timothy had thought went out of fashion a hundred years ago appeared to be alive and well among young people in England.

"No problem," he said.

"What? Are you feeding him real food?"

Timothy pointed at a book that lay open beside him.

"Apparently I should have been feeding him for two months now. My mom just said to start when he was ready, but how do I know when that is? She's all about *when you feel things*, but I'm not so good at figuring it out by feeling."

"Where'd you get that thing?"

"From the little local book store? Cool, eh?"

"I guess."

"I think this explains why he hasn't been sleeping so well at night. He's hungry."

"So you're feeding him potato curry."

"Yes. Do you think that's bad?"

"No, I mean, what do I know?" Linus said. "But my sister started with bananas."

"Bananas!" Timothy said. "I didn't think of bananas."

Linus pulled a chair over to the table and called to Sagar that he wanted a veg thali. He sat his guitar on the table. Isaac immediately reached for it, and Timothy moved it out of Isaac's reach. It was getting to be a reflex—rescuing things from little grasping hands.

"I'm worried about my dad," he said now to Linus.

"Your dad? Why? He's doing great."

"Don't you think he's doing a little too great?"

"How can anyone be doing too great? Great is great."

Timothy didn't know how to explain it. He had imagined, in the short time that he had to imagine anything about his dad's visit, that his father would come, only slightly enjoy himself, get freaked out a bit, and then go home.

Instead he had changed his flight dates so that he could stay another month. He was wholeheartedly involved in three projects: getting to know his grandson (which Timothy was grateful for), making Maria a set of kitchen cupboards, (against Timothy's protests that people didn't have kitchen cupboards here, it wasn't done) and handing out pamphlets with Ruth about the turtles. He couldn't believe how sad his father had been when they missed the hatching of the eggs Ruth had been guarding when David, Linus, and Prema had met her. They had hatched in the nighttime, and immediately David had gone out and bought a cell phone, so that Ruth would be able to call him right away if anything went on with the new nest that she was guarding.

"I guess," Timothy began, then stopped. He didn't know what he thought, what he was trying to say. Sagar brought Linus's thali to the table and brushed some old crumbs off the table cloth with a flick of an old rag, then set the thali plate down. "I think it's as though I don't really recognize him here, in India. I'm almost afraid for him. What will happen when he gets back home? Will things be the same with my mom?"

"Maybe he wonders the same thing about you," Linus said.

"I'm sure he does. I don't know if I'm ever going back, to tell you the truth."

"You say that now," Linus said. "You'll feel differently later."

Sometimes David and Timothy went out on David's rented motorbike together, armed with binoculars David had brought from home, while Prema watched Isaac. They stopped near rice paddies and looked for birds. Up until his father had arrived, Timothy had mostly seen crows in coconut trees, maybe the odd hopping sparrow or two. But with his father's teaching, the world had exploded into some kind of bird paradise.

"Just look up," David had told Timothy after coming back from a solitary drive excited by the three different species of kingfisher he had spotted. Timothy had been stunned by his father's luck in finding birds, and felt slightly jealous, hearing about it while changing a wildly explosive diaper, the contents of which were spread from Isaac's thighs to the middle of his back. "Look at the power lines if you don't have time for a big search. They're always there."

The next time Timothy had gone for a drive on the scooter (lately he'd found that they relaxed him almost as much as swimming did) he took his father's advice and looked up at the power lines next to the fields. Sure enough, there one was, a kingfisher whose wings flashed bright, iridescent blue as it lifted off into the sky. He and his father began birdwatching together after that. Timothy had seen kites, brilliant green parrots, tiny bright bee catchers with their long tails, several types of kingfisher, egrets, herons, and daily he said hello to the large, white-headed brahminy kites that lived in a large pine tree at the beach. They reminded him of the bald eagles he had grown up with in Canada.

"How will he ever go back to normal birds?" he said to Linus.

"I think he doesn't think of anything as normal," Linus said, smiling at Isaac, who had yellow potato curry all around his mouth and was dancing for more.

"Babahbabhbabhamama," said Isaac.

A week later, Timothy and Prema sat on the porch when Linus and David were out on a day trip to search for wood trim in Mapusa, the nearby town. The cabinets were nearly finished, and Isaac was crawling. It had seemed to take a long time for him to learn, but according to Timothy's book, babies crawled at all different ages. For a few days, he had been able to get up on his knees and rock back and forth, but soon he learned to really take off, scooting along on his stomach for awhile, then crawling a real crawl on hands and knees, shifting back to his stomach when he got tired. Last week Timothy's dad had taken about five minutes and installed a baby gate on the porch so Isaac could crawl all around and not go down the steps. It was dark already and they weren't back. Timothy figured they had stopped at their favorite restaurant in Mapusa, one that served excellent naan, which wasn't easy to find in Arambol.

Timothy and Prema sat on the porch and watched Isaac crawl. Prema grabbed at his little legs moving under his tiny shirt. The baby was dressed in a shirt and diaper, with dirty knees from what he picked up from the floor, which seemed to happen no matter how much Timothy swept. Isaac was obsessed with an empty juice carton, and he rocked back and forth on his knees talking to it, then made a scoot that looked like a frog jumping, and Prema lifted her head and laughed, showing her lovely brown throat. They were sitting next to each other on the porch floor, leaning on the railing, knees up in front of them. A quarter moon shone bright in the dark sky beyond the porch awning. Prema planted a kiss on his son's head, then sat back up beside Timothy and met his eyes. There was a strange and lovely swooping in Timothy's chest, like he'd gone down a wave or an elevator, and he leaned over and caught her mouth with his.

If he had thought the swooping was wild before the kiss, it went off the charts when her face was against his. It wasn't a long kiss. Her mouth was warm and sweet. She smelled like the most beautiful flower garden, a garden of roses. Her mouth was so soft. He relaxed against her and put one hand up to her face, and she moved closer to him. He thought his heart would beat out of his chest. And Isaac sneezed.

They broke away from each other. He was sure he looked as stunned as she did.

"Sorry," he said, which was a stupid thing to say. There were too many thoughts, too many emotions going on, wrestling for prominence in his chest and in his mind and all he wanted was to kiss her again and also to lock himself in his room and never see her again.

He heard someone whistling a song in the distance. Linus. They were back. Relieved, he called to them before they even reached the porch.

"Did you get everything you need?" he asked, turning away from Prema with

Isaac, whom he had scooped up like a shield, in his arms, putting the line of his back between himself and her.

Linus and David came up out of the dark and emerged in the porch light. David looked from Timothy to Prema and then back to Timothy, while Linus fished for something in his bag. "Got you a poster!" he said. "You, too, Prema." He looked up. "Oh, whoa. Hey, should we come back later?"

"No, never mind, I'm just heading out," Prema said. Her voice sounded like something else, nothing like Prema's low, full voice. This one was bright as tin. Before anyone could say anything, she had her *chappals* on and was beyond the baby gate and out into the night.

"You really have to do something about this air between you," Linus said. "It's full, mate, full. And not in a good way."

Timothy felt his dad looking at him and refused to meet his eyes. He sighed.

"What's this about a poster?"

Linus unrolled the paper he had in his hands. It was a large photograph of a cruise ship in a harbor, with elaborate scalloping around the edges of the poster. A caption read, "Like ships passing in the night."

"That doesn't even make sense," he said.

"I know! That's the point! These Indian posters are priceless."

"Cool," he said. His heart felt heavy. He should have gone after Prema, but he couldn't bring himself to do it. It was his fault. He didn't have to kiss her.

His dad let himself onto the porch and sat on the one plastic chair.

"I have to work on the cupboards tomorrow in the morning, but do you want to go for a swim together in the afternoon? I can bring my new bodyboard."

"Sure."

David reached out and put his hand on Timothy's shoulder. Timothy heard Linus whistling as he walked away, out into the night. He felt the sick jealousy again, the feeling that everyone else had something he didn't— a better life, a better set of circumstances. Next came the familiar feeling of helplessness about changing anything in his own life.

"Were you always sure of what you wanted to do?" he asked his dad.

David looked up, surprised.

"It was laid out for me," he said. "I did what my dad did. I don't think I really questioned it. I got it into my head at one point, I suppose, that I might want to fix car engines. So my dad set me to work on the broken tractors around the property. I think I sweated that idea out of me. And I've always loved wood. I love trees, you know."

"I feel like I wasn't ready to be a grownup," Timothy said. He realized after he said it that it was the real truth, this was the truth behind many of his sluggish days, the fact that he didn't want to leave India, the jealousy, the hesitancy. He was jealous of people who either knew how to be a grownup or didn't have to be one, like Linus.

"You had it sprung on you, didn't you?" his dad said. His voice was soft, his hand still gentle on Timothy's shoulder. Timothy wondered why he never knew that his dad could be so understanding. He turned to him and smiled, a lump in his throat.

"It— it'll be nice to go for a swim," he said. The moon had risen beyond where he can see it. Out there it was only stars.

CHAPTER 28

The next day, they decided to take Isaac to the beach.

"We can take turns with him," David said. "I need to get a lot of baby time."

The water drew itself up into each wave, drops flinging themselves upward from the crest, into the sky. The sun was in the hesitant part of the afternoon, heading down now, but very slowly. In a few hours it would be ready to drop. The light made the waves and water a flat silver in color, so different from the mornings that Timothy came out here, when the sun shone into the waves, making them translucent and green.

He pulled Isaac's clothes off, wiped some sticky banana off his chin and underneath, where mushed banana was caught in a fold. Isaac had been putting on weight— he had become a round little guy with chubby knees. He smiled at Timothy and Timothy picked him up and kissed him in the space between his cheek and his neck. Isaac laughed, ticklish, so Timothy did it again.

"I think I'll sit out here for a bit," David said.

They had walked along the beach to get away from the crowd and it was quiet where they were, with only a few people passing on an afternoon walk.

"Ready to go, Isaac?" he said. "We're so sticky," he said to his dad. "We're heading right in."

They waded out, Isaac tight in the crook of Timothy's arm. A milk bag floated out beside them. Timothy kicked his feet at the sand. He wanted to forget how her mouth had tasted, how the side of her face was so soft against his hand. He could have cried from frustration. How could he be so shallow? To fall for the first girl he met after Isabel, just because the girl was beautiful and funny and nice and sweet and kind to his son?

They were in the sea, the water over Timothy's waist. He wondered if he could float with Isaac on his chest. He felt heavy, like he needed to be light for a minute, to get off his feet and forget what he had lost and what he may still have been losing. He kicked back and tried to float, keeping Isaac steady on his belly with one hand. He found he could float. Isaac stuffed a fist into his mouth and laid his head on Timothy's chest. The large eagle that lived at the top of the tallest tree on the beach flew into its nest and dropped something in. Isaac rubbed his face against Timothy's shoulder and this was it, he swore to himself, this was all he needed. He floated. He only needed to float, to rest here with his son. To float.

After a few minutes, Isaac fussed a bit and Timothy decided to stand up. He held Isaac up over his shoulder and tried to put his feet down, but to his shock he found that he if he stood he would be in water over his head. The current had carried him to deep water and he couldn't stand.

Shit, he thought. He treaded water with his legs and shifted Isaac to his left shoulder so he could try to swim with his right. He got Isaac a face full of water in the process and Isaac spluttered and then screamed. Timothy treaded water and tried to swim forward but he couldn't make any headway. He raised his right arm and waved at his father, who stood at the shore, shading his eyes to see them. Timothy saw that he had really floated far out. He swallowed.

"Shhhh, Isaac," he said. "It's okay. It's only a little bit of water."

David turned away from the water and Timothy cried out, but his dad was retrieving the bodyboard. He walked back to the water with it (so slowly, it seemed to Timothy) and waded in.

Later Timothy would reflect that although neither of them knew it, that was only the beginning. At the moment, it seemed that it was all right again—the relief that Timothy felt the minute his father's foot first hit the surf swelled in him and became the closest thing he had felt to being a child since he had grown up and gone away. He felt like a boy with a nightmare, his dad coming to him in the night, face pale against the moonlight from the window, tucking the blanket up farther around him, hands warm as he wiped the tears from Timothy's eyes.

Timothy could see the surprise on David's face as his feet left the ocean floor and he kicked his way out to Timothy and Isaac, both hands on the board.

"This really isn't safe," he said, as he reached them.

Timothy grasped at the board and threw an arm over it, exhausted.

"You think?" he said, his voice coming out sharper and more sarcastic than he meant it to be.

"Well, how did you get out here?"

"I was floating on my back, for only a minute or so." He shook his head. "It carried me."

"It's pulling us now," his dad said. "I can feel it. Let's go in."

They kicked together, each with a hand on the board, Timothy still holding Isaac over his shoulder. He wasn't sure which one of them noticed first that they weren't getting anywhere at all, but Timothy gradually became aware that the boats on the beach were getting more distant, if anything.

"This isn't working," David said, breathing hard. "We need to rest."

"What's wrong? What's happening?" Timothy said.

"It's a riptide. Not much use fighting it. We could just drift with it, no problem, but I'm worried about having this little guy out here."

Isaac was holding both hands up to his face and occasionally reaching an arm down to splash at the water. He was happy again, but he would get tired of this. Timothy was glad that the water was so warm. It felt like a warm bath, and though there was a breeze, he didn't think his baby would get cold.

This was the way they went. For how long? Minutes? Hours? The sun made its way across the sky and toward the distant horizon. Timothy's arm was cramping and he shifted Isaac to the other arm.

"Why don't you put him on the board?" David asked.

"I'm worried that he'll fall off."

"Put him on there and then put your arm around him," David said. "You can keep him on there and have more power for swimming."

They tried swimming again, but it brought them no further. They waved their arms, but they were specks now, far from the lifeguards who seemed to be busy with a large group of drunken Indian tourists. Timothy blinked back frustrated tears and hid his face in Isaac's leg. His son patted at his head, closed his fist on a few of Timothy's dreadlocks and yanked.

"Thanks, kiddo," Timothy said. "I needed that."

David had the steel face that Timothy knew meant he had gone deep inside. He was using all his reserves.

"We only need to swim parallel," he said. "To the end of this current. Then we'll be able to get in."

"I'm sorry," Timothy said. He shook his head and put it down on the board. His legs and arms were trembling and he felt waterlogged, like half the ocean had soaked into him. He was hungry with a gnawing pain.

"Don't be defeated, son," David said.

"I'm worried that we're not going to be able to get back."

"Don't even say that. Hope is what drives more strength into your body."

"Hope for what?"

"Hope for seeing your son walk to you. For Prema in your life. For years and years of joy to replace this year of sorrow."

Timothy stared into his father's face, so close to his own. Their blue eyes were so similar, it would be a little like looking into a mirror except for the lines in his father's face, etched there over time, like water on stone. Days in the sun, days of laughter. He thought of his parents in the garden together, harvesting tomatoes for the evening meal. His mother planting a kiss on the side of his dad's head. Right now his hair was standing up, thinning on top, wet and salty. His beard was fuller than Timothy's, something he had grown since being here. Timothy couldn't remember the last time his father had a beard, but it suited him, brown and even.

"Prema?" he said. "Oh, Dad. I'm a widower."

"I know that. But she loves you."

"I think she loves everybody."

"No, I mean, she loves you. Certainly. And she loves your son, too."

"Mom would kill me if she knew I put you in danger like this."

"She's going to kill you, you mean. Because we'll get out of this and your mother will then kill you, but not for putting me in danger." David looked at Isaac, who was whining now. "For putting him in danger."

Timothy kissed Isaac's face. Both of their arms were slung around the board, protecting Isaac from falling. They drifted as they talked.

"I can't think about it. I think I could let go of my life, but not his."

"Spoken like a father. Now you know why I'm not even entertaining the idea of not getting back. I have a son and a grandson in the water." His voice broke and he looked away for a minute. When he looked back, he had the steel face again.

"Dad?"

"Yes?"

"Thanks for coming out here." Timothy didn't specify which "out here" he meant, and he wasn't sure he knew, because they were all tangled up in each other. Either way, before his dad had come he was close to drowning.

"Let's try again."

They kicked with everything, but the current was like a wall. Isaac began crying, his screams sending arrows into Timothy's heart. The baby wanted off the board, out of the water, this wasn't fun anymore. He was ready for something to eat, he was thirsty and tired. He cried for a long time, his wails echoing in the air. The men kicked the whole time, the wall of tide not giving way for them. Eventually Isaac fell asleep, his cheek pillowed on the body board, his thumb in his mouth.

"Let's rest, then give another push," David said.

"Please don't let me go, Dad," Timothy said.

"I would never. You know that."

Timothy knew then just how badly he wanted to walk out of this. He didn't feel despair anymore, he wanted it to work, which only made the fact that they couldn't get out of the current harder to take. He wanted to scream, but the pain in his stomach, reminding him that he forgot to eat lunch, told him he should reserve every bit of energy he had. He was also terribly thirsty.

David started to pray, and then he began singing a song in a thin, wavery voice. "Hosanna, hosanna in the highest." Timothy remembered that his father had told him that hosanna meant *save us*. Timothy began singing along, but found that his mouth was too dry. He swallowed hard and tried again. He had loved singing with Linus's hands flying on the guitar, the words flowing from his mouth like water. The water around him now was unfamiliar and vast, the underneath full of sound and fear, and this was what it came back to, to sing like water or open his mouth and drown. He sang it hard, along with his father. *God, if you are there, come and save us.* All the bodies of water in this whole long journey seemed to line up before him. If he got out of this, he would be reborn, he would not despair again, he would move toward Prema because she deserved someone who loved her wholeheartedly. He would choose life.

The sun had lowered enough to turn the waves into metallic shades of gray and green. They had drifted so far along the beach that Timothy didn't recognize the shore he could see from the board. David opened his eyes and they both stopped singing.

"Wait, what's that?" he asked.

Timothy looked in the direction his father was pointing.

"It's a river," he said.

"That's our spot, son. We wait until we get there and we hope for a change of current."

"We need to get out of this water, Dad."

"I know we do, Timmy."

Timothy put his head on the board to rest, taking care to keep his arm curved around Isaac. He was living a sort of slideshow in his head. Isabel kissing him in Rajasthan, Isabel dead on the floor, Sunita nursing Isaac, blessing Timothy as he left, Prema the first day on the train, the chai in its cup in the morning, Prema in her red dress, the jungle whirring by as they drove on the scooter, a flock of white birds, vomiting on the bank of the Ganga, feeding Isaac bottles on the train, Isaac laughing when Maria tickled him, Isaac's eyes on him in the morning, the smell of Prema as he leaned over and kissed her.

"We need to do this, Dad," he said, lifting his head to look at his dad. "I want to go back, I want to go home to Mom." His dad looked up at the sky, ran a wet hand over his face, blinked tears away.

"I think I love her too," Timothy said, not talking about his mom.

If we get out of this, he thought. I'm doing everything differently. He meant it.

"I want to go back to school," he said. "I want to play music. I'm sorry if that makes you disappointed."

David looked at him, shock on his face. His hair was standing on end, full of salt. Timothy could see where his scalp was burned a bright pink. His father lifted one hand and put it on the side of Timothy's face.

"I'm the farthest thing from disappointed," he said.

"I always thought you were upset that I left the business," Timothy said.

"Maybe a long time ago I felt sad, when I had a dream about passing the shop on to you— but there's Matt and Ryan now, and soon Joel will be ready to start working. It doesn't matter anyway. I realized a long time ago, and even more, being here with you—maybe I've never told you this, but your music is the most beautiful I've ever heard. You sing like—" his voice broke and he tightened his hand on Timothy's face for just a moment before pulling it away. "You sing like an angel. How could I want you to be different?"

"Let's go, okay?" Timothy said. "Let's get my baby home. Let's go back to Prema, back to Mom."

This time Timothy reached farther than he had ever reached, even in all those months of pressing, of hard work and tears and unknown fears. He reached, they were both praying, he stuffed the tears back into himself and sang. Then he stopped singing and swam with everything he had.

The trees on the shore began to grow the tiniest bit larger. Timothy forced himself to look down at the water and stop watching the shore, to focus with everything he had on the swimming. He put all his love for his son into his feet, his legs. His arm was cramping around the baby, still asleep on the body board. Timothy felt the strong push of the current against them subside—now it felt like they were flying forward. Another minute and his feet bumped the sandy ocean floor. He gasped and sighed with relief. They waded in, Timothy picking Isaac up and holding him close to his chest. He turned to his father, who held his arms open. Timothy collapsed into them. His father held him, he held Isaac. The sun was a red orb hovering over the horizon. Soon it would be dark. They had been so close to being stuck out in the sea in the deep dark night.

Timothy had only heard his father cry once before, and that was through the door, his father locked in his room after Timothy's grandfather, David's father, died. But now that they were back on shore, now that the ocean had released the three of them, tears flowed from David's eyes.

They stumbled onto the sand and sat down. Isaac woke up and started wailing again, so they stumbled up the beach to a beach shack restaurant. Timothy asked for a mashed banana and fed it to his hungry baby. They both drank water. It was like a dream, they were in an unfamiliar shack, in an unfamiliar place. They weren't sure how to proceed. Timothy ate a sandwich with egg. David said he would eat when they got back to the house. They told the men in the restaurant what had happened, and promised to come back the next day and pay their bill before they left to find a taxi that would bring them back to Arambol. Once they were in the car, night fell quickly and Timothy was exhausted. His legs hurt, his eyes hurt. Isaac was asleep in Timothy's arms again. Timothy wouldn't let Isaac go, though he knew David would happily hold him. Timothy tried to turn his brain off. He couldn't think about what might have happened. He couldn't wait to sleep. He would have to save the thinking about it for some other time.

When they got home, Timothy walked up to the house to get his wallet so he could pay the driver. Linus was pacing on the porch, in front of the door. When he saw Timothy, he ran both hands through his hair, then he grabbed Timothy and pulled him into a hug. Timothy was shocked to see tears in his eyes when he drew back.

"You look like hell," Linus said.

"You have no idea." Timothy said. *We nearly drowned*, he thought, but he didn't say it. There would be time for stories later.

"I have to go tell Prema," Linus said. "She's been pacing to and fro on the beach, sure that you've drowned."

"She was nearly right." Timothy did say this.

"I'm going," Linus said. He put his hands on Timothy's shoulders. "But I have to say this. You're a damn lucky guy, Tim. She loves you. A girl like her," his voice broke and he looked at the ground. Timothy thought suddenly that maybe the tears were not for him. "A son like Isaac," Linus shook his head. "You're a lucky man."

Linus didn't know what it was like to see your wife die on the floor in front of you, or he wouldn't be throwing words like lucky around. But tonight, with the moon coming up and the salt still on his skin, still alive, Timothy felt exhausted and tingling with life. He was lucky. Lucky, no, blessed. Yes. Blessed. And he suddenly saw, for the first time, that his circumstances were enviable. Linus envied him. Free, easy-going Linus. Timothy held Isaac a little more tightly as he walked through his front door.

When Prema arrived she was shivering. Timothy was drying a very sleepy Isaac off after a feeding him some water with electrolyte powder and giving him a bath. He put a T shirt on him while the baby's eyes closed on their own. Timothy reached a hand to Prema standing in his doorway. Her eyes were dark and moist. She swiped at them with her palms, walked over to him on the bed. When she sat, he could see that her chin was quivering despite how tightly she was holding her mouth. Her thin shoulders were up, rigid. He set Isaac on the side of the bed and put a blanket on him. Isaac sighed a little but barely moved. Timothy turned to Prema. She was looking down at her hands, which were tightly closed.

"I have your towel and your shoes," she said. "They were on the beach."

He leaned over and put a hand on each of her cheeks. She closed her eyes. He moved closer, then kissed each of her eyelids, wet from tears, and then her mouth, which was still trembling.

He pulled back and looked at her. She opened her eyes. She smiled a small smile, but her eyes were worried.

"I love you," he said.

She laughed and it turned into a sob.

"I love you too," she said. "I always have."

"Always these last three months?" he asked, teasing a little.

She shook her head. "Always," she said. "What about you? Did you need to nearly drown to figure it out?"

"Have I mentioned I'm not the sharpest twig on the branch?"

She laughed, then rubbed her hands on her face, her beautiful hands with the delicate wrists. She leaned over and kissed Isaac on the head, straightening again.

"I love him, too," she said.

Timothy caught one of her hands and held it in his, rubbing his thumb across her palm, and sighed. "We're here now. We're going to be fine." And he moved closer to her again, reaching for her face in the still evening.

CHAPTER 29

The cabinets were finished. Prema stood near Maria as David put the finishing touches on his cleaning job. He rubbed at each cabinet with a cloth until it shone. Prema had her arms crossed in front of her. All during that terrible afternoon she had really thought they were gone and she still had to hold herself together sometimes, physically grabbing her stomach. It often felt like it wanted to drop out, and her dreams were terrifying.

She could feel happiness coming off Maria in waves. Maria was very proud of her new kitchen and all the spaces for pots and pans and plates. Prema thought about how often they had to drive back and forth to Mapusa with David, helping him to find the wood and tools he needed. It had been difficult for him. The men in the market had nothing like what he was used to, and she remembered him standing there in frustration as they tried to buy a hammer.

"Where's the handle?" he asked. The hammer was a piece of iron sold alone.

"You have to buy it separately," Prema had said. She shrugged. She was no longer accepting responsibility for every Indian idiosyncratic idea. But somehow, they had found the wood, the tools, the varnish, and this was what he had made. She was continually impressed with Timothy's father. He overcame every single obstacle. He never gave up. She wasn't accustomed to thinking of Timothy as someone who never gave up, but now she thought of the bubble of love he had formed around Isaac despite the circumstances, Isaac's good health, his happiness, and she had to admit she couldn't wait to see Timothy in a different time, when things weren't as difficult and she could really see him shine.

Just this morning they had booked their tickets to leave, just two weeks after David's flight. They would be home in early January. David was leaving in time to be home for Christmas, but Timothy thought that Christmas at home would be too much for him after the two and a half years in India. He and Prema would go to Delhi to get a passport for Isaac, and then they would visit Sunita in the mountains before Timothy flew home. Sunita and Gopal needed to see Isaac—the big happy baby that he had become. David had stayed in Goa a month longer than he planned. He said he regretted leaving. He wanted to come back with Timothy's mom and really see India.

"It will be good to see the place where Isaac was born," he said. "And Isabel died," he added. He glanced at Prema.

"You could plant some flowers," she said, encouraging him.

Timothy was ready for home, but nervous as well. He wanted them to go back together. He told Prema that the months before she arrived, and even after, before David arrived, felt like a long lonely dream that he had woken from. He didn't want to return to it.

Timothy came in to see the finished work, just as David moved aside from polishing the last cabinet. Maria turned and said something to Prema in a mixture of Hindi and Konkani. Prema had been picking up more Konkani and she caught the gist of what Maria said. "She says you clean up a lot better than Indian carpenters, and I have to agree," Prema told David. She had seen the way builders left their spaces in India. It was just the way it was, cleaning was not part of their job description, that was a job for someone else. It was another part of the great big work ethic in India: a job for everyone.

"It's amazing, Dad," Timothy said.

Maria's eyes filled with tears as David turned and gestured to the cupboards. Prema half expected him to say something deep and meaningful, but all he said was "All yours."

"Thank you," Maria said. She didn't hug him or even take his hands, but her eyes spoke it for her. She walked over to the living room and picked up a basket filled with fake flowers, carried it back into the kitchen and tenderly placed it in the first cupboard, the very spot where Prema would have put all those steel tumblers.

The four of them were drinking tea on Timothy's porch when David's phone rang.

"I think that's you," Prema said when he didn't show signs of picking it up.

"Oh!" he said. He reached into the pocket of the shirt he had hung over the rail when he arrived in the morning. "I'm going to finally get used to this ring and it'll be time to go home. Who can this be, anyway?"

"Likely a spam call," Linus said, just as David punched the button and said, "Hello?"

Prema was trying not to look at Timothy, who was giving her little smiles out of the side of his mouth that made her warm to her very toes. Something in her didn't want this dynamic to change, though, the ease of the four of them hanging out, this unlikely group. Three twenty-somethings, a forty-something and an infant. She nudged Timothy with her foot. Linus was looking at David anyway.

"Oh!" Comprehension washed over David's face. "Ruth! What's happening?"

"Not spam," Linus said to Prema.

"No, definitely not," she said, curious.

"Yes! Yes, we'll come right away. Okay, right, thank you!" He punched the button on the phone again and leapt to his feet.

"This is it, guys, we're having babies! Let's go!"

They had missed the first turtle hatching, which happened in the middle of the night. Even Ruth hadn't been there for it, but she had soon set up another watch, a miraculous watch. The turtle, their turtle on Arambol beach had laid her eggs and the forestry workers had come out to place a sign and a protective barrier around the nest, away from the busyness of the rest of the beach, near the cliffs, where Prema lived.

"They're hatching?" Timothy said. He looked toward Isaac, sleeping in the bedroom. "I don't know if I should go."

"Timmy! You're leaving India. You've never seen turtles hatch before. You have to come!" David said.

Timothy shook his head as he walked into the room to collect Isaac. "Never wake a sleeping baby," he said. "Mom told me that. But I guess, for turtles, I can do it."

"Even your mom would wake a sleeping baby for turtle eggs hatching," David said.

There weren't many people on the section of the beach with the turtles. Most people were way down the beach, far away from the cliffs, at the sunset circle. Ruth, a few Russians, and a whole Dutch family stood near the fenced area that sheltered the turtles. Prema waited beside the Dutch family. Both the father and the oldest daughter were holding cameras. The owner of Morjim's largest club had also come to watch—Ruth had wrestled him out to Arambol from Morjim with the intention of showing him just how beautiful this event was, that the turtles needed protection more than Goa needed another party.

"Even more than you need any more money lining your pockets and corrupting your soul," she scolded him now.

He stared at the tiny eggs, which were moving and writhing with the effort of the turtles to get to the outside world, harsh and wild though it may have been. His Russian girlfriend crouched beside him. She gasped as a turtle poked his head out of the soft shell.

Timothy stood a little to the side of the large group, hovering over Isaac, who was sitting in the sand, trying to shove handfuls of it into his mouth. The crowd gasped as the small turtle left its shell, then another wriggled out, and Prema walked over to Timothy.

"Go," she said. "I'll watch Isaac. You go stand with your dad."

"Are you sure? Don't you want to see it?"

"I can see it from here... and I want to spend some time with this guy."

Isaac looked up at her and smiled a big gummy grin when his eyes met hers, bits of sand sticking to his wet chin. He bobbed his head, then smashed his hand back down into the sand. Prema caught his fist before he could shove the sand into his mouth.

"Okay. Thanks," Timothy said.

Prema sat on the sand beside the baby. She wiped sand and drool from his chin, stroked his damp head. The turtles were beginning to waddle down the beach, out to the sea. Somehow they reminded her of the baby beside her. They brought tears to her eyes. She reached down to pick Isaac up so he could stand while holding onto her arm. He turned his head to look at her, clutching her arm and smiling his drooly grin even wider. She kissed the top of his warm, sandy head. Why did the turtles remind her of him? He was motherless like the turtles, maybe, but no, she shook her head. He had always had Timothy. A father.

It was just because they were made like this, she realized. Made so you wanted to reach out and protect them, to take care of the baby things. She kissed him again and laughed as he reached up and rubbed his head with a fistful of sand. Timothy and David were smiling as they walked to the sea beside the first turtles, making it into the surf with their tiny short legs. The sun drifted down to the horizon, they were nearly silhouettes. It was one more sunset on the beach, with Linus flapping his arms to try to scare away the crows that would have loved to swoop in on the turtles. Ruth was shushing everyone. "They need focus," she said. "This is their most important job."

Prema was happy where she was, with Isaac's hands patting at her face.

She had come to India looking for belonging and it had reached out to her in a way she couldn't have expected. Her people were Indian; her people were also Timothy, Linus, and David. She and Timothy could do things a different way, she realized, watching him follow the turtles to the sea. She had been born to do things a different way, as a second-generation immigrant. She had been fighting it, but this was who she was, this was how she was born. The world was changing and there wasn't really a category for a girl like her— she had wanted to find one that she fit in neatly, she had wanted to control her own destiny, but control had been denied. Indo-Canadian, traveler, explorer, wild girl, she had fallen in love, not once, but twice, three times. With a country, with a man, and with this small, incredible boy. It was more love than she could have expected. Timothy was in the sea now and she saw that she didn't have to label him as white, herself as someone who betrayed her culture. He was the man she loved. The way people perceived her was out of her control, she couldn't guess what category they would put her in. For every label she wanted to apply, Indian culture could apply a hundred more, but she was sitting barefaced before God now, like during the mornings of singing on the beach, when she had showed up without knowing beforehand what it would all be like, simply allowing it to be what it would be, simply finding beauty without suspicion, not looking sideways at it. Her country, her questions, her parents' decisions, all out of her control. She sighed and felt a great weight lift from her as she let it go. She saw Isaac, stopped labeling him in her head as someone else's baby. He was just Isaac and she loved him. She pulled the baby to her, kissed him under his chin. He laughed his squeak-toy laugh and her heart swooped. The squeaky laugh sounded like bells waking her up, welcoming her home.

Bio

Rachel Devenish Ford is the wife of one Superstar Husband and the mother of five incredible children. Originally from British Columbia, Canada, she spent seven years working with homeless youth in California before moving to India to help start a meditation center in the Christian tradition. She can be found eating street food or smelling flowers in many cities in Asia. She currently lives in Northern Thailand, inhaling books, morning air, and seasonal fruit.

Other works by Rachel Devenish Ford:

The Eve Tree: A Novel
Trees Tall as Mountains: The Journey Mama Writings- Book One
Oceans Bright With Stars: The Journey Mama Writings- Book Two
A Home as Wide as the Earth: The Journey Mama Writings- Book Three

Reviews

Recommendations and reviews are such an important part of the success of a book. If you enjoyed this book, please take the time to leave a review at Amazon.com or your site of choice.

Don't be afraid of leaving a short review! Even a couple lines will help and will overwhelm the author with waves of gratitude.

Contact

* * *

Email: racheldevenishford@gmail.com
Blog: http://journeymama.com
Facebook: http://www.facebook.com/racheldevenishford
Twitter: http://www.twitter.com/journeymama
Instagram: http://instagram.com/journeymama

Thanks so much for reading.

Thank you so much to Leaf Reilly for your understanding and knowledge about life in India. Thanks to Sara J Henry for your wonderful encouragement and sharp-eyed editing. Thanks to my kids for being so patient with a writing mother, and to Chinua as always, for unending support.

Made in the USA
Lexington, KY
12 December 2015